Angel's Back:
What's Next
By Brenda G. Wright

Library of Congress Control Number:		2012911139
ISBN:	Hardcover	978-1-4771-3154-1
	Softcover	978-1-4771-3153-4
	Ebook	978-1-4771-3155-8

To order additional copies of this book, contact:
Xlibris Corporation
1-888-795-4274
www.Xlibris.com
Orders@Xlibris.com
115093

Table of Contents

Chapter 1
Angel's Back for Revenge

ANGEL AND RAMON moved back to Columbia after their baby turned three months old. Things to Angel hadn't changed that much, but deep down inside, she knew that it would never be the same. She also knew she had to stay on alert and keep her eyes and ears open to everything that was going on around her. Angel had six more months before her daughter Baby Girl could join her in her mast of destruction that she had been put on high alert from Uncle Joe and his brothers that Josh, the late Mr. Sanchez's brother, and his four sons were gunning for her head.

Angel wasn't worried about Josh and his sons; she had been mapping out their demise for six months, so she was ready to get the war started. She just wanted her son to be somewhere safe and out of harm's way. Angel talked with Ramon that night, and she told him about her Aunt Marie. She wanted their son to be with her aunt because she knew he would be safe with her. Ramon wasn't too sure about letting his only child go so far away from home, he was still an infant, but he also knew the danger he would be in if he stayed in Columbia with the war that was taking place.

Ramon asked Angel if he could sleep on it, and he would give her an answer in the morning. Angel said, 'fine,' but in reality, she knew Ramon loved his son, but she also knew that he wanted their son to be somewhere safe. The next morning, Ramon woke up early to go to sit in the nursery with their son. He was rocking him in his arms, telling him how much he loved him and that he would miss him with all his heart and soul; he promised his son as soon as the war was over, he would be at Aunt Marie's house to pick him up. The baby made a little giggling sound that came from his mouth as if he knew what his father was saying. That made Ramon feel a little bit worst about what he decided to do;

1

he knew Angel wouldn't send their child to anyone that she wasn't one hundred percent sure that he would be protected by their life.

Angel called Aunt Marie to explain to her what was going on; she told Angel to bring the baby to her, and that she would guard her son with her life; she also told Angel to handle her business, and when she returned to pick up her son, he would be fine. The next day, Angel packed up the baby things. She and Ramon got in the helicopter and flew their son to Aunt Marie's house in Ohio.

When Angel and Ramon arrived back in Columbia, Uncle Leo had plenty of news for the two of them; he knew exactly where the Sanchez brothers were spending their time. He wanted them to be dealt with as soon as possible; he didn't like the fact that his competition was still hanging around, hurting his business. He wanted their existence wiped off the face of the earth. The Sanchez brothers and their father were messing around with Uncle Leo and his brothers reputation, even though Uncle Leo and his brothers were into all kinds of illegal activities such as extortion, loan sharking, murder, drug trafficking, money laundering, black-market agreements, and committing violent crimes; their reputation is valuable to the Columbia mafia. Uncle Leo and his brothers couldn't handle a series of failures; it can completely ruin the mafia reputation, and they definitely weren't having that.

After the meeting was over with Angel and Ramon that Uncle Leo and his brothers had set for that night, Angel decided it was time to put her own personal dream team together to take these Sanchez brothers off the map. She knew that her daughter, Baby Girl, would be the muscle of the team when she wasn't around. She also knew that Baby Girl and her friends were coming to Columbia on their summer break, and that would be a good time to put her dream team together, but first, she had to put Baby Girl's friends under a microscope. She wanted to make sure that her daughter wasn't fraternizing with the enemy; she knew they came at you in all shapes, sizes, and color, and being in the life that they were living, hard-core killers didn't discriminate.

Two days before, Baby Girl and her associates decided to leave Spellman for their summer break; they all went to the mall shopping to take clothes back to Columbia all the name brand clothing they could find. You know the expression shop to you drop. They hit every name brand store in the mall such as Prada, Christian Dior, Donna Karen, Baby Phat, and Channel. They had one more store to hit before they left the mall, and that was Victoria's Secret; they all had nice hips, big asses, and ample breast, so they knew that they were going to rock the shit out of Victoria's Secret lingerie department. When Baby Girl and her girlfriends left Victoria's Secret, they had to restock the store; the only things that were left were perfumes, oils, and plus-size lingerie.

While Baby Girl and her friends were walking the mall, she noticed this tall, dark-skin brother watching her. She knew he was checking her out because she had him on her radar as well. He had long black French braids going down his back; he had on a pair of Roca Wear jeans with a white wife beater with a pair of Nike Air Jordan XII playoffs. He looked like he had been pumping major weights. Homeboy's body was chisel from head to toe; he had six-pack abs, and he had the sexiest swagger Baby Girl had ever seen. She was rocking the hell out of this short-ass Donna Karen red mini dress with her six-inch stilettos to match, so she knew he was looking, and to make sure he was, she dropped her purse on purpose and bent over, so he could get a peep at her fat ample ass.

Baby Girl made it her business to walk over and introduce herself to this dark-skin brother who gained her attention; she had never seen a brother who was as dark as a Hershey bar—the brother in Baby Girl's mind was fine as blackberry wine. She introduced herself to him as Baby Girl; he told her, "Hold on, ma', I know that's not your government name, is it?" She said, "I'm sorry, boo. My name is Gloria. All right baby girl that sounds better."

Baby Girl asked him his name. He told her, "My name is Rodney. My friends call me Cash." Baby Girl kept staring at Cash's eyes because he looked familiar to someone she used to date, but she couldn't place them right then only if she knew Cash was the brother of Raymond. He was Raymond's younger brother from the same mother but different father; he knew all about Baby Girl from his brother. He knew that his brother was the one who got Baby Girl hooked on cocaine. What Cash didn't know was that Baby Girl didn't kill his brother; her mother Angel killed Raymond.

She admitted Baby Girl in a rehab and went back in the hood where Raymond hung out, selling drugs; he walked up to Angel's car, thinking that she was a junkie and stuck his head in her car window, and she shot his damn brains out and drove smooth—the fuck off didn't know body see nothing.

Cash knew that Baby Girl was the last person to see his brother alive, and he wanted to wreck havoc on her life; he didn't have any idea that he was treading on thin ice. He was about to ignite a fire that he wouldn't be able to put out. He exchanged numbers with Baby Girl, so they could meet up later that evening; they said their good-byes to each other, and Baby Girl left the mall, but she couldn't get the thought of Cash's eyes out of her head. It kept playing over and over; it interrupted her thoughts. Her and her girls were talking about how sexy Cash was, but they all agreed that his eyes made him look like the devil. Baby Girl wasn't threatened by him at all because she was an assassin. She stayed strapped even in class; she would take her .38 and keep it tucked in her backpack.

When Baby Girl and her friends made it back on campus, her cell phone started to vibrate on her side. She looked at it and saw it was her mother Angel calling. She picked it up and said, "Hi, Mom, what's up?" Angel asked her if she was still coming to Columbia on her summer vacation. She told Angel 'yes' and that her friends Olivia, Michelle, Ava, and Sophia would be there in three weeks as planned. Angel told Baby Girl that she would have everything ready when they arrived. She also told her daughter that she had something very important that she wanted to talk to her about once she got to Columbia because she didn't want to talk to her about business over the phone.

Baby Girl knew exactly where Angel was going with the conversation, so they cut it short. Before Angel hung up, she asked her daughter whether she was sure that Sophia and Michelle were coming with her to Columbia. She assured her mother that they were; when Angel met Sophia and Michelle for the first time, she knew they looked very familiar to her. They look like they could be related. The two young ladies also looked like her used-to-be best friends Abby and Gabriel. She wasn't sure, but she was most definitely going to find out.

Rodney a.k.a. Cash called Baby Girl that evening, and as planned he asked her if he could come and pick her up so they could go out to eat. She told Cash, "I don't get in cars with brothers. I don't know. How about we just meet up at the restaurant of your choice." He agreed to meet her at the crab shack at eight thirty. She said, "Cool, I'll see you there." What Baby Girl didn't know was Cash was bringing his partner, Crazy Red with him. Crazy Red and Cash was in the dope game together; they had just got a million dollar's worth of cocaine from their connect. This guy was a Dominican cat they called Steele. He was a multimillionaire; he had houses in Hawaii and the Caribbeans. He was well established. Cash knew that dealing with Crazy Red was a bad move, knowing he smoked crack and he loved showboating for the ladies, which was his downfall. He had pussy on the brains; he was the type of guy who would fuck a snake if you held his head still.

Baby Girl showed up at the crab shack at eight fifteen. Cash was impressed that she was on time; as soon as she walked in, Crazy Red started drooling at the mouth like a hungry pit bull. Cash said, "Damn man, put your tongue back in your damn mouth." Crazy Red told Cash that bitch there is fine as a T-bone steak; before Crazy Red could say another word, Cash told him to shut the fuck up before he messed up his plans.

Baby Girl sat down next to Cash, and he introduced her to Crazy Red; he asked Baby Girl whether she had any friends who were sexy like her. She told him, "Of course, I do."

"All right, so when can I meet one of your homegirls?"

She said, "I tell you what, come on campus with Cash Friday, and I'll see what I can do for you." Crazy Red was smiling like he had just hit the jackpot because in his mind if they looked halfway as fine as Baby Girl, he was going to make sure he spent a grip of his hustling money on her to make sure he kept her happy.

Gloria a.k.a. Baby Girl went to class the next morning with Cash on her mind; she had the feeling that she knew him somehow, but where she didn't know. As Baby Girl was leaving class, there were a lot of people standing around on the parking lot, screaming as if it was a fight or something, and she was hoping it was one of her friends, so she could put some hot lead in somebody. She and her friends were tight; Baby Girl had formed a clique. She called her crew the H&H, which stands for heavy hitters; even though she and her friends come from money, they robbed dope guys just for general principle.

When Baby Girl made it to the circle, where everyone was standing, it was a fight with this girl named Denise; she had been attending Spellman for two months. Baby Girl knew her from one of her classes; she didn't like what was going down. Denise was getting her ass whipped by four girls, who weren't even going to Spellman, over some nigga they called black that she had been sneaking around with. Baby Girl started pulling the girls one by one off Denise; she had been stomped so badly until she looked like she was black and blue. Denise was so glad to see somebody pull those bitches off her because she was losing consciousness fast. She told Baby Girl, "Thank you, I would always be grateful to you. Those crazy bitches tried to kill me."

Baby Girl told Denise she had to be careful because she was getting ready to go to Columbia for summer vacation; she wasn't going to be around to help her next time. Denise was a Puerto Rican; she stood five-feet six inches, weighing 145 pounds with a caramel complexion and shoulder-length red hair. She had ample breast and no ass in the ass department.

Both of Denise's parents worked for the Dominican Republic. Denise used to go to school in Puerto Rico; she went to the Universidad del sag ado Corazon in English. It is Sacred Heart University and one of the oldest and largest most prestigious institutions in Puerto Rico. Her parents wanted Denise to become a lawyer, but she disagreed with them on what they wanted her to be. She wanted to go to Spellman; she had a gift in contemporary arts.

Denise begged Baby Girl to let her come to Columbia with her; she told Denise she had to call her mom to get permission. Baby Girl called Angel to get permission, and Angel wanted all of Denise's information so she could investigate her as well. When Denise gave Baby Girl her info, Angel hung up, turned on her computer, and found out that Denise's parents worked for the

Dominican Republic; she said, "That's cool, I might be able to use them on down the line." She also found that Denise had a sister named Suzanne Mendez.

Angel had made her mind up that Abby and Gabriel would soon find out how she really felt about them; she wanted them dead in the worst kind of way. They would soon feel the destruction of Angel Carter for real. Before Baby Girl made it to Columbia with her friends, Angel had reports on all of them; she found out that Abby and Gabriel's daughters were Sophia and Michelle—only things that were different were their last names. Angel knew that they were her ex-man Mike Trivet's daughters. Mike was also Angel's brother from her father Cane, the Hawaiian kingpin, which would make his daughters Angel's nieces.

Angel was glad to see her daughter when she arrived in Columbia with her friends; she had sat up all night, thinking of regrouping a team of female soldiers. She even came up with a name for them; she was going to call them her own personal dream team. She first had to convince the girls that they would be making a shitload of money first and that she would supply them with everything they needed for their mast of destruction.

Angel asked Baby Girl if she could have a talk with her in private after breakfast; she also told Baby Girl's friends she had a proposition for them as well. They all were very curious to know what Angel had in mind for them, so they started eating breakfast very quickly, so they could get on with the proposition. After breakfast, all the girls headed to the den where Angel told them to come. Angel had reports on all the girls; she told them she was going to assemble a female dream team and if they were interested in being hired assassins; before she could finish what she was saying, all the girls agreed to help Angel in her mast of destruction on the rest of the Columbia cartel. She told the girls that they would be making a substantial amount of money on this job; she had already mapped things out. She had descriptions on each one of the men, and their hangouts—the Sanchez brothers and their father would hang out in a brothel called the baby doll.

Angel wanted the girls to get close enough to the Sanchez brothers to gain their trust; she knew every man's weakness was a female, so she wanted them to use their feminine side to get control over them and gain entrance into their villa. She explained to the girls every detail of what their job consisted of, and they all agreed that they could handle the situation, but Angel wanted the girls to have some training in handling the heavy artillery. Uncle Leo set up the shooting range near his artillery compound, so the girls could learn how to shoot first hand; he was shocked to see that Olivia could handle weapons of any kind very well. He asked her how and where she got her skills. She told Uncle Leo that her father was in the military; he taught her everything there was about guns. She even knew how to break them down and clean them.

While the girls were getting their training, Angel and Baby Girl were in the house, discussing how they were going to kill the Sanchez brothers with this poisonous plant that she picked up from an old lady she met, who came to visit Columbia from South America. The plant was called Brugmansia; the effects of this plant could cause paralysis of smooth muscles, confusion, diarrhea, migraine headaches, visual and auditory hallucinations, rapid onset cyclopedia, and death.

Angel wanted to use the {Brugmansia} plant in decongestant form; if concentrated in a refined form, derivatives of Brugmansia were also used for murder, seduction, and robbery. Angel and Baby Girl decided to boil the plant and mix its juices with a homemade blackberry wine. Angel had two identical bottles. She had one preserved for the brothers and one for her dream team; only difference between the two bottles was that Baby Girl marked an x on the bottle that she and the girls would be drinking from; the poisonous bottle would have a p under the bottom for poison. Once Angel got the wine bottles together, it was time to get the girls attire ready for the seduction and the murder of the Sanchez brothers.

Angel called one last meeting with her dream team before she got them ready for their dates. She had a serious sex 101 with them; she let the girls know that men think with one side of their brains—men like to see things and visualize, men hunt—whereas on the other hand women think with the other side of their brain—we like to feel comfortable and nest. She asked them have they ever experienced sex with a man. In the whole group, Baby Girl was the only one that wasn't a virgin. Angel was in awe that her daughter had her cherry popped without her knowing; the girls' adrenaline was racing, waiting to hear what Angel had to say about sex that they already knew. They just hadn't demonstrated it yet. I need you girls to be rough riders tonight. Don't let the guys talk you into the missionary position that is too personal, and it could get really intense. If you're not riding him, go into the vertical position. That way, you can stimulate his dick and wear him out.

Angel had the girls to go and get ready for their night out on the town; the Sanchez brothers were waiting but didn't have a clue that their demise was closer than they thought. All the girls came out, looking just like they stepped-off America's top model; they were gorgeous, and they all were rocking seven jeans with bra tops and leather jackets, all in different colors; they had on six-inch stilettos, and all were carrying mp 5 submachine guns that was strapped to their holsters under their jackets. Baby Girl also had some silver haze weed; it had the ability to go overboard with your sexual appetite. Baby Girl had a secret weapon of her own; she had twenty milligrams of cyanide. She knew the effect of the cyanide was a nerve-damaging disorder that would render any person unsteady and uncoordinated, and if the twenty milligrams didn't do the trick, she had her machete as backup as well.

Angel rolled behind the girls on the way to the brothel baby doll where the Sanchez brothers hung out. When Angel's dream team walked in the brothel, it was like time completely stopped all eyes were on them. That's exactly how the dream team wanted it; they all went straight to the bar. They ordered five apple martinis. As soon as their drinks were put in front of them, this tall dark and handsome guy with dark curly hair told the bartender I got this man their drinks on me. It was Josh Sanchez, the father of John, Daniel, Charles, and Anthony Sanchez; all the Sanchez brothers were accounted for and their father. All the dream team could think about was let the party begin. All the brothers came over to the bar and introduced themselves, and two drinks later, everyone was headed back to the Sanchez villa. They were all split up into couples: Baby Girl was with Josh, the father, in the den. She wanted to take him down personally herself because she knew he was the head nigga in charge; he might be more of a challenge than his sons.

Baby Girl went into the kitchen to get the wine and the wine glasses; she poured all the men a full glass of the poisonous wine. They rolled up some of the silver haze weed, and you could smell the aroma from the weed all through the house. They were all over the house, fucking like rabbits. When Baby Girl came down the hallway, she could see Olivia having sex with Anthony on top of the dining room table; he had her in the linguini position. He was teasing her g-spot while reaching around her and playing with her clitoris—covering all her pressure points. When Baby Girl was on her way back into the den, she saw some rocking in one of the bedrooms, so she decided to peep into the room. It was Charles and Sophia. They were in a slow and sensuous lovemaking move called the canoe canoodle position; the rocking motion of the boat will intensify each of his internal strokes. Baby Girl said to herself, "Shit, the whole house is getting their freak on, and it's time to shut this party down." When she made it back to the den, Josh was nodding like a junkie who had just hit the pipe. Baby Girl had already put a little cyanide in josh's wine, so she knew he was going to be a easy target, but when she saw him shaking his head and trying to call one of his sons, she got behind him, took out her machete, and cut his head clean off.

When Baby Girl went back in the front of the house to see how the other girls were doing, she saw that they were piling the rest of the Sanchez men in the middle of the floor. They weren't even dead; they were just unconscious. What they did next was unreal: they poured gasoline all over their bodies and sat the house on fire. They burned the Sanchez men alive; the house went up in flames. Angel was sitting outside while the girls were walking back to their car. She was proud that they hit their targets so fast. She gave each one of her soldiers fifty thousand dollars apiece. Angel had two more weeks to spend with her daughter, so she decided to take them to Jamaica for some fun in the sun. She needed a break herself, plus she wanted to get to know her personal dream team and to establish some personal ground rules as her assassins.

Chapter 2
Abby and Gabriel Striking Back

ABBY AND GABRIEL left Hawaii and headed to Spellman; they were going there to surprise their daughters, only to find out that their daughters weren't there and they didn't even know where they could be found. They were so upset because their daughters never missed a day of calling their mothers and checking in. Abby told Gabriel, "Let's go to the dean's office to see if he has any information on their whereabouts." When they made it to the dean's office, he was coming out of the door. He was leaving for the evening when Abby asked if she could have a word with him, concerning her daughter Sophia Smith. Gabriel also asked where was her daughter Michelle Jones. The dean told Gabriel that he had passed the girl in the hallway when they were leaving; he told them that they were with a friend of theirs named Gloria Carter.

Abby and Gabriel looked like they had swallowed a canary because they both knew if their daughters were with Angel's daughter, then they were headed for trouble, and they were not about to let Angel get her mitts on their daughters. Abby and Gabriel went and checked into the Hilton inn; they weren't leaving until their daughters returned. Abby was so angry that she started to tremble because she knew personally that Angel was dangerous with a capital D. Gabriel, on the other hand, was deep in thought. She was coming up with a solution to get rid of Angel once and for all. While Gabriel was deep in thought, a light switched pop on in her head about two of her father's friends that was up state in Rikers islands prison. They both were serving time on some chomped up charges; they happen to be at the wrong place at the wrong time. They happen to be at a bar one night flirting with a woman only to find out that the woman was really a man dressed in women clothing. When Montana Blackwell a.k.a king was hugged up tongue kissing the woman and reach down between her legs only to find out that he was packing the same kind of hardware as him, he jumped up, burst a beer bottle, acrossed his head. Brandon Lewis a.k.a. the candy man was sitting back in the cut when another gay guy came from behind and hit Montana with a right hook; he stumbled backward and Brandon caught him before he could hit the floor.

Montana and Brandon were supposed to be on the other side of town on a job site; both men were on a three-year probation period. When the bartender called the police, they were rolled back to do their three-year sentences. Gabriel went to the prison to pay Montana and Brandon a visit; they had been in prison for two and a half years. They were going to be released in two weeks for good behavior. When the guard called their names for a visit, they were shocked because no one came to visit them the whole time they were inside the walls. When they looked up to see Gabriel with this look of concern on her face, they knew something was wrong, and it really had her spooked. Montana asked Gabriel what had her spooked and was everything all right with her daughter. She gave the two men the whole run down on Angel; she also told them that she would pay both of them a hundred thousand dollars if they took Angel Carter off the map.

Brandon and Montana agreed to help Gabriel and Abby out of the sticky situation they were in with Angel. Gabriel told Montana that she would be there to pick them up when they got released in two weeks. When Gabriel made it back to the hotel and told Abby that their worries will be over soon, she wanted to know what Gabriel was talking about, so she discussed the details to Abby about the hit she just took out on Angel.

Abby and Gabriel left their numbers with the dean, just in case their daughters came back to school before their summer break was over. While Abby and Gabriel were waiting on their daughters to show up at Spellman, the girl'swere sunbathing in Jamaica. The girls had three more days before their mother would see them. Angel had Ramon to get the jet fueled, so when they got to Columbia, the dream team would be headed straight back to Spellman. Meanwhile Gabriel had two days left before she went to pick up Brandon and Montana from Rikers prison. Abby told Gabriel since these guys are going to be our hired guns, we could at least go to the mall and buy them at least a dress out outfit, so they won't look so suspicious.

Baby Girl and the dream team made it back to Columbia and were getting ready to go back to Atlanta to school. The dean was on the lookout for Sophia and Michelle. Abby had given the dean five thousand dollars to call her as soon as the girls got there. While the girls were on their way to Spellman, Abby and Gabriel were on their way to pick up Montana and Brandon; their timing was on point because Gabriel wanted them to stalk Baby Girl, so she could lead them back to her mother Angel.

Abby rented Montana and Brandon a black impala; she also took the men on Spellman campus, so they could sit and watch Baby Girl's every move. Gabriel gave them pictures of Angel. The only picture they had of Baby Girl was the picture that the dean gave them. When the girls rolled up on campus, Montana and Brandon were already sitting three rows back from Baby Girl's 2011 burgundy ford excursion with cream color leather seats, sitting on 26-inch spinners. Baby Girl was going to class the next morning and spotted the black Impala sitting three rows down from her truck. She was a trained assassin; she knew when shit was out of order, so she thought that she would pull these fool cord to see what was up.

Baby Girl had Denise to run out the dorm room, screaming to get their attention. When Brandon heard the screaming, he was the first one to get out of the car, and Montana followed suit. While they were trying to find out what was going on, Baby Girl snuck into their car and put a recorder under the seat. She wanted to know why these two men were hanging around campus, taking pictures of her and watching her every move. When she got back into her dormroom Olivia was telling the dream team that they were invited to a party off campus, and they all agreed to go. When Baby Girl and her friends pulled off the parking lot, so did the black impala. When they got to the party, Cash and Crazy Red were there, so she asked Crazy Red would he do her a favor and start an argument with Denise. For her, he would do anything; he didn't ask any question and did what he was told only because he had his antennas up soon as he saw Denise, when he grabbed Denise and told her to play along, she did. Montana and Brandon got out of the car again because they were there to protect Sophia and Michelle as well.

While Montana and Brandon were out of their car, Baby Girl snuck in and got the recorder. When she ran inside the party, she went straight to the bathroom to listen to the recorder, only to find out that Abby and Gabriel had hired these two men to kill her mother and follow her to see if she would lead them to her mother. When Baby Girl heard the recorder, she called her mother immediately. she cut it up loud enough so that Angel could hear the names Abby and Gabriel. She got so angry; she told her daughter to keep her composure and that she would be in Atlanta the first thing tomorrow morning. The next morning, Abby and Gabriel were in the dean's office, waiting on Sophia and Michelle to come to the dean's office; they were glad to see their daughters were fine, but after the happy reunion was over, they lit into them like flies on shit, but when it was all said and done, they remembered what Angel told them never give up your location.

Abby and Gabriel knew that Angel had her hands in what was going on with their daughters. They knew firsthand how Angel worked; they wanted Angel wiped out sooner than later because they weren't about to let her destroy their daughters' lives. When Abby and Gabriel left Spellman defeated because their daughters wouldn't give up any information on their whereabouts, they decided to stick around a little while longer to keep a closer eye on them. While Abby and Gabriel were on their way to have breakfast, Angel and Ramon was fueling up the jet to head to Spellman after Baby Girl called Angel last night and gave her the heads up on the two men in the Impala who were sitting outside on Spellman's campus ground and were sent to kill her, and they were hired by Abby and Gabriel; she was more than happy to oblige them in their quest.

Angel went to the gun house to get her artillery she was taking with her. She wanted something that will take a nigga down with one shot; she came up with her strategy and tactics to approach the situation. She wanted to use some characteristic of guerrilla warfare but on a smaller scale. She was about to give Brandon and Montana the element of surprise. While Angel was in the gun house looking for her weapon of choice, she looked up on the wall to see a machine pistol Steyr M1912. She like the way it felt in her hand. She loved the fully automatic pistol. She also pick the Tec 9; she chose these two weapons because they had armor-piercing rounds instead of pistol ammunition. Angel also decided to take the flamethrower just in case she had to set fire to a nigga's ass; she didn't want the flammable liquid, the one she took with her was the one with the long gas flame.

When Angel and Ramon loaded up the jet with their artillery, they were headed to Atlanta; she had already called ahead to check in to the Ramada inn. What Angel didn't know was Gabriel had checked Montana and Brandon into the same hotel, but in reality, they only went there to shower because they slept in their car on Spellman campus ground, which would be to Angel's advantage because she would soon catch them, slipping up. When they made it to Atlanta, they went to enterprise and rented a black-on-black charger with tinted windows. Angel texted Baby Girl to let her know that she had made it to Atlanta, and She and Ramon were sitting two rows back from the hired killers. She also let Baby Girl know that they would be going to home depot to purchase an electric saw because she had very different plans for Abby and Gabriel. She wanted them to feel the fire from fucking with Angel Carter.

Angel decided to rent a boat to carry out her demise for Abby and Gabriel. She first wanted to take care of their hit men. She came up with a plan to sneak up on them. When it got dark, she knew their stupid assess would fall asleep sooner or later, and when they did, she was going to be their last nightmare. Angel and Ramon purchased the saw and made it back on campus in record time. Montana and Brandon were just pulling back up; they had gone to Kentucky Fried Chicken to pick them up some lunch. Angel told Ramon this is going to be easier than I thought because soon as they finish eating they are going to fall asleep, but I want to wait until it gets dark, so we can kidnap them because I'm not going to kill them where my daughter goes to school at.

While Angel and Ramon were sitting on campus ground, watching their targets, Abby and Gabriel were spending their time shopping at the mall enjoying their free time, because they knew sooner or later Baby Girl was going to trip up and lead the two killers to her mother. What their dum assess didn't know was Angel taught her daughter well. She could spot targets a mile away, and Montana and Brandon didn't have a chance. They would soon find out that Brandon and Montana weren't a match for an assassin like Angel.

Angel waited to six that evening; the sun was whining down. It started to get dark. She wanted to kill them so badly that she could taste their blood in her mouth. She noticed this spot that was an empty apartment complex that was being worked on, on the south side of home depot when she and Ramon were there, buying the saw. She told Ramon that would be a good place to dispose off their bodies. Angel had even bought some chloroform; she wanted to make sure once they snuck up behind them that they would stay asleep until they made it to their destination, breathing in the chemical put them at a greater risk of being exposed to contamination.

Two hours later, the sun had gone completely down, and Montana and Brandon were sitting in the car, smoking silver haze—the weed had the men high as kites. They both were getting the munchies; they were about to make a snack run when they heard a loud boom sound. When they turned around to see what was going on, it was too late. Ramon threw a smoke bomb in the back window of their car. It was smoke everywhere; they couldn't see, so they crawled out of the car. Angel jumped on Brandon's back, wrapped her hand over his nose with the chloroform towel, and his body went limp. Ramon followed suit; he had a rough time with Montana because he tried to wrestle Ramon down with him, but Angel hit him in the side with her stun-gun, and he went out like a light switch.

Ramon put both men in the trunk on top of each other; they slept the whole time, while Angel was driving to the empty apartment complex. When they pulled up to the complex, they drugged the men out of the trunk and tied them up. Angel slapped them to wake them up. She wanted to hear them say who sent them. She got their attention quick. When she said, "if you tell me who was gunning for my head, I promise you I'll let you live, but if you lie to me, I will take your testicles and torture them electrically," Angel sent Ramon to the car to take the battery out. She told him to bring the jumper cables also. When Brandon heard her say battery and jumper cables, he was the first one to speak. Montana wasn't going out like no bitch he wanted to die holding on to his manhood and without his balls.

Angel asked the question only once. When Ramon returned with the battery and jumper cables, Brandon started singing like Freddie Jackson at live concert. Ramon was happy he was on the opposite side because when it came to torturing a man, Angel showed no sympathy. She did shit to men that gave Ramon nightmares; he just knew not to ever threaten Angel's life. Angel hooked the cables to Montana's balls first since he wanted to play hard. She wanted to see if his ass pumped kool-aid or blood; it was later that he spilled blood from his balls like tomato sauce. You could hear him screaming from under the tape. Angel had cover his mouth with tape and that scared Brandon shit-less; he knew he was next because assassins used whatever tactics they wanted to get information. He knew at the end of the day you were going to be just another fucking body with a tag on your toe. Montana bleed to death from the electric shock Angel was putting on his ass. Brandon gave up Abby and Gabriel. He also told Angel their room numbers at the Hilton inn. Right after he gave up their location, Ramon looked at him as being a snitch, he told Angel to take his bitch ass out of his misery. Angel shot Brandon with her Tec 9 until it was empty. After both men were dead, Angel took the flamethrower and burned their bodies completely up; their bones were even charred.

Chapter 3
The Murder of Abby and Gabriel

ANGEL AND RAMON were sitting outside the Hilton, waiting to catch Abby and Gabriel. Stalking her targets was Angel's favorite part of the job. She knew one day she would cross paths with her so-called friends again, and it wasn't going to be a pretty sight. Abby felt kind of strange that day because they haven't heard anything from Montana or Brandon; she suggested to Gabriel that they should give them a call to see if they made any progress in the whereabouts of Angel. What Abby and Gabriel didn't know was that Angel was closer than they thought. When Gabriel called Montana's cell phone, it went straight to his voicemail, so she tried Brandon's cell, and his phone did the same thing. She knew something was terribly wrong because they would always answer their phone.

Gabriel looked at Abby with the scariest look on her face that made Abby's heart skip a beat. Abby knew all too well where the look was coming from. She personally didn't want to cross paths with Angel, but they will soon find out that Angel Carter will soon be their last nightmare. Abby came up with the idea to go up on Spellman's campus grounds to see if Montana and Brandon's car was still sitting there. If it was and they wasn't in it, that will let them know for sure that Angel had gotten wind that they were camped out stalking Baby Girl to get to her. When Abby and Gabriel drove up and saw the car was still there, and it was vacant, their assumptions were right; something had happened to them, and it frighten Abby to death.

Gabriel and Abby wanted to go snatch their daughters out of class and disappear but that wasn't going to be easy because Angel and Ramon were hot on their trail; they were following them the whole time. Abby and Gabriel were smart; they knew one day that Angel would catch up to them, so they had all the information on Angel stashed in their safes, just in case one day they meet their demise. When Abby and Gabriel got back in their car to leave the parking lot, Angel told Ramon she was going to force them to a dead in street and kidnap both of them. While Abby was driving, she had a funny feeling that they were being followed, so she looked up into her rearview mirror, and she spotted this black charger coming up behind them, so she speeded up. She came to an alley sitting to her right, and she turn down the alley, only to hit a big dumpster someone left sitting right in the middle of the alley. She hit the dumpster so hard that the air-bag knocked Gabriel out-cold, and Abby's head hit the steering wheel and busted her forehead. She wasn't out, but her head hurt like hell.

Angel and Ramon jumped out of the car and ran up to the car where Abby and Gabriel were slumped over in and grabbed both of them out and put them in the backseat of the charger. Ramon sat in the backseat with them; he told Abby if she said anything, he would shoot her in the head. Gabriel was still out from the blow of the airbag, so they didn't have a problem with her. Angel headed straight to the boat arena; she had it set up because she had big plans for her so-called friends. She wanted them to suffer a slow-and-agonizing death. She and Ramon set them up and duct taped their legs arms and mouth; she then poured water on Gabriel to wake her up. When she opened her eyes and saw Angel, she tried to scream, but she couldn't her mouth was taped up, so she started, squirming around trying to get a loose.

Angel snatched the tape off their mouth, so she could tell them what was going to happen to them; she wanted to hear what they had to say about sending two hit men after her. Angel bent down to eye level with them, so they could see the seriousness she had in her eyes before she killed them. She had two questions to ask them. She said, "I can't believe, I let you two bitches live and leave town, and you two stupid bitches had the nerve to come back for revenge. My first question is why were you sitting up in court, gloating at my trial? My second question is why did you guys hire some hit men to kill me? When you should have tried to take me out yourselves." Abby was so afraid that she blamed Gabriel for everything. Angel told her to shut the fuck up because you share just as much blame as she does, so you both are going to share the same fate.

When Angel told Ramon to go get the electric saw, Abby literally passed out because she knew Angel was going to make them suffer in the worst way. Angel started up the saw; she cut off Gabriel's legs first and then she just started cutting her body up piece by piece until she got to her head. She was like a different person to Ramon; it fucked him up to see Angel in that kind of light; he knew she was assassin, but he never saw her in full form before. When Angel was through with Gabriel, she tossed her body over board, so the sharks could eat her flesh. She then started on Abby. Abby was still unconscious; she didn't see what happen to Gabriel. She did notice a lot of blood running on the floor of the boat; she automatically started pissing on herself because Angel had a death grip on the saw she had in her hands.

Angel looked at Abby and said, "Bitch, you're next. I will kill you just like I did Gabriel." Abby said, "Please, Angel, I have nothing to do with the hit men coming after you." Angel said, "Oh, but you did. You two bitches have been a thorn in my ass, and after today, I'm not going to have to worry about finding you and killing you as of today it's a wrap. Now shut up, bitch." Abby was hysterical she couldn't be still, so Ramon knocked her out with one punch, and he went down on the lower level of the boat; he didn't want to see Angel in action again; this time Angel started with Abby's head. She cut her head smooth off and then she cut her in half. Once she was done, she threw Abby over board as well. She and Ramon cleaned up the boat, wiped it down clean, and took it back to the arena.

Angel and Ramon headed back to Spellman to let Baby Girl know that they took care of the situation, and she didn't have to watch her back as far as the two hit men. Angel didn't tell her daughter that Abby and Gabriel were dead; she wanted to tell her later on. She was exhausted and ready to go back to Columbia and rest up because next week she and Ramon would be headed to Ohio to pick up little Ramon at Aunt Marie's house.

Angel knew she would one day deal with her nieces, once they found out about their mothers' disappearance; the only thing about that situation was that they would never find their bodies unless a shark turn up dead on dry land, and they cut it open to find the remains of Abby and Gabriel. That she wasn't worry about because by the time the sharks get through eating up their flesh, nothing would be left but a few human bones. A couple of days had passed since Sophia and Michelle had talked to their mothers; they were starting to worry because their cell phones were turned off. They knew their mothers had rooms at the Hilton, so they decided to go check on them, only to find out that they hadn't been in their rooms for two day since the last time they talked with them. Michelle broke down in tears because she felt in her heart that something had happen to them. While they were still there at the Hilton, the police came by because they found the car in the alley that Abby and Gabriel had rented from enterprise, and they were no where to be found. That really shuck them up; they both were in tears because they couldn't come up with explanation for what had happen to their parents. They made a police report and went back to campus, but both girls stayed up all night talking to the other members of the dream team, trying to make sense out of their mothers' disappearance. Baby Girl had a good idea of what happened, but she wasn't about to let them in on her mother killing their parents. She just wished her mother would have told her beforehand that she killed Abby and Gabriel.

Chapter 4
Angel and Ramon Going to Ohio

ANGEL AND RAMON flew out to Aunt Marie's house in Ohio to pick up little Ramon; he had been staying with Angel's Aunt until the war was over in Columbia with the Columbia cartel. Now that they were dead, it was time to bring their son back home. Angel had been calling Aunt Marie for the last couple of days, and she hadn't been answering her phone. She didn't want to tell Ramon; she felt something was wrong. She had called her a couple of times last week, and she got the same response, so she wasn't going to say anything this time either because they were about to land in two hours, so she thought time will tell sooner than later. When they got to the airport and rented a car, they headed straight to Aunt Marie's house, only to find the house empty, so she went next door to Aunt Marie's friend's house to see if she knew what was going on because the house was vacant by this time. Angel and Ramon had gotten angry; they wanted to know where the hell was their son.

When Mrs. Mary told Angel that her Aunt Marie had a heart attack and died two weeks ago, she was stunned. She couldn't believe that no one contacted her about her son, but then it dawned on her didn't anyone know about her and her Aunt Marie. Angel asked Mrs. Mary whether she know what happened to her son. She told Angel that she took care of him until social services came and took him away from her. Angel asked her whether she happened to have the address or phone number to social services. She said, "sure." This lady named Cynthia Green left her card for anyone who came looking for the baby. Angel took the card and dialed the number to find out that Miss Green was out of the office for lunch, so her and Ramon went to the social services to wait until she came back in from lunch.

When Miss Green was out for lunch, she went by the daycare center to check up on whether the baby was kept clean . She wanted to adopt the baby herself; she was hoping no one would come to look for him. She thought, *he was the prettiest little baby she had ever seen*; she spent a lot of time with the baby because instead of putting him in foster care, she kept the baby at her house. She fell in love with the baby at first sight. When she came back from lunch, Angel and Ramon were waiting in her office. She asked them if she could help them with anything, and Angel told her sure you can. My Aunt Marie Black died two weeks ago, and she was taking care of my son Raj Ramon Carter. He turned six months old today, and we were told social services came and picked him up from Mary Joseph, a friend of my aunt who stayed next door.

Miss Green knew exactly who they were talking about because Aunt Marie had told Mrs. Mary if anything ever happened to her, take care of the baby until Angel came to pick him up, and that's what she told Miss Green that his mother was away on business, and she would be back to pick her son up soon. Mrs. Green looked at Angel and said, "What kind of mother drops their son off with a sickly old lady?" Angel told her, "First of all my Aunt didn't show any signs of being sick. She was always healthy as a horse." She told Angel, "Well, according to my report that I received from her neighbors, she had been suffering from heart problems for two years." Angel told Miss Green, "I didn't come here to discuss my personal family business with you. I came here to get my son."

Miss Green gave Angel hell. She wanted to take her through all the red tape there was before she turned over little Ramon to her. She asked Angel, "How do I know that you are his biological parents. All I see is a birth certificate with your names on it. I would have to discuss this with my supervisor." Angel stood up; she was ready to attack Miss Green until Ramon grabbed her hand. He said, "Wrong place, wrong time, baby. Wait, just think about our son. After we get our son back, you can whip her ass if that's what you want to do, but right now this is about our son, all right. Now let's just do what she wants."

"I need you two to go downstairs to the lab to take a blood test. If it comes back that you are Ramon's parent, he will be here waiting to go home with you in the morning." But to be honest she didn't really want to hand little Ramon over to Angel. She didn't like the way Angel just up and left her baby with her sick aunt.

The next morning wasn't coming fast enough for Angel. She couldn't sleep. She and Ramon had been up all night. Ramon even told Angel, "I don't like that bitch. She's up to something. I can feel it. If she doesn't have our son at that office in the morning, I'm going to strangle that bitch with my bare hands until she tells us where he is." Angel took a shower and was ready to go back to social services. She looked in the bedroom to see if Ramon was dressed, but he was already waiting in the car; he was more ready to get there than Angel was. He wasn't taking any chances; he felt that Miss Green was trying to pull the wool over their eyes, and he wasn't having it.

When Angel and Ramon walked into social services, Miss Green was standing there with her supervisor. She had this look on her face like "yeah you two think you are just going to walk in here and take little Ramon without an explanation." What Miss Green didn't know was the test came back in favor of Angel and Ramon; they were little Ramon's parents, and there was nothing she could do about. Her supervisor, Mrs. Porter, had the results in her files; she also had their son waiting in the other room. She had only one request for Angel because she was a dear friend of Angel's Aunt Marie. She knew all the details behind Angel's leaving her baby with her Aunt. She just wanted to make sure that Angel gave her Aunt a proper funeral.

Angel told Mrs. Porter that she intended on sending her Aunt home in a special way; she loved her Aunt because she was there for her more ways than one, so she owed her more than that, and she will be missed in her heart forever. Angel and Ramon got their son back and made funeral arrangements for Aunt Marie; they also paid for it to go in the town's newspaper in Ohio, just in case any of her friends wanted to attend her home going. She was a sweet person to anyone who needed her help. Angel was in awe when she saw the turnout at Aunt Marie's funeral. It was packed; she was known for her good deeds from a whole lot of people, and they thanked Angel for including them in her home-going services.

After the funeral was over, they went to the cemetery and went back home to Columbia, angel gave money to a lot of Marie's friends; they knew their lives would never be the same without her. She would forever be missed by everyone in her town that knew her as mother Marie. She kept a lot of runaway teens off the street when they had no place else to go she kept them safe. Angel was heartless, but she felt guilty for what happen to her Aunt, so before she left Ohio, she opened up a group home for runaways in her Aunt Marie's name. That turn of events surprised the hell out of Ramon, but he still thought that it was a good gesture on Angel's part.

Chapter 5
Baby Girl and Her H&H Team

GLORIA A.K.A. BABY Girl met up with Cash on another date. She was one step ahead of him this time. Since their first date, he had his friend Crazy Red with him on their date, so this time, she took Denise with her since Crazy Red was falling for her. When Cash saw Baby Girl walking in the restaurant with Denise, he knew Crazy Red was going to be all over her like flies on shit. Cash and Crazy Red had been together all day, cooking and cutting up cocaine, plus they had been smoking blunts too, so both of them were as hungry as a hostage. Crazy Red asked Denise what she was going to be doing after they finished dinner. She said, "Nothing. What's up? What do you want to do?"

"I want to take you to some place with me if you're free tonight."

She said, "Cool, let's go." Denise was feeling good about Crazy Red because he kept her laughing at his crazy ass jokes, so she really didn't mind spending time with him.

What Denise didn't know was she was in for a ride of her life. Crazy Red was a for-real freak. He looked at Denise as if she was a steak dinner with two side orders. Crazy Red took Denise to his crib for a lovemaking session. When Denise walked in his crib, he offered her a glass of Cristal, and she accepted; he lit up a blunt, and they started smoking. Next thing you know Crazy Red was dancing around in Denise face. He started stripping; she looked up, and his dick was swinging in her face like an eight-inch polish sausage.

Denise couldn't control her vagina; she was getting wet just looking at his chiseled hard body, and Crazy Red felt the heat her body was throwing off. One thing leads to another, and they wind up in Crazy Red's bedroom, having the most hot and intense sex Denise had ever had. She was screaming Crazy Red's name in tongue, and he was enjoying every minute of it until he flipped her ass

25

over to enter her asshole. She almost slid right from under him; he said, "Come on girl, stop tripping. You know what time it is."

Denise told Crazy Red, "I don't know what type of bitches you've been with, but, nigga, it hurts me to shit, so since you are not my doctor, and I'm not scheduled to get a colonoscopy, you can get on with that shit."

Crazy Red told Denise, "I thought that you were down for whatever."

"Well, sweetie, you thought wrong. I'm not upping, no ass unless I'm married to you, and I'm still going be tripping then."

Crazy Red was so distraught about what went down with him and Denise; he tried to get her to calm down, but she didn't want to hear it. She was ready to go until he went into his closet and pulled out a duffle bag of money. He knew if nothing else, this would get her attention, and he was definitely right. She sat there quiet to see what this crazy ass nigga's next move would be. He told her all of him and Cash's business; he even told her how much money they had in the duffle bag. It was at least one million dollars in that bag and five ki's of cocaine in the closet.

Denise knew this fool was crazy for real; you never bring your product where you lay your head, but it's cool because he is going to hate that he ever dropped that kind of information on Denise. That night with Crazy Red was enough for Denise; she decided to go back on campus.

Crazy Red said, "Hold up, Denise. I thought you were going to spend the night with me."

"If you thought that, you were seriously mistaking." Denise grabbed her clothes, put them back on, and left.

Baby Girl got to class the next morning, looking for Denise. When she didn't see her, she wanted to know what happened with her and Crazy Red. Denise didn't show up at class that day, and Baby Girl got worried about her because she heard from Cash that he earned that name Crazy Red for a reason. When Baby Girl's class was over, she went looking for Denise. She found her sitting in her car, smoking a blunt and crying. She gave her every detail of the event with Crazy Red. She even told her about the money, when all of a sudden a light pop on in Baby Girl's head.

She said, "I'm sorry that nigga played you like that, but don't worry, it's time for him to pay the piper."

Baby Girl called a meeting with the dream team; she knew she was the muscle of the team, so she came up with a name for them outside of the dream team. She came into the idea of them robbing dope boys and taking everything they had from dope to money, guns, and their life if they didn't release their shit. When Baby Girl told her crew that she was starting up a new crew for them while they were in Atlanta, they were down with it. That way they could keep their skills on point. Olivia asked Baby Girl what was their name going to be.

She said, "H&H."

Ava said, "What the hell do that shit stand for?"

Baby Girl said, "Heavy hitters."

She said, "All right, I like that. Are we going to wear ski mask like the jump out boys?"

She said, "Yes, we are, and we all are going to carry 9 mm with shoulder holsters."

Gloria a.k.a. Baby Girl came up with the idea to rob Crazy Red for his million dollars and his dope, and the H&H crew decided to go along with Baby Girl for the big haul. Denise wanted to pay Crazy Red back for what he tried to do to her, so Baby Girl put her in motion for the setup. Denise was to set up another date with Crazy Red and make him believe that she was down with the anal sex. After class, the next day Denise called Crazy Red to make a date with him for that night; first they were to go to dinner like they did before, and while they were at dinner, Baby Girl and her crew would be posted up outside the restaurant, waiting to follow them back to Crazy Red's crib. Baby Girl told Denise to ask Crazy Red if she could drive to the restaurant; that way she could leave the alarm off the car. While they were in the restaurant, she could sneak into the back of the car and lay down on the floor, so when they made it back to Crazy Red's house, she could knock him out from behind as soon as they pulled up and parked in his driveway.

Baby Girl knew how weak Crazy Red was from listening to how Cash would degrade him about women, so she knew he was a natural-born sucker. What Baby Girl and her crew didn't know was Crazy Red had made plans to have a threesome; he already had a girl at his crib, a girl named candy who was a porn star. He hired her before Denise made plans to go to dinner with him. As soon as they pulled up to Crazy Red's crib, Denise noticed the lights were on. She said, "Did you leave your lights on?"

He said, "No, that's what I wanted to tell you. I have a surprise inside my house for you if you are game for it."

What Crazy Red didn't know was that Denise had surprise waiting for him as well.

When Baby Girl heard that, she rose up from off the backseat of the car and hit Crazy Red so hard in the back of his head with a Billy club she retrieved from the security guard at their school. The H&H crew was parked down the street from Crazy Red's crib. Baby Girl had texted them to let them know that she was ready. Crazy Red was out cold, lying up against the window of his car;

the only thing they had to do next was to get his keys out of his pocket and carry him inside his crib. All five members of the team had to carry him inside. Baby Girl took the keys and opened the door when they got inside, Candy didn't even come out of the bedroom to see who was entering the house because she just knew it was Crazy Red, but when she heard a female voice, she came out of the bedroom buck naked, thinking that the party was going to get started until she saw a group of women holding guns with face masks. Baby Girl told Candy, "Bitch, if you make a sound, I'll blow your fucking brains all over the wall." Candy froze right in her tracks. Baby Girl told Sophia to take Candy in the bedroom to get her clothes and bring her back into the living room where they had already tied up Crazy Red.

When Sophia made it back in the living room with Candy, they tied her up also, so Baby Girl told the H&H girls to go look for the money and the dope. Denise was the ring leader because she saw where Crazy Red kept the money. When they went to the closet, the money and drugs had been moved, so they had to wake Crazy Red up. When Baby Girl threw that ice-cold water in Crazy Red's face, he woke up screaming, "Bitch, I'm going to fuck you up. What do you bitches want?" He didn't even remember being knocked out. He looked up at Denise and said, "Bitch, you set me up. I'll kill you and every one, who's some kin to you, bitch." Baby Girl said, "Listen here, bitch ass nigga, you're not going to make it out of here alive if you don't tell us where the money is, and I'm only going to ask once, so you better not lie you know what time it is." Crazy Red looked at Baby Girl and said, "Bitch, you just going to have kill me because I'm not telling you bitches shit." Baby Girl told Denise, Sophia, and Ava to strip Crazy Red out of his clothes. When they untied him, he came up swinging. Baby Girl took the butt end of her 9 mm and broke Crazy Red's jaw; he went down like a ton of bricks.

They stripped him out of his clothes, put him back in the chair, and tied him back up with his dick hanging; he was in so much pain from the blow Baby Girl gave him until he could barely talk. When he saw that Baby Girl wasn't playing, he started to sing like Keith Sweat at a live concert. Baby Girl had the girls to go look in the floor safe, and the million dollars was there, but the dope wasn't there, so she went up and got between Crazy Red's legs and asked him where are the drugs; he spit blood in Baby Girl's face. She got up, went in his kitchen, and got a butcher knife and cut Crazy Red's dick wide open; he was screaming like a banshee. When he finally stopped screaming, he told Baby Girl that the drugs were in the couch. She told her girls to flip the couch over. When they did, they saw where the couch had been ripped and sewed back up; they ripped it back open, and the drugs were right where Crazy Red said they were.

Baby Girl looked at Crazy Red and said, "You made a good decision, but by you giving us shit, you are going to die, but before we kill you, Denise wants to show you how it feel to get fucked in the ass." Crazy Red looked at Denise with fear in his eyes because he really didn't know which way she was going with her thoughts until he saw her with a big ass dildo. They pulled him out of that chair, flipped him over, and Denise shoved that dildo up Crazy Red's ass without any grease, and he literally passed out. When she was done ramming that dildo in his ass, he begged them to kill him, but that was short-lived because Baby Girl took her 9 mm and shot Crazy Red twice in the head. As soon as she shot Crazy Red, Candy started trying to get free because she knew that they weren't going to leave her alive, knowing that she witnessed the whole thing. She was right. Baby Girl turned around and shot Candy straight in the heart, and she dropped right there, still tied to the chair.

Chapter 6
Angel the Columbian Assassin

ANGEL WAS WORKING overtime in Columbia; she was the madam of Uncle Leo's new whore house. She had established all new females from India. She also changed the name to sexy ladies; she kept the girls' routine of going to the doctor to be checked for diseases on a regular basis. She liked them all, but it was one, in particular, that she called Praia Angel like her because she was trained to run sexy ladies. When Angel went out on hits for the mafia, Praia was so good with handling business. Angel made her, her assistant; they became very close. Angel had another job that Uncle Leo wanted her to go on. She was headed to Charlotte, North Carolina. Angel made reservations to stay at the Hyatt place hotel in Charlotte. She would be leaving in two days. She had her pictures ready of this guy named Rico Davenport, who ran off the grid with over a half million dollars of Uncle Leo's money. When Angel found out Rico was in Charlotte North Carolina, she knew that she would be arriving there soon. Angel went to the gun house to retrieve her weapons of choice; she knew she was taking some C4 with her because he owned a big house, and it was locked down like fort Knox's, and she wanted nothing to stop her from getting at her target.

Angel wanted something different in the guns department for this trip; she picked up a waltherp99 Glock, and she also picked a Glock 17. She liked the adrenaline she felt from these two guns, when she held them in her hands. Angel wasn't leaving without her two switch blades; she kept them tucked away safely under her breast, just in case she had to cut a bitch up real quick. She took extra clips to her Glocks and extra bullets, so she was ready for whatever; the morning was coming fast, and Angel wanted to get her freak on with her man before she left, so she got her artillery out of the gun house and headed back to the villa for some much-needed sex. When she walked into the bedroom,

Ramon was laying in bed buck naked; he stood up, grabbed Angel around the waist, and kissed her. He looked in her eyes and said, "Baby, aren't you ready for some of this." She said, "You better know I am." Before Angel could get undressed, Ramon had snatched off Angel's clothes, and they started kissing again; this time it was more intense. She laid back on the bed and wrapped her legs around Ramon pulling him in between her legs. He stopped Angel because his mind was on eating her out first; he stopped kissing Angel and stuck his head between Angel's legs. He stuck his tongue deep inside Angel's pussy. She closed her eyes and was squirming underneath his touch; that shit was feeling so good to Angel. She was pulling her own hair out.

Angel was screaming "oh, my god." Ramon was putting his tongue, licking down so good. Angel was cooing just like a baby. Ramon obliged Angel in lifting her legs; he centered both of her legs on his shoulder, so he could have more of access to her pussy, but before he could position her up a little bit, he slid his finger in and out of her pussy, which started her to quiver uncontrollably. Her orgasm was coming fast and quick, and she started screaming her way to ecstasy when Ramon was finished. His erection had grown eight inches long. Angel reclined her legs back, and Ramon went in for the kill. He was so deep inside Angel until he could feel her pussy throbbing. She met Ramon stroke for stroke; the lovemaking was so intense until they both had another orgasm. They both collapsed in each other's arms until they fell asleep.

The next morning, Angel was on their jet, headed for Charlotte North Carolina. She got there checked into her hotel, and she headed over to enterprise to rent her a car with a GPS set up on it. She was on her way to a club that Rico Davenport owned called the trap. When Angel put the location into her GPS system, it took her straight to the trap. She went in and cased the bar for escape routes, just in case she had to take Rico out in his own bar. Angel was sitting at the bar in the trap, when Rico walked in. He spotted Angel sitting at the bar. Sexy as hell, he definitely wanted to meet her, so he told the bartender to send Angel a drink on him. The bartender gave Angel the drink and told her that the owner has sent her the drink on him. She raised her glass to Rico and said thank you. Rico in return asked Angel to join him at his table. She agreed. When she sat down at his table, he introduced himself as Rico, the owner of the trap. Angel told Rico her name was Kyra. He said, "That's a name I never heard before, but that name fits you well. Kyra, you are a beautiful woman, and if you were my woman, I wouldn't let you come to a bar by yourself. Let me ask you a question, Kyra. Are you married?" Angel told Rico no that she wasn't married.

He said, "That's good because I don't hit on other men's wives."

She said, "That's good because that will get you killed."

Rico was so into Angel that he kept her sitting at his table for two hours before she decided that she was tired of listening to his weak ass game. When Angel told Rico that she was getting ready to go, he looked like she had just stuck a dagger in his heart; he didn't want to let Angel out of his sight, so he invited her back to his house that night for a nightcap.

Angel said, "That would be fine, but I have no idea where you stay."

He said, "Here is my address, and this is my cell number, so when you get ready to come by, call me, so I can have my security to let you through the gate."

Angel said to herself, "this nigga got it hooked up, but it's all good because I'm going to blow his shit up."

Angel arrived at Rico's at eight thirty; she had left the trap, went back to the hotel, took a shower, and changed clothes. She had put on a cream-colored staples dress with the five-inch stilettos with her hand bag to match. When she called Rico to let him know that she was at the gate, he had his security to let her in. When Angel made it to Rico's front door, he was looking at Angel like she had just stepped off a modeling magazine. Angel knew she was the shit; she just wanted Rico to drool all over himself before she killed him. When Angel stepped inside Rico's house, it was beautiful; he had five bedrooms with five bathrooms. His whole house had marble floors; he had a lot of expensive artwork on every wall. Angel asked Rico who decorated his house.

He said, "My sister. She's an interior decorator."

Angel said, "She did a good job because this is nice." Rico thanked Angel for her sincerity; he didn't want to tell her that he never met a female that he let come to his house, but with Angel, it was an exception.

Rico thought that he hit the jackpot with Angel; she was pulling on his heart strings. He never met a woman that had him open that fast before. With Angel, he felt something deep with her; he wanted Angel to be his. What Rico didn't know was Angel was assassin sent there to take his life; she wasn't there to be his woman. Angel could tell by the way he admired her that it was love at first sight for him, and she was going to make sure before she killed him, he understood that it wasn't personal. It was business.

Rico asked Angel, "if she wanted anything to drink."

She said, "Of course, do you have any Cristal?" Rico said sure and went behind his bar in his den and poured both of them a glass of Cristal. Angel was sitting there looking around his house. When he caught her looking, he said, "You want me to give you a tour of my house." She said, "Yes." Angel was thinking to herself, *this nigga don't have a clue. I need to know how many security men he has around here, and I need to find my escape routes out of here.*

Time was winding down, and Angel wanted to get this job over with and head back to Columbia. Before she went to Rico's house, she stopped off and stole a money green Cadillac. She didn't want Rico to see her in her rental. Rico was beginning to feel the after effects behind the Cristal; he started looking at Angel, licking his lips, so she thought this is as good of a time as any. She slipped Rico a pill of ecstasy; he started to feel a little hot. He begin taking off his shirt, asking Angel did she feel hot; all of a sudden, Rico was coming out of his pants. When Angel looked down, Rico's dick was rock hard. She knew then that the ecstasy had kicked in; she was about to have Rico right where she wanted him.

Rico broke out sweating; he was running water off his body like a faucet. He told Angel that his body wanted her; he couldn't control the feelings he had for her. He grabbed Angel by her hand and led her over toward his bed. When he did that, Angel took a piece of piano wire she had in her bra and held it in her hand until Rico laid down on his stomach for a message. Angel said she was going to give him. When Rico rolled over, Angel started massaging his neck and shoulders first, before she took the piano wire and slowly wrapped it around Rico's neck. She was pulling the wire so hard that Rico started bleeding from his eyes. When Rico didn't have any more movement in his body, Angel knew her job was done, but she still had to get passed Rico's security, which was going to be a challenge because Rico had to walk her back out of the house. When she went to open the door to leave, Rico's bodyguard asked Angel, was Rico in his bedroom because he had an emergency phone call that he had to take.

Angel told him, "Yes, but he was sleeping." The bodyguard knew something was wrong because Rico was a night person; he stayed up to the wee hours of the morning. When Angel was about to run to the door, the bodyguard hit the alarm, and Rico'S security came rushing in the door, only to be hit with Angel's Glock 17; she was spitting hollow point bullets out her Glock like she had a license to carry the Glocks.

Angel was sliding across the floor on her back, shooting everything moving. She was shooting so fast that she didn't even notice that she got hit in the arm by the bodyguard that found Rico dead lying across his bed. When Angel stopped shooting, she realized nobody was left; the floor was full of dead bodies, so she took the C4 out of her purse and start placing it around the house. When she made it back to her car and got two blocks away, she ignited the C4 from a remote control device she had in her hand.

Angel got away from the crime scene without anyone seeing her; she made it back to her hotel room. She went in the bathroom to get a towel; she was bleeding bad—the bullet went in and out of her arm. She called for Ramon to pick her up in the jet because she didn't want anyone to notice blood coming through her clothes, plus she couldn't stop the blood on her own. Ramon told Angel that he was on his way. When Ramon hung up, Angel wrapped her arm up and went downstairs across the parking lot to take the rental car back. As Angel was returning to the hotel, she heard people talking about a house blowing up twenty minutes away from the hotel. One lady said that the firemen thought that it was a gas leak, but Angel knew she set off a hell of an explosion on that block; she even knew with all the C4 she used, they weren't going to even find bones, let alone human parts.

Ramon picked Angel up around five, the next morning; he came with a doctor on board of the jet. He took care of Angel before they made it back to Columbia. She had a clean bill of health; she just had to keep her arm clean and still for a couple of weeks, and she would be back to normal in no time. Uncle Leo thanked her for another job well done, paid her two hundred thousand, and Angel went straight to sleep because her pain medication knocked her out.

Chapter 7
Baby Girl and Cash

RODNEY A.K.A. CASH was beginning to feel like something was definitely wrong because it seems like right after Crazy Red met up with Denise for a second date, he winds up missing the same night, then he goes over to Crazy Red's crib to check on him, only to find him inside his house dead alongside an unidentified female he had never seen before. That sent up all kinds of red flags because the scene looked like a robbery gone bad, and that terrified the shit out of Cash because he and Crazy Red were partners in the drug game, and if Crazy Red got robbed and killed, that meant that their connect would soon be out for Cash's ass. Cash was trying to figure out who setup Crazy Red up; he knew the only people could get that close to him were females. He would sell his soul to the devil for a piece of ass.

Cash couldn't wrap his head around the trouble he was in by their connect; he knew once he saw the news with Crazy Red's picture flashing across the television screen, his right hand man is going to be looking for Cash in the day time with a flashlight. Cash had to come up with some answers quick; he also knew the robbery was an inside job. Someone knew exactly how to get at Crazy Red; he was weak when it came to females, but he wasn't a punk by a long shot, so this person had to know him in order to have access to his crib. Baby Girl was sitting in class, thinking about Cash, so she decided once class was over, she would give Cash a call to see if he wanted to have dinner at the crab shack that she liked so much.

Baby Girl gave Cash a call after class; he answered on the first ring. He didn't agree to go out to dinner, but he did agree to have dinner at his place. Cash was really paranoid; he didn't want to take any chances getting caught up, tripping in the streets, if Mr. Steele was sending his right-hand man, the butcher, after him, because one thing he knew for sure it was more than a million dollars that was gone; the key's of dope that was missing would bring at least a quarter of a million dollars in street value. Baby Girl told Cash she would bring the food from the grab shack to his place; he said cool and hung up.

Baby Girl noticed Cash had something on his mind; she just hoped he didn't bring up the murder of Crazy Red. It had flashed on the news stations all day, so she knew he knew about Crazy Red's murder. Baby Girl wasn't worried about looking suspicious; she learned from her mother early don't ever let your opponent see you sweat. When Baby Girl arrived at Cash's apartment, he was sitting down in the living room, watching the news. When the newscaster said that Crazy Red had been raped, Cash started to throw up, because while he was in prison, he had gotten raped himself by three other inmates, so he knew how his partner felt. To this day, Cash still hasn't been able to accept being raped by three men; he's never been able to sleep a whole night because the terror of being snatched up out of his bed with a pillow case thrown over his head and knocked out and left in the shower bleeding from his rectum still frightens the shit out of cash.

When Baby Girl heard what the news reporter said about Crazy Red, she said to herself, "That's what his punk ass get for trying to stick his dick in my friend's ass." Cash was still in the bathroom, empting his guts out in the toilet, when Baby Girl knocked on the bathroom door. He told her that he would be out in a minute. She asked Cash if he was all right.

He responded, "Get the fuck away from the door. I'll be out in a minute."

Baby Girl said, "You know what, Cash, fuck you. I'm gone." She knew he was upset, but to take his anger out on her—she wasn't that type of female.

Cash came out of the bathroom and apologized to Baby Girl. He really wasn't himself; his stomach was in knots because he knew that it wasn't going to be long before he would be dodging bullets himself trying to stay alive. Baby Girl accepted Cash's apology, and they went into the living room, cut the television off, and started talking, but Cash was still too upset to eat, so Baby Girl just opened up a bottle of Absolut Envy. Cash went into his kitchen, retrieved two glasses with ice, and returned back into the living room. Cash and Baby Girl sat up in Cash's living room, drinking until wee hours of the morning. Cash looked at Baby Girl, picturing her naked; he wanted to get to know her sexually. She didn't mind because it had been a while since she had her salad tossed, so she was up for taking Cash on a ride he would never forget.

Cash started kissing and caressing Baby Girl's neck. She started moaning, letting Cash know she was on the same page. Baby Girl started sexy dancing in front of Cash; she pulled off her top and unsnapped her bra. She had slid out of her pants before Cash could pull his shirt over his head; by the time Cash got fully undressed, Baby Girl was buck naked, rubbing on her nipples, waiting for Cash to ravish her body.

When Cash laid Baby Girl down on the bed, he split her legs open like the Red Sea, bent down between her legs, and started teasing her clit with his tongue; she started moving with the rhythm of Cash's tongue. She then came up off the bed with her hips going into a circular motion. She began rubbing the side of Cash's head, begging him to go deeper. When Cash felt Baby Girl's clitoris throbbing, he knew he hit more than just her pressure points.

Baby Girl and Cash was sucking each other like they were bomb pops on a hot summer day; she was expanding her muscle walls to meet each stroke that Cash was throwing her way. She wanted to feel Cash's dick inside her. When she told Cash she wanted to feel him deep inside her walls, he quickly obliged her. When he went in raw, Baby Girl didn't even notice that Cash didn't strap up. She was so into the rhythm of lovemaking that she didn't care what was taking place that; she was feeling more heat than she had ever experienced with any man that she had been with before.

Baby Girl and Cash were in the zone; they made love until ten thirty the next morning. Baby Girl missed going to class because she was too caught up with making love to Cash all night. When she returned to her dorm room, all the H&H crew was sitting there, waiting to find out why she wasn't at class; they knew she was all right because she was taught how to handle herself at an early age. When Baby Girl started laughing at all the questions the crew was shooting at her about what went down with her and Cash, she was sitting there glowing like a pregnant woman.

Ava said out loud, "oh, shit, our girl done went and got her back cracked."

Baby Girl was more giddy than they ever seen her; before she was always the serious one out of the crew, but this time they saw her for who she could be. For once, she got her freak on. Cash knew that one day, he would have to take Baby Girl out, but right now it wouldn't be in his best interest because he had too much on his plate right now, but what Cash couldn't get out of his mind was Baby Girl put some shit on him. He thought she had kryptonite in her pussy; he thought to himself, *if I didn't have to kill that bitch, she would definitely be a keeper.* She was a different kind of pedigree plus. Cash knew Baby Girl was to secretive for his taste; she always hid her eyes behind a pair of sunglasses. Cash also knew she had a hidden agenda; she was too intelligent, and she had the confidence of ten men. He couldn't believe she had balls as big as his.

Cash had to come up with a sting to get back the money and drugs that was took from Crazy Red; he had been getting phone calls from Mr. Steele, but Cash wasn't returning any of his calls. He didn't want to admit to himself that he was as much at fault to what happen to Crazy Red because he knew that he and Crazy Red should have never took that money and drugs to Crazy Red's crib. Cash started calculating some drug spots he could go and hit, trying to come up on a good lick before Mr. Steele sent the butcher after him. While he was sitting in his car, thinking, he got a cold chill. He thought about this guy on the north side of Atlanta named Cool who sold major drugs, so he thought as soon as it get dark he was going to go and strong arm Cool out of his shit.

Baby Girl and her crew, the H&H girls, already had Cool on lock; they were waiting on the sun to go down as well. They had Cool on lock for two days; she heard about Cool while she was in class listening to some girls, talking about how rich he was, so Baby Girl said "Oh, that nigga is going to be sucking out of a straw if he doesn't up his shit when I tell him to." Baby Girl found out Cool's location from a girl in her class they call Big bootie Katie; she was always boasting on how Cool's crib was setup. He even showed her stupid ass he had, a safe built outside under his pool with a sliding door that slid the water back, so you could walk up under it like it was a waterfall.

Cash parked down the street from Cool's crib, waiting to catch him coming home, so he could run up on him and hit in the head with his 9 mm, but what Cash didn't know was Baby Girl and her crew were two steps ahead of him; they had been parked down the street also, a block up the street in front of Cool's crib, also a block up from Cash, so from where Cash was sitting, he could see everything Baby Girl and her crew did. Cash really didn't know Baby Girl and her friends were the ones, robbing nigga's because everybody would always say it was niggas in ski mask.

Cash was sitting in his car when he saw a black range rover pull up with the license plate reading Cool printed in big bold letters. Cash said, "Oh, shit, it's show time" and opened his car door to get out, but he looked up in Cool's direction and saw dark figures run up behind him and hit him across the head.

Cash said, "It's some crazy shit going on," and I'm about to find out what the hell is going on. After Baby Girl and her crew jumped Cool and made him open his front door, he started screaming, "Look, man, I'll give y'all whatever y'all want, just don't take my life, please. I have three kids."

Baby Girl said, "Shut up, mother fucker, you knew you had three kids when you started distributing that bullshit to other people's kids, so I don't want to hear that bullshit." When he heard her voice and knew that they were females, he turned on his testosterone booster and tried to be hard because in his mind, wasn't no bitches going to make him bow down.

When Baby Girl saw him rise up, she kicked him so hard in his balls; he balled up on the floor, screaming like a bitch. She told Denise and Michelle to tie his punk ass up all while they were in Cool's crib, demonstrating tactics on Cool. Cash was in the window, watching everything unfold right before his eyes. He put two and two together, thinking this bitch is heartless; she and her crew been the culprits the whole time right up under my nose, and I didn't have a damn clue.

Cash said, "All right, things are looking brighter for me." He took his cell phone out, so he could take pictures of every move they made, so he could black mail them into giving him back what they took from Crazy Red.

Baby Girl asked Cool, "All right nigga, you're not a rookie to the drug game. Nigga, you know what time it is." When Baby Girl said that, Cool went into stupid mode. She told Cool, "Everything will be fine if you don't try and be no hero. Just give us what we want, and we will be out."

Cool said, "I don't keep anything at my crib. Haven't you ever heard, you don't keep your shit where you lay your head."

Baby Girl said, "You know you may be right, but you have yours close by."

She said, "Grab his ass. We're going to the pool area." when Cool heard pool, he went into a convulsion. He knew loose lips sinked ships, but it was his own fault bringing bitches to his crib, boasting about his money and his crib.

When Baby Girl and her crew took Cool out back to the pool area. Cash was standing behind the bushes with his cell phone snapping pictures. He saw how they had handcuffed Cool with his hands behind his back.

Baby Girl said, "Now Cool give us the combination to let the pool slid back, so we could go down in your safe. Get's what's there and bounce."

Cool said, "I told you, bitches. I don't keep shit at my crib." When he said that, Baby Girl shot Cool in his right knee. He dropped to the ground.

He said, "Bitch, you shot me. What the fuck is wrong with you?"

Baby Girl told Cool this time, "When I ask you to slid the water back, you are going to do it or we are going to started firing bullets in your ass until you look like Swiss cheese, so what's it's going to be."

Cool said, "All right, damn."

Sophia sat Cool up, and he said the combination. The water slid back for them to go under to some steps that led to Cool's underground safe.

When Baby Girl and her crew entered the safe; they was in awe they had never seen that much money in one place. He had his safe setup like a bank. Cool had money stacked in piles already counted up with money bands around it. He also had ten keys of uncut heroine; they knew they had hit the mother lode, so Baby Girl told her crew to look around for some duffle bags because there was no way they could carry that kind of money in pillow cases. Cool looked at Baby Girl and told her, "All right y'all have everything I own. Now get the fuck out my crib." That made Denise angry because she was still having flashbacks from Crazy Red's killing, so before Baby Girl could respond to what Cool said. Denise went behind Cool with her switch blade and cut Cool's throat from ear to ear. Blood was gushing out his neck like a soda fountain; they took what they got from Cool and got the hell out of dodge.

Cash had witnessed Baby Girl and her crew robbing and murdering Cool. He had evidence to prove that they were the H&H crew that everyone had been talking about. He had enough pictures and conversations to put them behind bars for the rest of their life. Cash also had a smile on his face because his blackmailing scam could payback Mr. Steele and make him rich in the process, so his life was looking much better in his eyes.

Chapter 8
Sophia and Michelle

SOPHIA AND MICHELLE still hadn't heard anything from the police concerning their parents whereabouts. They wanted to know if the police found any leads since they found their rental in the alley a couple of weeks ago, so Michelle decided to call the police officer who left them his card to contact him to find out any information leading up to the accident. Officer Cole Washington answered on the second ring when Michelle called his private line; he told Michelle that they had a witness who was a homeless guy, who was in the alley sleeping under a cardboard box, but he was also a drunk. The man who they call John Doe is a very sickly man, and he vividly remembers what he saw that day, but he could tell that someone was carrying your parents away from the wreckage, putting them in another car, so he knew they were alive at the time of the accident.

Michelle told Sophia what Officer Cole told her, so they would have a little satisfaction in knowing that their parents weren't dead but still alive somewhere, but the truth was neither one of the girls could get the idea out of their minds that something was definitely wrong. This whole scenario was something out of a movie scene, but Sophia and Michelle wanted to go home to Hawaii to their parents' house to see if they could find something that could help them uncover this mystery they were in. They made plans to leave Spellman the weekend to fly home to their mothers' house. Michelle told Baby Girl and the rest of their crew that they were going home to Hawaii to see if anything was left behind for them. Sophia and Michelle were feeling lost; they felt in their hearts that their mothers weren't coming back.

The weekend was approaching fast, and Friday was right around the corner. Baby Girl had called the airlines to get tickets for the whole crew to go along with Sophia and Michelle to Hawaii. They were part of her crew, and whatever they were facing, they all were going to be there to support them in their time of need. Baby Girl felt their pain because she knew what it felt like when Angel was in her car accident a while back. It literally took the wind out of her seeing her mother in a coma. Baby Girl knew deep down inside she was housing her own darkest secrets. She knew Angel had killed their parents; she was just hoping that they didn't find out any time soon.

Friday had finally come, and the girls got out of class and headed to the airport. They had packed up their clothes the night before, so the only thing they had to do was get to the airport. Baby Girl called Cash to let him know that she would be out of town for the weekend. Cash was happy to hear that because he was going to try and sneak into their dorms and search for the money. Michelle and Sophia and the rest of the crew boarded the plane and headed for Hawaii. The flight was a quiet one; nobody said anything. Baby Girl slept the whole flight. She was tossing and turning in her sleep; she was dreaming about what happened to Abby and Gabriel. She saw the whole scenario playing over and over in her head. She saw what her mother and Ramon did to Abby and Gabriel. It didn't really bother her because they put a hit out on her mother first, so she felt that it was better Abby and Gabriel died than her mother.

Baby Girl started talking in her sleep, and Denise woke her up. She jumped up, ready for war. Denise said, "Hold on, Baby Girl. It's me, Denise. You were talking in your sleep, so I took the initiative to wake you up before you said something that we all would regret." The plane landed three hours later, and they rented a car from Avis and went straight to Sophia's mother's house first. When she entered the house, it smelt kind of funny. There was an envelope sitting on the table, and the mail was stacked up on the floor. Sophia found a letter that her mother had written to her, which she forgot to mail it to her. She was explaining to Sophia about how much she loved her, and she wanted nothing but the best for her daughter.

Sophia started to cry because she knew her mother wanted the best for her, and she knew her mother had a lot of secrets she was keeping from her also, but today she was going to find out what all the secrets were about. As soon as she opened her safe to retrieve the contents, Sophia asked the crew if she could have sometime alone, and they agreed to give her some space. Sophia went into her mother's room and removed her big picture from the wall to open her safe. When she put in the combination, the safe popped open, and Sophia reached in and pulled out everything that was in there. The first thing she noticed was pictures of Angel and Baby Girl. She didn't know why her mother had pictures of them because she was under the impression that her mother didn't know them, because her mother never mentioned Angel or Baby Girl's names. Sophia opened up a folder that had information on Angel that said Angel was a cold-blooded killer. Abby even had a picture of Mike Trivet. Sophia had Mike's eyes, so she knew right away that he was her father.

Sophia found out her mother's secrets; she knew Angel killed her father, and she might be responsible for the death of her mother as well. She knew Angel was an assassin for the Columbia mafia, and she also knew Angel would kill you if you looked at her cross-eyed. Sophia found a bank certificate that left her with four million dollars. If anything was to happen to her mother, she would be wealthy. When she saw pictures of Baby Girl from the time she was an infant until she was about ten, she knew her mother had been keeping a close tab on Angel, but why was the question she didn't have the answer to until this folded-up piece of paper fell to the floor, and she picked it up to see that Angel's father was a kingpin named Cane who was a killer as well and that Sophia's mother was also a daughter of a mafia family. Her own parents were killed by the hands of Angel Carter. Sophia was angry; she was terrified because she knew if she went up against Angel or Baby Girl without a full-proof plan, she would become another dead body missing in action, and she didn't want that so she had to prepare herself and her sister for the battle between them and Angel.

Michelle knocked on the bedroom door to ask her sister Sophia if she was all right. When Sophia opened the door to let her in, she told Michelle to be quiet and look at the information she had given to her. When she took the information out of Sophia's hand, she almost screamed. When she saw Angel's picture and the other contents of the safe, she asked Sophia, "Do you think that Angel was behind what happened to our mothers?" Sophia said, "Yes, I do, and I believe Baby Girl knows as well." When Sophia said that Michelle lost it. She grabbed her gun and wanted to go out in the living room and kill Baby Girl right there on the spot, but Sophia stopped her.

She said, "No, not right now. We have to act as if we don't know anything for now okay."

Sophia and Michelle went back into the other room with the rest of the crew. When Baby Girl asked them was everything all right. They said "yes" in unison, but Baby Girl knew they found something because they were acting very strange. Michelle was ready to go to her mother's, Gabriel, house to fine some information as well. When she opened the front door, there were stacks and stacks of mail, but she didn't notice a letter for her left on the table, but she did find a set of keys to a mailbox that her mother had setup for her at the post office. Under the keys was the name and social security number she was supposed to use, when she got there. They all headed to the post office. When Michelle arrived at the post office, she went up to the desk clerk and showed her the keys to the lockbox, and the clerk took Michelle in the back. They both had to put the keys in the lockbox together. Once that was done, the clerk left Michelle in the back with lockbox.

Michelle opened the box, and she had the same information her sister found in her mother's safe, but Michelle's mother, Gabriel, had left her a voice-activated recorder. She told Michelle that if she was listening to the tape, that meant she was dead, killed by her nemesis Angel Carter. She went on to tell Michelle about how she and Abby grew up with Angel, and Mike Trivet was her and Sophia's father, but she went behind Angel's back to sleep with her man, Mike. Later on, she and Abby found out that Mike was Angel's brother from her father Cane, the Hawaiian kingpin. Gabriel also went on to tell Michelle all the criminating information she left her about Angel that could send Angel to the chair with a lethal injection, a death sentence for sure. All Michelle had to do was to take the recorder to the prosecutor attorney in Chicago, and they would know exactly who Angel Carter is.

Michelle felt that all the information her mother left for her was very disturbing news to her, but now things were adding up. She knew that her mother and Abby had slept with Angel's boyfriend, and as a result, her mother and her friend got pregnant. Angel killed their father; now she was holding Angel's faith in her hands. Only thing she had to do was blow the whistle on her, and that wasn't going to be easy, knowing she had the Columbia mafia behind her, plus her daughter is an assassin as well.

Michelle was left four million dollars as well. She was set for life as well; she decided to leave the tape locked up in the lockbox at the post office for safekeeping. It would come in handy when and if she needed it. Sophia and Michelle and the rest of the crew left the post office and went to lunch before they headed back to Atlanta. Baby Girl knew she seen the difference in how shady Sophia and Michelle was acting after they found the information that their parents had left for them. That kicked Baby Girl gear shift in overdrive. She knew that maybe they found something containing to her mother because she knew that Abby and Gabriel grew up together, and they went off to college together as well.

After lunch, the girls headed back to Avis to drop the rental car off. The next flight to Atlanta was in an hour so they stayed camped out at the airport. The whole time they were there, Sophia and Michelle didn't say anything to Baby Girl. They were throwing shade her way like she was the one who killed their parents. Then, it hit Michelle about what her mother said, "Don't act suspicious because you and your sister could become a liability, and Angel or her daughter wouldn't think twice about taking you out." Michelle knew how dangerous Angel and Baby Girl were. She knew first hand; she also knew if she crossed Angel what would happen to her and Sophia.

Chapter 9
Angel's Thirty-ninth Birthday Party

ANGEL'S BIRTHDAY HAD arrived, and Ramon wanted to give her a birthday she would never forget; he arranged for Baby Girl and dream team to meet them in Vegas. Angel knew Ramon was up to something because he had been sneaking around for two weeks. Ramon thought that *it would be nice to take Angel out of her element for a while*. He had the honeymoon suite set up for them; he was going to ask Angel to marry him, once Baby Girl and the dream team arrived. He had already bought the ring he purchased, a ten-carat platinum ring, for Angel. Angel wanted to marry Ramon, but she wasn't ready to just yet. She had unfinished business in Chicago with her companies. Baby Girl and the dream team arrived before Angel and Ramon did. Uncle Leo, along with his two brothers, had reserved the whole casino for Angel and the dream team, plus the sexy ladies they had. One side of the casino was set up with a buffet offering foods from all over the world. Baby Girl knew that Ramon was going to propose to her mother, but he wanted Baby Girl to be there.

When Angel and Ramon pulled up, they were in a long-stretch white Cadillac limo. They were dressed to kill. Ramon had on a silver Armani suit with the Armani silver banisters; Angel was dressed in pearl white Armani as well. She had on a pair of two-thousand-dollar pearls that Uncle Leo gave her for a birthday present. Ramon's other two uncles gave Angel her own personal artillery shed with every weapon known to man to carry out her hits. Angel was happier than she had been in a while, but when she looked up and saw the dream team, she went ballistic because her party was going to be off the chain literally; all the dream team showed up in Vegas with their own dates. Baby Girl's guy friend was a Jamaican cat named Cuba. He was dark as night and was mean as a rattlesnake. Denise had a guy name Richard a.k.a. Baby Face; Ava had this

47

bad ass piece of chocolate on her arm named Will, a.k.a. Sporty. Sophia was with a guy who adored her. She felt he really wasn't her cup of tea, but she took him with her; anyway, his name was Malcolm a.k.a. Pike. Michelle had met this hustler named Jordan a.k.a. Blood. He was a beast in the sheets, and she loved how he got down when it came to the streets.

The party was in full swing when two men burst through the door carrying machine guns, stating that everybody get down. Angel and Ramon went straight into attack mode, so did the dream team. Angel thought that *it seemed weird that these two guys would try and rob the place when everyone at the party was strapped,* but when the guy grabbed Angel and said, "Bitch, you are the one we were sent here to get," all hell broke loose. Guns were being fired all over the room. Baby Girl and Denise hit one of the guys in the forehead with 45 mm, sending him straight to the floor. The other guy was hiding behind a slot machine, trying to shoot his way out of the casino until a bullet struck in the leg, making him drop to the floor.

Angel told Ramon and Baby Girl to take him to the bathroom. Angel said, "I want to know who sent this bitch after me at my fucking birthday party." When Michelle and Sophia saw Angel going in the bathroom with the shooter they hired to take Angel out, they started sweating because they knew they were in deep shit, but once Angel questioned the gunman and he gave her the information she wanted, Ramon stuck the barrel of his Glock 17 in his mouth and shot the man's brains all over the bathroom mirror. When Sophia and Michelle heard the gun go off, they were scared to death because they knew they were next, but it didn't go the way they thought Angel had a plan of her own for them. She was going to make them pay for trying to cross Angel Carter. She couldn't believe they had the audacity to come at her like armatures, so for that they will pay for being stupid.

Just when Angel thought everything was over back inside the casino, Pike and Baby Face were going at it about a gambling bet. Baby Face said Pike lost on the dice game, and he owed Baby Face five thousand dollars, but instead he told Baby Face to kiss his ass. That's when Baby Face punched Pike in the eye, and in return, Pike drew his pistol and shot Baby Face in his face. When Angel heard the shot, they came running out of the bathroom just in time because Pike was going to put two more rounds in Baby Face's head. Angel said to everyone that if there would be anymore killing going on at her party, it's going to be by her gun. Angel didn't even look Sophia's and Michelle's way; they knew she was on to them. They just didn't know how she was coming at them, so after the party, when everyone went to their own rooms, Sophia and Michelle decided to leave Vegas once everyone went to bed for the night; their dates wanted to leave as well.

Angel made it clear to Baby Girl to keep the code of silence with Sophia and Michelle and not let on that they were the ones who paid Joe Blow to kill Angel. Joe Blow was so scared of dying that he gave Angel the fifty thousand that Michelle had given them. She still owed fifty more when the job was completed. Angel didn't get the proposal from Ramon that night, but she did get the ride of her life for sure. Ramon had Angel in so many different positions that night until she lost count, but she did remember her favorite the doggy-style position; she could feel Ramon so deep in her that she swear she could taste his cum. The next morning when everyone came down to breakfast, Sophia and Michelle were missing in action. Angel saw the fear in the two girls, but she wanted them to sweat a little bit before she decided what she really wanted to do with them because she understood why they did what they did because Baby Girl gave her the scoop on going to Hawaii with them to their parents' house.

Angel was assassin from the heart, and it wouldn't be in her nature to let Sophia and Michelle get away with what they pulled at her party. She was going to take her time with ending their lives when she was ready; she knew they were going to hide out, but it didn't matter where they hid from Angel, she was going to turn over stone after stone looking for them.

While Angel was deciding what to do with Sophia and Michelle, they were on the plane thinking about going to Columbia to kidnap Angel's son little Ramon. What Sophia and Michelle didn't know was that if they even breathed on Angel's son, she and Ramon would hunt both of them down like dogs. Angel was thinking about letting her nieces live, but they would be disfigured. She just wanted to shut the two beauties down. She wanted them both to feel bitter that would make their animosity build up toward her so they could try and take her out again. Then she could dispose of them for good. Sophia and Michelle vowed that one day they would have their revenge on Angel. She will slip up, and they would be waiting in the shadows.

Angel and Ramon went back to Columbia, and he surprised her with her own personal party on the beach. He had a proposal to make, and nothing was going to interfere this time because they were alone. Ramon had the decor setup, lovely along the table. He also had vanilla candles, gracing the table with beautiful lavender and white roses. He had champagne chilling in a bucket of ice. Angel's heart was protruding in her chest because she knew what Ramon was up to, and she didn't want to hurt his feeling by telling him she just wasn't ready for marriage. Maybe one day Angel knew she would fold and marry Ramon, but right now wasn't the right time.

Angel agreed to, at least, get engaged to Ramon; That way she would have time to think the marriage proposal over for awhile. Angel loved Ramon; he had all the qualities she need in a man. He was business-oriented; he was good in the sheets, and he loved and treated her with respect. For that she would forever be thankful. Ramon scored major points with Angel, and he would forever be her nigga in crime and in her bed.

Chapter 10
The Disfiguration of Sophia and Michelle

SOPHIA AND MICHELLE didn't go back to school; they stayed camped out at a hotel in Atlanta, trying to regroup. They didn't think that the men they hired to kill Angel would whine up dead so fast. They thought that *they were smart enough not to move on Angel at her birthday party full with bitches with guns including them.* Angel had Baby Girl on the lookout for Sophia and Michelle. She was to call her as soon as she spotted them. While Baby Girl was looking out for Sophia and Michelle, they were stalking Baby Girl's every move; they thought *if they couldn't kidnap her little brother, then they would kidnap baby girl instead.* Sophia had come up with the idea that Cash should know about what happened to his friend Crazy Red. Sophia wanted to know if he was interested in where his money and dope was, so Michelle and Sophia left their hotel room to go camp out where they knew Cash frequently hung out at. It was a park on twenty third that he would bet on basketball games with some of the young cats up there who he knew.

When Michelle spotted Cash, she called his name, and he immediately went over to them to see what was up with them, especially knowing he had enough evidence to bury all of them for the murder of Cool, but Cool really wasn't his problem; his problem was with them for the robbery of Crazy Red. He wanted back what they took from Crazy Red—the money and the dope—so he could set things straight with Mr. Steele. Michelle told Cash they had a proposition for him if he was interested. He looked at both Michelle and Sophia as if they had just sprouted two heads; he said, "Look here, why should I trust you two? First y'all apart of a click called the H&H, am I right? If y'all lie to me, there's no reason for me to trust you because I know what's been popping off around here. Everybody is talking about the robberies and murder that's being done by a group of females wearing ski masks."

Sophia told Cash, "We don't care if you trust us or not. I'm just stating that we could help each other out of a bad situation."

Cash thought long and hard before he asked his next question, "All right, let's hear what this proposal is." Sophia explained to Cash that they wanted him to kidnap Baby Girl so that they could bring her mother Angel out in the open so they could kill her.

Cash looked at them and asked, "If I do this, I want everything y'all took from Crazy Red before y'all killed him." Sophia and Michelle looked at Cash as if he was stupid because neither one of them said anything about Crazy Red, so how could he know that they were the ones who robbed and killed him. What Sophia and Michelle didn't know was Denise was sitting across the park, watching everything unfold between Cash, Sophia, and Michelle. She already gave Baby Girl a call to let her know what was up.

Sophia and Michelle told Cash that they didn't have what he was asking for, but they could give him the money to pay Mr. Steele back. He thought to himself, *if these two bitches got this kind of cash, I'm going to take their shit and bounce that way. I could pay Mr. Steele and have a substantial amount of cash for myself to set myself up somewhere else.* While Cash was contemplating taking the money from Michelle and Sophia, Denise's trigger finger was itching. She was still sitting across the park, watching them with her .380 automatic locked and loaded. Once cash agreed to help them with his own agenda in mind, he was to call Baby Girl and setup another dinner date with her. Cash thought, *maybe I could kill two birds with one stone and get rich in the process.*

Baby Girl was ready for whatever went down because now she knew Cash was becoming her enemy; he was next on her target hit list. They wanted to play hard ball, and that's what they were going to get. Denise followed Sophia and Michelle back to the hotel where they were hiding out in. She wanted to be able to find them when the time was right. Once she saw them get out of their car and going inside the hotel, she called Baby Girl to let her know where they were staying.

She said, "Cool, stay there. Don't let them out of your sight."

Baby Girl called Angel to let her know the details of Sophia and Michelle whereabouts; she told her daughter that she would be there shortly and not to do anything but wait for her arrival. Angel had plans for them; she was going to make them afraid to look in the mirror. She wanted them to regret ever trying to go up against her, but first Baby Girl had to tell her mother about Cash talking with Sophia and Michelle about the team. She wasn't sure as of yet what the conversation was about, but she did know that Sophia and Michelle have definitely changed teams.

Angel arrived in Atlanta as promised. She called Baby Girl and told her that she would be staying at the regency hotel and asked her and the remaining dream team to come by after class. Angel really didn't want to hurt her nieces physically because she had taken them through enough by killing their mothers, but when they hired hit men to kill her at her own birthday party, they cross the line big time, so they were going to be made an example out of, so no one else on the team would try and cross her again. When Angel settled into her hotel, she rented her an Eddie Bauer Explorer floor runner equipped with tinted windows and a GPS system. She didn't want anyone out side of the dream team to know she was in Atlanta.

While Baby Girl was still in class, Angel went shopping around for a bullwhip. She thought, *what Sophia and Michelle needed was a good old-fashioned ass whipping*, and she knew she was the right person for the job. Angel wind up going to a Rodeo store for cowboys. When she first entered the store, she noticed the bullwhip's display running across the top of the store. She asked the sales clerk if she could see a couple of them to see which one felt the lightest in her hand. She also wanted some heavy rope. The lady in the store thought Angel was crazy or she had some serious issues. Angel noticed the clerk looking at her, so she asked her was there a problem. The young lady said no, so Angel paid her for her merchandise and kept it moving. Angel's next move was to go driving around, looking for a old barn or a vacant house that set out in the boondocks somewhere far. When she found this old beat up empty barn on the outskirts of Atlanta, she knew this would be her spot for what she was about to do; all she had to do was go set her trap with cheese and watch how the mice would scramble for the cheese. Meanwhile Sophia and Michelle were meeting with Cash about the kidnapping of Baby Girl, not knowing that Cash wasn't going to see daylight now that Angel knew he was conspiring with Sophia and Michelle.

Angel also found out from Denise where Cash laid his head at night so Angel was definitely going to snatch him up, but first she wanted to break into his apartment to get some information on him to make sure he wasn't an undercover agent. Angel was outside Cash house when he exited the building; he was smiling like he had a winning ticket in his hand. As soon as he left, Angel went to his door and jammed her credit card into Cash's door and jimmied it open. She went in and started searching through Cash's things when a picture of Raymond and Cash sent Angel's mind into overdrive. She wanted to know what this Cash person was up to, and if he was there to harm her daughter, he was going to wish he was never born.

Baby Girl was out of class, and the dream team was headed to Angel's hotel room when Baby Girl got a phone call from Angel, telling them to meet her at the McDonald's down the street from Cash's apartment. She knew where it was because she went there a few times to get Cash some breakfast, but what Baby Girl wanted to know was why was her mother over in Cash's hood. When Baby Girl and the crew pulled up, Angel had a lot to discuss with them. She wanted to tell Baby Girl about what she found out about Cash. She believed that Cash came to kill her; she also explained to Baby Girl that Raymond didn't leave town, but she killed Raymond herself while Baby Girl was in rehab. Baby Girl knew something happened to Raymond, but she really didn't think he was dead. She thought that he just moved on.

Angel asked Baby Girl, "I know you know him, but where do you know him from." She told her mother that she met Cash at the mall when they were shopping, getting ready to go to Columbia for their summer break. Angel told her daughter that he was planted there because he knew you were the last one to see his brother alive so he was banking on setting you up for the kill. Baby Girl was looking defeated. She couldn't believe Cash wanted her dead until Angel showed Baby Girl a letter that Raymond had sent Cash. He also sent a picture of him and Baby Girl standing in sand at the beach. She knew the picture that Angel showed her was right on the money because they stopped a girl that was passing by to take the picture of the two of them.

Baby Girl was angry at the fact that she didn't pick up on Cash. She could have got caught slipping, but her mother was there in time to stop Cash right in his damn tracks. After Angel gave Baby Girl the run down on Cash, she wanted to put his ass in the dirt. He was going to pay for leading her on. Angel had the girls to sit across the street from Cash's apartment until he came home, while she and Baby Girl waited on him inside his apartment. Baby Girl wanted Cash's head as a trophy. When Cash came home, he didn't even notice that his front door lock had been jimmied. He was so deep in thought about robbing Sophia and Michelle. He didn't notice the shadow of a dark figure standing in front of him when he walked in his door. By the time he noticed, Angel hit him in the face with a glass; he instantly started rubbing his eyes because blood was running down his face from a cut that was three inches deep across eye.

Angel hit Cash again with the butt end of her 9 mm; he dropped to the floor. He didn't even look up because he really thought that it was Mr. Steele's right-hand man, the butcher, that caught him slipping, until Baby Girl said, "Open your eyes bitch ass, nigga. I'm taking your heart out and make you eat it." But before Baby Girl could launch forward toward Cash, he came up off the floor with his .380 and started shooting. Angel and Baby Girl got behind his couch until they heard his gun clicking, so they both started firing Cash ass up. He was hit some many times with their 9 mm until his body could be used as a pin cushion. When Baby Girl and Angel came out of Cash's apartment, people were running out of the building because they didn't know where the shooting was coming from, but they weren't taking any chances; they were getting the hell out of dodge.

Angel and Baby Girl made a clean get away out of Cash's building because people were running all over the place. Angel and Baby Girl kept moving through the crowd until they reached Denise's car sitting across the street. Now that Cash was dead, it was on to their next targets Sophia and Michelle. They were sitting down the street, watching Angel and her crew get into Cash's house that made them want to kill Angel and Baby Girl so badly until they wanted to get the law involved, but how where they going to do that without implicating themselves so they would have to come up with another strategy hopefully one that wouldn't cause them their life. Angel stayed in Atlanta for a week, waiting to give Sophia and Michelle the element of surprise, but that wasn't going to happen as quick as Angel thought because Sophia and Michelle knew that Angel was in town.

Denise gave Angel the address to the hotel where Sophia and Michelle were staying, but when Angel got there, they were long gone; they knew Angel was going to be gunning for them, and they weren't going down without a fight. Angel was at the restaurant having lunch when Pike came strolling in. He noticed Angel right away, and he headed over to her table to speak to her. Pike was a ladies' man. He had a crush on Angel when he first met her at her birthday party so he thought that since Angel was out of her comfort zone, he might have a chance to indulge her appetite a little on some Pike master. Angel saw how Pike was coming at her so she thought she would have a little fun with him and find the location of Sophia and Michelle from him. Angel invited Pike to sit and have lunch with her in Pike mine. He thought, *he was going to throw his net out there to catch him a cougar.* Pike didn't know he was stepping in very dangerous water. Angel was going to eat him up and spit him out. Pike was sitting across from Angel, looking at her and licking his lips. He was thinking about doing some serious fucking if he got the opportunity. He kept thinking to himself, *I never had no season pussy but old. Well, first time for everything I'm going to tear that ass up. She gone drop that Columbian nigga she fucking.*

Pike was so deep in thought about having sex with Angel that he didn't even hear her calling out his name twice. Angel asked Pike if he wanted to go someplace else where they could be more comfortable.

Pike said, "Hell, yeah, let's go."

Angel said to herself, *this kid don't have a clue about the danger he's in, but he's about to find out after I get my information.* Angel took Pike to her hotel room; she pulled out a bottle of Hennessy.

Pike said, "I didn't know you get down with the hard shit, ma."

Angel told Pike, "Sweetie, you don't know me, but are you ready to get to know me." Pike looked at Angel with this gleam in his eyes. Angel handed Pike his drink; she had already put an ecstasy pill in his drink. Pike swallowed his drink down fast, hoping to get the party started quicker. Angel stripped down to her panties and bra when Pike saw that hot pink up against Angel's caramel-colored skin, he lost it. His dick was standing up hard, saluting in Angel's direction.

Angel said, "Not so quick, big boy. I want to see this python you were telling me about on the way over here." Angel pushed Pike down on the bed; he ripped his own underwear off, and Angel's eyes bucked wide open because Pike didn't lie. He had ten inches of steel.

Angel was in awe because this was the second time she had seen a guy who was standing at the front of the line when God was creating men's body parts. All Angel could do was tell Pike how blessed he was in the dick department. Angel immediately jumped on top of Pike. She had to test the water on this young stud before she killed him. Pike felt the heat from Angel's pussy and almost busted his nut right then and there, but he held his own. He was matching Angel's stroke for strokes until Angel eased down a little and came back up slow, bringing the tip of Pike's dick to a tight squeeze. The next thing she heard was a piercing high-pitch scream; it was Pike. He was trembling and sweating like a nigga on death's row. Right when Pike was about to bust off, Angel jump up, leaving Pike a wet and nasty mess, and Pike enjoyed every minute. He was ready to tell Angel anything she wanted to know.

Angel asked Pike if he knew where Sophia and Michelle were staying.

He said, 'yes' and that they rented a condo in midtown Atlanta in colony square. Pike gave Angel their address along with Sophia's new cell phone number. He gave up the information so fast. Angel decided to let Pike go on with his life, but she told him not to contact Sophia to let her know that Angel was looking for her. Angel also gave Pike fair warning that if he did, she will come back for his head. Pike laughed because he thought, *she was playing.* Angel drove Pike back to the restaurant where he left his car. She also followed Pike to see where he hung out, just in case she had to back track to find him. Angel started feeling like she was getting soft. She put it on her age. She thought, *maybe because she was feeling exhausted at times, her body was changing.* She decided when she got back to Columbia that she would go and get checked out.

Angel found Sophia and Michelle's condo. Pike was right on the money with the address he gave Angel. She liked the community that they chose to stay in; it was beautiful. It was a community of Italian people who stayed around their neighborhood. Angel sat down the street, watching their condo. She was waiting on them to come home. She called Baby Girl to let her know that she was sitting outside their condo. She also told Baby Girl she needed her to come join her after class. Baby Girl told Angel that they had early dismissal, and she would be there within the hour. While Angel was sitting there waiting, she thought about how Sophia and Michelle tried to play her at her birthday party. She was screaming obscenities to herself; she was just that angry at the two of her nieces.

Angel continued to wait for their arrival. Then she saw them pull up and park; they got out of the car carrying grocery bags. Angel pulled her hood over her head to hide her identity. She wanted them to think that she was a jogger passing by. When she got close to Sophia and Michelle, she bent over to tie her shoes. When she came up slow, pulling her .38 revolver out of her leg holster. She grabbed Sophia, and Michelle dropped the grocery bag to the ground. She told both of them if they screamed, she would drop them where they stood. Sophia and Michelle were scared shitless. Angel told Michelle to walk in front of them slowly because Angel was still holding Sophia in front of her with her gun pointed to her rib cage.

Michelle did exactly what Angel told her to do. She opened up the door, and they all went inside. Angel had duct tape, hidden inside the pocket of her hood she was wearing. Angel knew that they were very scared, but she didn't care. She was going to put a little heat to their assess, just to make sure they won't try to cross her again. Angel made them sit down in a chair while she duct taped their arms and legs; they were shacking so badly that Angel had to put her knee in their laps to hold them still. After she duct taped their mouths, she called Baby Girl to inform her that the mice ate the cheese and that their heads were caught in the trap. Baby Girl knew what that meant so she headed to the address her mother gave her.

Angel sat down on Sophia and Michelle's sofa, waiting for Baby Girl. She had something to say that the girls needed to know, but she wanted her daughter to be present as well because she wasn't going to repeat what she was going to say ever again. When Baby Girl finally made it to Sophia and Michelle's condo, she was in awe as well because for them to have something that nice they had a nice piece of change. Angel opened the door to let Baby Girl in. She asked her to have a seat; she had something to get off her chest. She told all three girls her history with Abby and Gabriel. She wanted them to get an understanding to why she did what she did. She told them about the mafia and the killing of Abby and Gabriel. She didn't leave any stone unturned. She just felt the need to purify her soul.

Sophia and Michelle were crying so hard until they were chocking on their own mucus. Angel snatched the tape off their mouth so that they could talk. Sophia coughed up some spit, and she spit directly in Angel's face. She didn't care if Angel killed her right there; she couldn't believe that Angel had just admitted to killing their mothers. Angel was a monster in Sophia's eyes, and she wanted Angel dead. Angel told Sophia and Michelle she knew how they felt because she knew the pain of losing a parent. That's what made her the bitter person she is today. Sophia and Michelle didn't give a damn how Angel felt; they knew one day for sure that they would be spitting on her grave. Angel told Baby Girl now that I got that out of the way, let's get them ready for transportation. Baby Girl went into the kitchen to get a towel. She soaked it with some chloroform. She knew they would be knocked out for a while from the strong vapors from the chloroform. When Angel saw that the girls were completely on cloud nine, they checked the outside surroundings to make sure no one would see them when they bought them out of the house.

Angel and Baby Girl loaded Sophia and Michelle in the back of Angel's rented Explorer. They covered them up so that if they happen to get pulled over; they wouldn't see anything but folded up comforters. When Angel made it to the vacant farmhouse she found earlier that day, she pulled the heavy rope she had inside . She found a beam and threw the rope over the beam and tied a tight knot in it. Angel and Baby Girl went back out to the Explorer to get Sophia and Michelle; they were still knocked out from the chloroform so it was easy to get them inside the farmhouse. Angel strung both of them up to the beam; she had the rope tied tight; she stripped both of them down to their underwear. She pulled out her bullwhip that she was going to use on Sophia, but first she had to wake her up. She didn't want her to miss the show. Angel woke her up when she swung the whip, striking Sophia across her back with the bullwhip. She hit her over and over with bullwhip, cutting into her flesh like a switchblade.

Sophia was screaming so loud that you could hear her a mile away; she was bleeding like she had just given birth to twins. Sophia couldn't take it anymore; she passed out from the pain. She had scars on her that would make her shame of her body the rest of her life. Michelle woke up vocally; she was screaming at what was happening to her sister. The expression she was throwing off let Angel know that if she got loose, she would kill her with her bare hands.

Michelle wanted whatever Angel wanted to do to her to get it over with because she was getting nauseated, watching her sister hanging from a beam bleeding to death. Angel had a pot a sitting to the side; she had bought a thermos that holds cold and hot products. Angel wanted to keep things moving so she got a ladder and positioned it next to Michelle. She went up the ladder with the thermos, opened it up, and poured lye all over Michelle's head. She burned the hair off her head and the skin off her face, ears, and neck. She was screaming as loud as Sophia. She could feel her skin sizzling from her flesh; it wasn't a minute later before Michelle passed out as well. Angel and Baby Girl left them still tied to the beam; they left them there bleeding and unconscious. Angel dropped Baby Girl back off where her car was parked outside Sophia and Michelle's condo. She followed her back to her dorm, and Angel went back to her hotel room where she stayed for two more days. She took her rental back, got on a plane, and went back to Columbia.

Three days later, a man was cutting the grass outside around the vacant farmhouse when he noticed two bodies, hanging from a beam. He went inside to see if they were still alive. When he heard a squeaking sound coming from one of them, he immediately called the police and an ambulance; the two bodies were in bad shape. When the police arrived, the ambulance was close behind. When they got Sophia and Michelle down, they were barely breathing; they needed oxygen badly. The EMS hooked them up to some fluids, and their pulses returned to normal.

When Sophia and Michelle arrived at the hospital, they were rushed straight to surgery. Sophia was going to have extensive stitches over a major part of her body. Michelle was going to have extensive skin grafts from her head to her neck, so they would be laid up for a while in the intensive care unit.

Chapter 11
Baby Girl's Double Murder

BABY GIRL'S NAME started ringing around campus that she was the chick to see if you wanted to purchase a key of cocaine or heroin. She let this dude named Big Scotty know that she had some pure shit to sell. He on the other hand told a couple of other people, and word of mouth shot up the charts like diarrhea. Baby Girl was being watched by the dean because drugs weren't sold on his campus; he also alerted the authorities to let them know that she might be distributing drugs on campus grounds. The authorities were already looking into the death of Cash a.k.a. Rodney Anderson. They were informed that Baby Girl was his leading lady, so she may know something about what happened to him. Cash had sent the tape that Baby Girl starred in killing Cool to his girlfriend out of town two weeks before he got killed. Just in case something happened to him, he also had informed her of Mr. Steele. Cash's girlfriend didn't know rather to send the tape to the authorities in Atlanta or not. She was really scared because if this girl and her crew had this kind of power, they could easily find her in New Jersey, but when she looked at her son and realized that he would be growing up without a father, she decided to take her chances. Cash's girlfriend, Lisa Chandler, sent the tape to the police department in Atlanta; she didn't put any address on it because she didn't want them to ask her where she got the tapes from. When the tape arrived at the station, an officer in the mail room took it straight up to the homicide department. He handed it to two detectives who were on the Rodney Anderson case, not knowing that they were also on the case of Cool a.k.a. Reginald Willis.

Detective Cotton told his partner Caldwell, "Don't it seem strange that we get a call from the dean at Spellman College right before this tape was hand delivered to our department. I think we should go pick this Baby Girl person up and bring her in for questioning. We have information showing us that she committed murder. She also has a crew that we see here on this tape. What the hell we're haul all their assesses in to be questioned." When Detective Cotton and his partner arrived at Spellman, Baby Girl and her crew were still in class; the two detectives pulled Baby Girl and her crew from class and hauled them down to the station.

They had each one of the crew members in separate rooms, questioning them about their whereabouts the night Cool was murdered. They had all the crew members, but Sophia and Michelle were still in the hospital in intensive care. Detective Cotton asked Baby Girl did she know Cool.

She said, "I have never seen that guy before in my life." They all told the detectives the same story, but they had the tape to prove differently. The detectives told Baby Girl that he advise them to call an attorney because they were in deep shit; they were being charged with the murder of Cool and possibly with the murder of Crazy Red as well if their witness show up who saw them leaving Crazy Red's house on the night of his murder.

Crazy Red had an old lady who stayed next door to him who he called Gladys. She was nosey like the women Gladys who played in the series "Bewitched"; her nosiness came in handy for a change. She might be the one to send his killers away for a long time. Baby Girl made her one phone call to Angel to let her know that she had been arrested for a double murder. Angel knew with the lifestyle they lived, they would be caught up one day, but she wanted it to be her rather than her daughter. When Baby Girl hung up with her mother, Angel couldn't get packed fast enough. She and Ramon flew back to Atlanta in their jet; she wanted to get to her daughter before those sharks detectives ate her alive. While Angel was on the jet, she found a top notch attorney. He was known for winning murder trials; he charged a hundred thousand dollars to even accept the case.

Angel hired an attorney name Mark Murdock; he was a beast of an attorney everyone in Atlanta called him killer Murdock because he had won at least eighty percent of his cases. Angel had planned on hiring him long time ago, but she forgot about it. She didn't want to deal with the attorney they had for the mafia. She wanted someone else who knew Atlanta's prosecuting attorney. She wanted the best. When Angel walked in Atlanta's police department with killer Murdock, all you could hear was "oh" shit; he walked up in the station as if he was a black goddess. The man was sharp; he had on a five thousand dollar Armani cream-color suit with some Armani three thousand dollars loafers to match. Angel knew this man knew his shit; he had a watch on his arm called a sea-gull automatic 18 k rose gold plated that cost about sixteen thousand dollars. When killer Murdock walked in the station and asked to see his client, they directed him in the back room where Cotton was threatening Baby Girl with a life sentence. Cotton looked up and saw killer Murdock and excused himself from the room. Murdock introduced himself as Baby Girl's attorney and told her that he would be getting her released within the hour.

While Murdock was working on getting Baby Girl released, he started getting the other girls released; also their bond was sat at half a million dollars. Angel paid their bond, and they were released with a pending court date. When Baby Girl and her crew came out, Angel and Ramon were ready to take them to a hotel, so they could find out what was going on. They never did shit out in the open that would get them caught up. Baby Girl was afraid to let her mother know that she had started another click outside of the dream team that she called the H&H crew and that they robbed and killed for money and drugs. She really didn't have a choice but to tell Angel because she was going to find out anyway when they went in to talk with killer Murdock the next morning. Angel was pissed when Baby Girl told her what had been going on in Atlanta. She knew her daughter was just as much as vicious as she was, but to form a crew with her own personal dream team was a no-no. She let Baby Girl know how angry she was; she was really out of bounds, and Angel let her know that too.

That next morning came fast, and Angel and Baby Girl and the crew along with Ramon headed to the attorney's office; they had a nine thirty appointment, and they were there on time. Murdock was waiting in his office going over the evidence the detectives had of the murder of Cool. Even though they had Baby Girl and her crew on tape, he told them that he still thought it was circumstantial because if nothing else, he could get the detectives for not reading them their Miranda rights before hauling them off to jail. Murdock showed Angel and everyone else the tape with the evidence on it. In reality, they were caught dead to right for the murder of Cool; he also explained to Angel that the detectives were trying to charge them with the murder of Crazy Red a.k.a. Patrick Stewart. They have a witness who saw them running from his house on the night of his murder. Some female name Candy was also shot to death inside Patrick's house.

Angel was fuming when she saw all the evidence building up against her daughter; she knew she had created a monster for real; now she may lose her to the judicial system. Murdock assured Angel that he could get them off because he was owed favors. The prosecutor owed him big time, and he would be having lunch with her today, so she could pay up, but he told Angel if he got them off, she would have to pay him a million dollars because he would be putting his life on the line as being the most powerful attorney Atlanta had ever seen.

Chapter 12
Baby Girl and the Crew Murder Trial

BABY GIRL AND her crew were set for trial on October 22, which was one month and ten days. They had been kicked out of Spellman for all the trouble and publicity that they have around them; the school board wanted them out. They couldn't leave town so Angel rented them a condo big enough for all of them to stay in. Angel even stayed with them the whole time. Ramon went back to Columbia to let his uncles know what went down with the dream team, so they understood why Angel stayed in Atlanta. She had her assistance well trained to fill her shoes while she was in Atlanta, so her job as Uncle Leo's assassin was on hold as well which was a good thing for Angel because her plate was full at the time.

Baby Girl didn't know what she was going to do after getting kicked out of school. She really was trying hard with a grad average of 4.0; she had one year left, and now it was gone. She knew by having the publicity that this trial was going to bring that she probably wasn't going to get a chance anywhere else to finish getting her degree. When Angel saw her daughter sitting alone in deep thoughts, she went over to her and put her arms around her to let her know that it would be okay even when she really didn't think it would be. Angel had called attorney Murdock for a meeting; she also wanted to pay him half of the million dollars she promised him. She wanted to know who this witness was who saw Baby Girl and the crew running out of Crazy Red's house on the night of the murder.

Murdock asked Angel why she wanted to know. She looked him square in the eyes and told him that I'm going to do everything that's possible to save my daughter. He knew she meant every word she said, so he gave her the information with one stipulation that she didn't get it from him. Angel went to the old lady's house who said she saw Baby Girl and the crew when they came out of the house that night. She wanted to question her to see what she really knew. When Angel knocked on Ms. Grey's door, she cracked it just enough for her to peak out of it.

She asked Angel, "Who are you and what do you want?" Angel told Ms. Grey that she was an investigator from the prosecution office; she needed to ask her a couple of questions about the murder that took place next door. Ms. Grey opened the door and let Angel in, without asking her for identification. Angel went in, and Ms. Grey asked her did she want anything to drink, and Angel said a glass of water would be nice.

When Ms. Grey went into the kitchen to get Angel a glass of water, Angel was digging in her purse for a pill that she got from an old lady in Columbia who she met awhile back. The pill will put her in the state of a right hemispheric stroke; it attacks the right side of your brain. It also affects your speech and language. When Ms. Grey handed Angel her water, she had a cup of tea she was drinking when Angel knocked on the door, so while she was out of the room, Angel dropped the pill in Ms. Grey's cup of tea. After three hours, Angel left Ms. Grey's house. Her caregiver found Ms. Grey stretched out on the floor. She was having problems in breathing and swallowing. Ms. Grey was rushed to the hospital by ambulance and admitted. The doctors worked on her as soon as she arrived there. Dr. Smith told her caregiver that she wouldn't be able to remember her; she had also lost movement on the right side of her body. The caregiver wanted to know what happened to her that fast; she was only gone to pick her medicine up from the pharmacies. She wasn't gone an hour. Dr. Smith explained to the caregiver that it attacked her body very quickly. She didn't even know what happened that it hit her so fast.

Angel was sitting down the street when she saw the caregiver going into the house; she was still sitting there when the ambulance pulled up and took Ms. Grey out on a gurney. She said to herself my job here is done on to the next victim. She was counting down the days before Baby Girl's trial began; she didn't have that much time to find this Lisa person, who sent the detectives the tapes. Angel knew she was going to be like a grey hound dog, trying to sniff Lisa out. It was going to be well worth it to save her daughter and the dream team.

Attorney Murdock was having lunch with the prosecuting attorney; she was sitting there smiling like a school girl because secretly she loved Murdock, but she didn't think he felt that way about her, but she was going to make him love her one way or the other. Prosecuting attorney Ms. Adonis Carlotta was an Italian sister with long black hair, a caramel completion, and pretty hazel-brown eyes. She stood 5'6, weighing 135 pounds; she had a flat stomach and 38B sized breast, and her ass wasn't flat. She came into the restaurant rocking the hell out of a white pinstripe suit made by Armani. She had a snakeskin purse made by Armani as well. When she walked in, every man in the room was staring as if she had just been handed an award of being a bad ass bitch. Adonis knew on a scale to one to ten that she was most definitely a ten.

Murdock knew she was a diamond in the ruff, and one day, he would give her a run for her money because one thing he knew for sure was she liked his style. When Adonis got close to the table where Murdock was sitting, he got up to pull out the chair for her to sit down. She said, "Thank you, you are quite the gentleman." He smiled and called the waitress over, so they could order their food and drinks. When the waitress took their order, she left them alone and returned to their table with their drinks. Murdock ordered a Crown Royal on the rocks, and Adonis ordered a Stolichnaya vodka with cranberry juice.

Adonis told Murdock, "All right, let's get down to business. I know you didn't invite me to lunch because I'm sexy as hell. This involves the murder case of Patrick Stewart and Reginald Willis. I want you to know that we have them dead to right. We have them on tape, plus we have their voices implicating the murder of Reginald Willis." Attorney Murdock told Adonis that shit wasn't going to hold water; they could have fabricated the facts. Whoever sent the tape might be the one who committed the murder's and trying to railroad his clients.

She told Murdock, "Stop bullshitting yourself. You know that they are guilty, and I'm going to prove it without a shadow of a doubt." He looked at Adonis with this sexy smile, and she got wet just looking at the fine specimen, sitting across from her.

He said, "Look, let's eat our lunch, and we will pick up where we left off after lunch. Do you agree?" She said "yes," and they started eating. After lunch was over, Murdock said, "Remember the case we had a couple of years back about this guy who molested his daughter? And he said he was out of town when the molestation took place. We had charged the man with the molestation case, and two weeks later, we found out that it was his identical twin brother that no one knew about because his mother had put him up for adoption." Adonis admitted that was a strange case, but he got released because we fought hard together to get his sentence over turn. She said that was the time when I was very impressed with your courtroom expression. You sat the room on fire that day; the media went wild.

Adonis knew where all of this was leading to; she owed Murdock some favors for helping her with some heavy case's she had before so he thought that this was as good of time as any for Adonis to pay up. Adonis said, "Come on, Murdock, stop beating around the bush and spit it out."

Murdock said, "I know this would be the case of the century for you, but I need my favor from you for this case." She said, "I really think these girls need to know that they can't take the law in their own hands running around, killing people like they have took an oath to do so." Murdock said, "I understand where you are coming from, but these girls have never been in trouble before, and none of them ever had a run in with the law at all."

Murdock looked at Adonis with his sexy ass eyes, and she fell for everything he was saying. She said the only thing we had was the tape and Lisa Chandler, and she kept moving around because she didn't want to get caught up in a long trial.

"So tell me, Attorney Murdock, what I'm going to get from you once this is over? Once all this madness is over how about we take a weekend on my boat. We can cruse the open sea and who knows nature can just take its own course, what you think?" What Murdock just said to Adonis was something she had been waiting to hear him say for two years, and he finally said it but at what price.

The trial was coming up fast, Baby Girl and her crew had two more weeks to worry; they knew for sure with that kind of evidence that the prosecutor had on them, they were going to be spending some time behind bars, but what they didn't know was killer Murdock had some shady shit up his sleeve. He wasn't about to let that million dollars get out of his reach if that meant he had to romance the prosecutor, then so be it. He wanted Adonis in his king-sized bed anyway but on his own time, but now that the time has arrived he was more than ready.

Angel gave Murdock a call to see if he made in progress with the prosecutor; he told Angel not to worry he had the case in the bag.

She said, "You sure, because this is my daughter's life we're talking about here." He told Angel that the kink's was being worked out as they speak. She said all right and hung up. When Angel hung up the phone from talking to Attorney Murdock, she wasn't restless anymore because she felt that he was handling the case, but if he let her down in any way, she was going to kill him and the prosecutor. Murdock said to himself, *Angel is a sexy ass bitch. She and Adonis have the same completion, and they both have that killer instincts—only Adonis take hers out in the courtroom, and Angel look like she will kill you at a drop of a hat.* Murdock knew street justice, and Angel had that capability just like her daughter and the rest of the crew; he knew for sure they were some dangerous females, and he wasn't trying to cross them.

The trial had begun, and the prosecuting attorney showed up without the evidence. She said she had it locked away for safekeeping in the evidence room.

When she went to get it, it wasn't there. She also told the judge that she sent a marshal to pick up Lisa Chandler; she too was missing. The marshal told the prosecuting attorney that Ms. Lisa Chandler had pack up in a hurry, leaving behind all her furniture. He told her it looked as if she wasn't coming back, no time soon. What they didn't know was Murdock flew out to meet Lisa in Connecticut and gave her fifty thousand dollars to disappear. She took the money. She and her son left Connecticut and went to stay with her mother in San Diego with no return address.

When Detective Cotton and his partner heard that, they went ballistic because they knew that was some bullshit. Even Mrs. Grey couldn't testify because she had a severe stroke; she couldn't remember who she was, let alone who the girls were running from the house the night of Crazy Red's murder. The prosecutor had no evidence, no witness, and the trial was dismissed. The media went wild; the case was over, and the H&H girls were free to go.

Chapter 13
Murdock and Adonis

AFTER THE TRIAL was over, Murdock stuck to his word. He and Adonis were leaving to go cruising the deep blue sea. He called Adonis to let her know that he was already at the marina, waiting her arrival. She said she had a few more things to pack, and she was on her way. Adonis pulled out all the stops she had and put all her sexy lingerie in her night bag. She wanted to seduce Murdock in ways he would never forget. When Adonis made it to the marina, she could see Murdock standing there with a glass of wine. She could see his physic ripping through his shirt; her nipples immediately grew hard. She was ready to test the waters very soon with Murdock; his body was sculptor to a T. Adonis wanted to squeeze every inch of his body; her mind was going a hundred miles a minute, thinking about Murdock being naked.

Adonis said, "I'm going to make him go blind looking at my fire-engine-red thong bikini bathing suit. I need his attention focused on me. We don't need to spend too much time drinking and talking. I've waited two years for this man to make love to me."

When Adonis approached the boat, Murdock was pouring them a glass of Cristal. She accepted the glass and he took her suitcases down below. She swallowed her first glass quick because she wanted to get into something more comfortable. She excused herself when Murdock came back capsize. When Adonis walked out with her fire-engine thong bathing suit on, just as she predicted, Murdock started chocking instantly; all he could say to Adonis was, "damn you look gorgeous."

She said, "thank you," and Murdock handed her another glass of Cristal. Murdock was trying to get control of his body parts; they were starting to get a mind of their own. He was continuously trying to keep his dick from going in the direction of Adonis so soon. He was savoring the taste for a little later. Murdock had stirred the boat out into the waters. Once he got it further out in the water, he was going to shut it down and head to the kitchen to cook a couple of lobsters he had picked up earlier for lunch. He was also going to steam some asparagus and a small green salad.

Adonis asked Murdock if he needed any help in preparing lunch, and he said, "No, you are my guest. I just need you to be comfortable and keep looking sexy." All the while Murdock was cooking, his mind was wondering in places; he knew that it had no business going, but Adonis's mind was going to the same places, thinking about him, where she wanted them to go with him being all over her. Murdock was basically thinking like any other man with a dick. He knew he wanted a shot of pussy from a gorgeous woman like Adonis. Adonis hadn't been with a man in a while. She wanted the affection; she needed to feel the touch of a man just holding her.

While Murdock and Adonis were having lunch, they were staring into each other's eyes. They knew they had a sexual chemistry together, and together they would explore their feelings of their sexual appetites. Murdock went to reach for the bottle of Cristal, and the bottle was empty. Adonis had finished the whole bottle. While he was cooking, he told her the only thing left to drink is the strong stuff.

He said, "I really don't think that you should be mixing wine with the strong stuff."

Adonis told Murdock, "I can handle whatever you throw my way, so what's its going to be, Mr. Attorney?"

Murdock said, "only thing we have to drink is Hennessey and patron." Adonis told Murdock to pour her glass of Patron.

He said, "All right, you are going to need some big girl panties for this drink because mixing wine with Patron is going to knock you on your ass."

Murdock held his glass of Patron up for a toast to Adonis. He said this is to a beautiful beginning, and then he looked at Adonis with lust in his eyes. She followed suit; she had the same kind of glare that Murdock had in his eyes. Murdock definitely turned on a switch in Adonis to make her feel comfortable enough to pursue him in the fight for his heart. She loved the fact that he was a strong man, and he had the body of a Greek god. Murdock went and stood right in front of Adonis; she exhaled deeply when he invaded her space. She could feel his warm breath on her skin; he went in for the kill. He kissed Adonis with passion and skill. He licked her lips slow and sexually. He made her feel like she was the last living female on earth.

Murdock was so into kissing and caressing Adonis that they didn't even notice the sun had went down; only thing they were thinking about at the time was going down in the bottom of the boat to the bedroom to fulfill their need of sexual pleasure. Adonis was feeling real good; she finally had the opportunity to embrace this man she dreamed so long about. Murdock had soft music playing; the lights were dim. He set the stage for romance perfectly. Murdock wasted no time caressing Adonis's big breast. Adonis stopped Murdock, and she told him to be gentle because it's been two years since she been with a man sexually. He told her not to worry; he would be as gentle as a lamb. The foreplay was getting juicy and electrifying; they were connecting in ways that they didn't think was possible for two people. They were more than ready to submit their bodies to one another.

When Murdock took off Adonis's bathing suit, he admired her beauty. She was flawless in all aspects of the word. He knew exactly what made her body tick. He knew kissing down the side of her neck was one of her pressure points because she was moaning and squirming to just the touch of his tongue. Murdock was on the verge of executing his plan; he wanted to take Adonis to the level of pleasure she alone ever dreamed of. He also wanted to touch Adonis in places she never been touched before. Murdock strapped up and was ready to dive in. Adonis wanted Murdock deep inside her, but Murdock had other plans. First, he started kissing down Adonis's stomach until he reached her pussy. He loved the Brazilian wax job; she also had a strawberry smell coming from her pussy that drove Murdock crazy.

Murdock was eating Adonis's pussy seductively, arousing his dick at the same time. He squatted down some more between Adonis's legs, so he could have a better thrashing going on with his tongue. She was feeling the warmth from Murdock's tongue going in a circular motion; he was working on sending Adonis into a convulsion. Adonis was feeling so good that she grabbed Murdock's head pushing his tongue deeper inside of her. Adonis started screaming; her body was doing jerks. She was trembling and calling Murdock's name out loud. She was telling Murdock that it felt so good. When she said that, Murdock sped up the process. He was eating Adonis pussy like it was his last meal.

Murdock's dick had got hard as Chinese arithmetic; he was ready for some serious fucking, but Adonis pushed him down on the bed because it was her turn to satisfy him. Adonis rubbed her hand down Murdock's dick. She teased the tip of his dick, licking up and down the shaft of it. She heard a moaning sound come from Murdock that's when she took his dick and deep throated it. She swallowed Murdock's dick with prestigious skills he couldn't hardly control himself. He realized he couldn't take it anymore and flipped Adonis over on her back, opening her legs wide. He started thrusting and pushing his dick into her womb until Adonis was screaming to the top of her lungs. She hadn't had sex like that before in her life. Murdock sat her ass on fire, and she was definitely going to make sure she kept him around.

Murdock and Adonis sexed each other all night until they felt asleep in each other's arms; they both were satisfied with each other's performance and they both thought the same thing about each other. Their bodies fit together like a glove; their lovemaking was very intense, and right then and there they knew they had something more than just having sex together. They had made a connection together that neither one of them was willing to give up. They had one more night together before they went back to work; they were going to make this last night count until they see each other again. Murdock had cooked breakfast and fed Adonis in bed; he wanted to spend their last day together, locked in the bedroom. He didn't know how good it felt making love while the boat was floating on water. After breakfast was over, Murdock clammed back in bed with Adonis; he was making plans to always be there for her whenever she needed him. He was dazed at how beautiful Adonis was; he couldn't keep his tongue out of her mouth. He crawled on top of her and got between her legs; he kissed her with deep passion. He noticed his dick had gotten extra hard; he stuck his dick inside Adonis's pussy and started long stroking her; the more they kissed, the more intense it got, and the more Adonis would tighten up her pussy walls to welcome his every stroke. Adonis was giving Murdock the full introduction to Ms. Kitty. She was opening and squeezing pussy muscles all over Murdock's dick.

That evening Murdock went ashore to get them something else to eat and drink; he decided to change their alcohol choice up a little bit. He bought two bottles of Grey Goose; he said to himself if Patron made Adonis as freaky as she had been the night before. He thought that the Grey Goose would probably make her stand on her head for big daddy. He smiled at the thought he had in his head. Murdock had been with a lot of females before, but none of them made him feel the comfort ability he had established in such a short time with Adonis; he couldn't believe he had dodged her for two years, only to have been missing out on the best sex he ever had.

When Murdock made it back with the food and drinks, Adonis was just coming out of the shower. They had fuck so much until her pussy was sore, but to Adonis it didn't matter because before she left Murdock to go home, she was going to have to soak in some Epsom salt. When she got home, Murdock was standing in the door way. When Adonis got out of the shower, she was glowing from the water that was sliding down off her body. Murdock was feeling things that he hadn't felt in a while. He didn't want to believe; he was pussy-whipped, but then again his heart strings were pulling at him. He was falling in love with Adonis; she had his nose open wide enough to drive a fifty-seven Chevy straight up his nose.

The sex between the both of them was like time had stopped for them both untill it was time for them to return back to work.

Adonis told Murdock, "I have a surprise for you tonight." She had a towel laid out where she wanted him to lay down, so she could give him a full-body massage. She had hot oils and a roller pin that slides up and down your back once the oil is applied. While Adonis was giving Murdock his massage, she didn't have on not one stitch of clothing, but she did have on a chocolate eatable thong—Murdock's favorite. When he spotted the chocolate thong, his lips got juicy. Just looking at it, he wanted to just dive into the chocolate treat with his tongue.

Adonis and Murdock knew this was their last night together, so as she was massaging him, they both turned their attention to the water. It was beautiful when they saw the sun coming down, sitting just above the water. Murdock stopped Adonis from massaging him; he raised up, pulled her face close to his, and started kissing her and rubbing his hands all over her body before she could stop him he had started eating on her chocolate eatable thongs. This time the way Murdock was eating her pussy was different; it was sensual. It had more meaning to it this time, and she knew he felt exactly how she was feeling. Murdock was licking and lapping the juices out of Adonis like his mouth and tongue were a suction cup. She was screaming "oh shittt." Murdock stopped and flipped Adonis over he was hitting it from the back; his dick was so deep in Adonis that they was clapping each other's pelvic bones. Murdock was shoving his big dick deep inside of Adonis's muscle walls, and she was clamping down on his dick like she was taking it home with her. Adonis breast were bouncing with the rhythm of the strokes Murdock was putting down; he picked up speed because he was about to cum. When Adonis felt the vein swell up on Murdock's dick, she pulled back, and Murdock shot off. He was trembling like a nigga going to the electric chair; they both had the most intense orgasm they had ever had. They both were whipped, and they knew that they would be spending the rest of their lives together.

Chapter 14
The Marriage of Murdock and Adonis

SUNDAY HAD ARRIVED, and it was time for Murdock and Adonis to return back to work. The next following morning, neither one of them wanted to leave each other, so they setup another date for Tuesday. Murdock figured since he was feeling so much love for Adonis, he didn't want to be without her, but they both knew they had to be cool once they got back because she had just help Murdock with a murder case; she knew those girls committed the crime, but she owed him a favor, and one she's glad she paid up. When Adonis made it to her office that morning, Detective Cotton was waiting on her; he straight up told Adonis that she was a shady prosecuting attorney, and he was going to see to it that she get's disbarred. Adonis told Cotton if you don't get your dirty ass out my office, I will be talking to your captain about harassment charges.

Adonis had a ten o clock trial that morning so she wasn't about to let Detective Cotton spoil her day. Cotton was trying to figure out what the hell happened with the murder case. He knew deep down inside that Adonis and Murdock were more than just colleagues. Cotton would soon find out that his assumptions were right because while Adonis was in court, Murdock was out shopping for an engagement ring. He was going to ask her to marry him; he didn't want to wait. He wanted Adonis with him; he wanted her to be Mrs. Murdock as soon as possible. He wasn't going to be without her one more night. When Adonis's trial case was over, she gave Murdock a call to see if he wanted to have lunch. He accepted; they had lunch at a restaurant called Ocean Over the Sea. It had an elegant setting, and you sure could feel the romance in the air.

While Murdock and Adonis were having lunch, he looked her in the eyes and held her stare; he asked Adonis will she marry him. Adonis thought she heard Murdock wrong.

She said, "Excuse me, Did you just ask me to marry you?" Before he could repeat the question, Murdock pulled out the five-carat engagement ring. Adonis started to cry because she really did love Murdock for a long time; she just didn't think they were on the same page. Murdock was getting ready to ask Adonis what was her answer when she reached down and pulled his head up and kissed him.

She said, "Yes, I would love to be your wife."

While Murdock and Adonis were waiting for their waitress to come over and take their order, Murdock told Adonis that he wanted to get married right away. He didn't want to be without her.

He said, "We can start making wedding plans right now." He asked Adonis did she want a small wedding or a large one. It didn't matter to him as long as she was happy. Adonis told Murdock that she had a large family, and she wanted at least two hundred people.

He said, "Well, we're going to have a large wedding because I have a large family as well." Before they went on to talk more about their wedding, Adonis cut Murdock off telling him about her unexpected visitor that was waiting in her office this morning. She told him that Detective Cotton was asking questions about what happened in the courtroom the day of the murder trial. He said that you and I hid the evidence, and he was going to prove it. Murdock told Adonis not to worry because the trial was dismissed, and they can't be tried again for the same murder. It's called double jeopardy; they can't be tried for the same case twice.

Once their lunch came to the table, they ate and made plans to meet up after lunch. They had a wedding to plan. Adonis let Murdock know she knew about the double jeopardy clause also, but she just didn't want Detective Cotton stirring up trouble. As soon as Adonis got back to her office, it was over a dozen of beautiful roses all over her office. Murdock had the flower shop to send them to her office while they were at lunch. Adonis was impressed. After work, Adonis headed home; she didn't have to call Murdock because he was already in route to her place. He wanted to get the ball rolling quickly; he had already talked to a minister about performing their vows. He knew if Cotton kept snooping around, he might find something, but he knew if they got married, they couldn't make his wife testify against her husband.

Murdock made it to Adonis house in record time. When she opened the door to let him in, she had on a robe with nothing on up under it. She had just got out of the shower; he could see her naked body through the sheer robe she was wearing. Murdock was reminiscing about the last time they were together sexually. He automatically rose to the occasion; he had begun to break out in a sweat. Before Adonis could close the door, he was kissing and rubbing all over her body. She let out a moan to let him know she was enjoying the taste of his tongue. Murdock picked Adonis up and carried her to the bedroom. He laid her down and rested his body on top of hers; they were intertwined in a kiss that sent both of them over the edge. She was moaning Murdock's name so softly in his ear, until he just started licking and sucking on Adonis big breast. He was sending Adonis straight to the place she wanted to be. He missed the warmth he felt being inside of Adonis; she knew just how to wrap Murdock up in her juices. He wanted to be able to wake up every morning next to Adonis. When Murdock and Adonis were finished making love, they jumped right back on their wedding plans. They set a date for that following Saturday. They had to call family, friends, and a wedding planner all in one day. Everything came together as planned. Murdock had a beautiful backyard so they decided to get married in his backyard.

Adonis had her wedding dress designed by Channel. The wedding gown she decided upon was a ten thousand dollar dress. Murdock spared no expense; he wanted his wife to be happy. Adonis chose to have two maids of honor—her sister, Carolyn, and her best friend, China. She had four bridesmaids. Murdock had two best men—both of his brothers, Charlie and Houston. He also had four groomsmen; he decided that he wanted his tucks to be designed by Armani. Their colors were lavender and white; they had three chefs from Italy, France, New Orleans, and Washington DC. Their menu consists of grilled lamb chops to arugula salad; their menu had enough food to feed a small country. They even had ice sculptor of Adonis and Murdock.

Their wedding day was right around the corner, and everyone was arriving. Adonis's sister and mother arrived three days before the wedding, helping her get things arranged. Murdock was going to surprise her with a honeymoon in the Virgin Islands; they were going to be there for a week. He was hoping that they spend most of their time in bed. When Adonis's gown arrived from Paris, it had a hundred foot train. It was white trimmed in lavender with beautiful diamonds studs going around the waist of the dress. It was the most gorgeous dress Adonis had ever seen. It looked more beautiful in person; the wedding took place Saturday evening at three. Everyone was glowing when Adonis came walking down the aisle—she was stunning. She couldn't wait for the minister to announce them husband and wife.

The wedding lasted for fifteen minutes. Adonis got her wish—she was Mrs. Mark Murdock and the happiest woman in the world.

Chapter 15
Olivia the Secret FBI Agent

OLIVIA HAD BEEN an FBI agent for four years; she was planted in Spellman College to find out information on the Columbia mafia. She had been checking in with her boss every chance she got. He told Olivia she had to do whatever it took to get the job done that included sleeping with men to murder. She was to become close to Gloria Carter a.k.a. Baby Girl. The FBI couldn't get anything on Angel. They knew she was notorious for her acts of crime, but they couldn't catch her in doing her dirt. They knew she moved in the night like a ninja so to find out what was really going on, they had to put someone on the inside of Angel's camp. Olivia almost got busted when they were being trained to shoot high-powered weapons by Ramon's Uncle Joe. He asked Olivia how she learned to shoot like that. She told Uncle Joe her father was in the military. Angel checked out all the girls before she accepted them as her own personal dream team, but what she didn't know was the FBI was good at covering their tracks as well. Olivia's parents were in the military, and she was a military brat. She was also born into money so she fit right in with the other girls; they made sure Olivia wouldn't look suspect.

Olivia had graduated from high school, joined the police department, applied for the FBI, and she made it on the first try. The FBI had thought of ways to info trade Angel's camp. They knew she did a lot of killings, and she was involved with the Columbia mafia. They didn't want to take any chances with Angel slipping through their hands, so they had to create Olivia as a college student and for her to become best friend with Baby Girl. She was to inform them of everything that went down with Angel and the Columbia mafia, but lately Olivia hadn't been staying in contact with her superior so he started to worry about Olivia crossing over to the other side. He knew she was a vibrate young woman, and he was hoping that she didn't straddle both sides of the fence because she was missing in action on more than one occasion, so he was going to have her hauled in to the office if she didn't answer his call this time.

Olivia was beginning to feel frighten. She saw Angel in rear form, and she didn't want to be caught up in Angel's web if she found out that she was deceiving her. When they got arrested for the murders of Cool and Crazy Red, her superior was the one to have them to place Olivia in the bull pen with the rest of the dream team. He didn't want anyone else to think that she was treated any differently than the rest of the girls. Her superior had already found out that she and the other members of the dream team had targeted big-time drug dealers; she was looking more and more like she had changed teams. He really didn't want to give up on Olivia. He wanted to have a face-to-face with her to see what the hell was going on with her.

Olivia knew she had to check in sooner or later; she wasn't able to be alone at the time. They had been kicked out of school so they were always around each other all the time, so she decided she was going out today by herself because if she didn't, she knew for sure that her superior would send someone out to pull her in, and she wasn't taking that chance of someone seeing her talking to a federal agent. Olivia found a store on the corner where they were staying so she could use the pay phone to call her boss to give him details on what was going on. They had a brief conversation before Ava walked in the store. Ava was standing outside the store, the whole time talking to this guy who was trying to score a date with her. She watched Olivia talking on the pay phone. She didn't know why she had to use the pay phone when she had a cell phone. To Ava that made her look very suspect. Ava made a mental note to ask Olivia what was wrong with her cell phone that she had to walk to the corner store to use the pay phone.

Olivia thought to herself, *I'm playing a very dangerous game if Angel ever find out that I'm an undercover agent I'll be dead before sunrise.* Now that Ava knew about Olivia using the pay phone, she wanted to know who she had to call so important that she had to do it in private. Olivia had started getting nervous since Ava brought to her attention about seeing her using the pay phone. Olivia tried to tell Ava she was talking to her cell phone provider about her phone; it wasn't working. Right after she told Ava that lie, her phone started ringing. Ava just looked at Olivia like she was up to something.

Ava was starting to keep an eye on Olivia. She wasn't going to get caught up in anything. Even though they still did out-of-town hits for Angel, she just felt in her heart that Olivia was acting suspect. She was hiding something, and Ava made it her business to find out what she was hiding. Even Olivia's attitude had changed. She didn't want to hang out with them as much anymore. The girls wanted to go out to have some drinks at this new club called the Center Stage. They all were pumped up to go and have some fun for a change, especially since they didn't have the murder cases hanging over their heads anymore, but Olivia didn't want to go. She had plans on meeting her superior, once they were gone.

When Baby Girl and the rest of the crew left to go to the new club, Olivia waited until she thought they were gone, but what she didn't know was Ava stayed behind, hiding in the shadows, following Olivia to meet her superior. When Olivia pulled in the parking lot of mercy hospital and got out of her car and into a black Crown Victorian. Ava knew she was working for the Feds as an informant or she was a federal agent herself. It didn't matter because the shit was going to hit the fan as soon as Ava told the other girls what she found out about Olivia.

Ava stood, parked three rows back, watching Olivia sitting inside the Crown Victorian. She sat there inside the car for at least forty-five minutes. She wanted to know was the dream team being set up by one of their own. When Olivia did get out of the car, she was fidgeting with her bra. Ava could see her getting something from a gentleman that was old enough to be her father. At that point, Ava was getting angry because she trusted Olivia more than anyone else in the crew; they were tight, and they shared a dorm room together.

Ava didn't know if she should tell the team first or bring it to Olivia to see if she was going to lie her way out of the situation she was now in. Ava waited to get Olivia alone so she can ask her straight out about the night she followed her to mercy hospital and saw her getting into a black crown Victorian. Olivia's mouth flew wide open because her cover was blown. She could try and lie her way out of it or tell Ava what her choices would be if she was to tell the team that she worked for the FBI.

Ava told Olivia, "Bitch, do you know what would happen to the both of us if Angel knew you were a federal agent. She would kill us in the worse way possible, and I don't think that I want to keep your secret a secret. I'm not going to lose my life for a federal agent that lied to all of us about being a friend and sister. You know enough shit about us to get us buried under the damn jail."

Ava said, "You know what, Olivia. I feel like killing you myself, but I'm going to be smart. I'm going to let Baby Girl decide on your fate because it's either you or me and trust me when I tell you this, Angel is not going to be happy about this."

Olivia knew she had to think quickly. She couldn't let Ava spill the beans. She had to stop her somehow. Before she could think things through, she pulled her revolver out, but she was too slow, Ava was quicker than Olivia.

Ava said, "Bitch, I knew you were going to pull some crazy shit. That's why I came prepared. Look out in the hallway." When Olivia opened the door, Baby Girl and Angel were standing there, listening the whole time. They had Ava hooked up to a small microphone, hidden in her ear. They had been on to Olivia since the first day Ava followed her to mercy hospital. Ava had called Angel and Baby Girl personally herself to let them know that there was a rat in their camp.

Chapter 16
The Murder of Olivia the FBI Agent

OLIVIA KNEW SHE was in deep shit. Once she opened the door, Angel and Baby Girl walked in. She looked like she was about to pass out. She had just taken off her tape recorder that her superior said she had to keep on her at all times. It was good that she did because Angel had Baby Girl and Ava to search Olivia's bedroom while she kept Olivia's company in the living room. Olivia knew they weren't going to find the tape recorder because she had hid it inside the back of the toilet stool. Angel told them to stop looking because Olivia was going back with her to Columbia. When Olivia heard Angel say she was going back to Columbia with her, she lost it. She heard from a few people while they were in Columbia how Uncle Joe did you when he found out you were a snitch. Angel told Baby Girl to tie that bitch down.

"You no longer exist, Olivia. You betrayed me and the Columbia mafia. Do you know what the mafia is going to do to you, once we make it back to Columbia. It's going to be lights out for you, but first you are going to be past around to every man that frequents the sexy ladies, whore house. Olivia was hoping that her superior heard what went down before she hid the recorder in the toilet. She was so scared that her heart was beating so fast. She thought her heart was going to bust out of her chest. She knew that Angel was going to make her pay. Angel had a needle set up with heroine. She shot Olivia up with enough heroin to keep her drugged up until they made it back to Columbia. She had Ramon outside waiting in the car; they flew down to Atlanta in their own personal jet. When Olivia passed out from the heroin, Ramon came in and picked her up and carried her to the car. When Olivia finally came to, she was tied up to a bed in Angel's whore house, the sexy ladies, in Columbia. Before Angel started to torture Olivia, she wanted to know what did the Feds know about her and the Columbia mafia. Did they have enough evidence to come after them? Olivia told Angel what she thought she wanted to hear, but Angel could see through all that Maybelline that Olivia was wearing. She knew Olivia was lying through her teeth.

But to add insult to injury, Olivia told Angel that she could do whatever she wanted to do with her because the Feds knew exactly where she was and that they should be raiding that place very soon. Angel, Ramon, and Uncle Leo were in the room with Olivia when Angel was questioning.

Her Uncle Leo said, "Now, we need to move up higher in the mountains in Calli Columbia. Angel, you take care of that bitch. I'll go get things moving, so we will be gone before the Feds arrive." When Uncle Leo told Angel to get rid of Olivia, she couldn't believe she let one slip through the cracks, but she knew one thing for sure that she had to get her shit in order. She had fucked up.

Olivia was tied to the bed laughing because she finally saw fear in Angel's eyes for a change. She said to Angel, "Bitch, you do have a heart 'huh.' Angel was so mad." When Olivia noticed the change in her eyes, she spit in Olivia's face this time causing Olivia to laugh even harder because she knew her time had finally come to have the last laugh before she died. Angel took out her machete because she wanted to send the Feds a souvenir; she wanted them to think twice next time about sending a child to do a grown man's job. Angel swung her machete real quick and fast. She cut Olivia's leg clean off her body. The sight of Olivia seeing her leg being disconnected from her body sent Olivia into a coma state. She just closed her eyes like she had fallen asleep. Angel left the room to go to shed. She had a heavy duty aluminum box out there that she needed for shipment her intentions With the aluminum box was detrimental. She took the box back into the room where Olivia was still asleep. Angel took her machete; she went to work on Olivia like she was a side of beef. She took her head off last because she wanted her head to be delivered to the Feds in Atlanta; she was making a statement to the Feds, "do not fuck with the Columbian mafia."

Once Angel was done cutting up Olivia, she took her remains behind the shed and burned them. The aroma that was coming from Olivia's burned body smelt like Angel was burning rubber. When everyone were gathering their things to get the hell out of dodge, they caught a glimpse of the black smoke coming from behind the shed, but Ramon had got their things and was waiting on Angel to hop in the truck. They were moving so fast that Uncle Leo forgot to retrieve all the artillery out of the gun house; they had already loaded the truck up twice so he had to call for another truck to come to pick up the other remaining guns.

Angel took the aluminum box to the post office to have it delivered in one day by airmail. She wanted the Feds to get it the very next day. Uncle Leo, the head of the Columbian mafia, was proud of the way Angel handle her business with the Feds. He said she learned acceptably well. He knew when he chose Angel to be their personal assassin, she wasn't going to let them down. Angel and the Columbia mafia drove all night when they reached the top of the mountain; everyone was tired. They had one big house with eight bedrooms and five bathrooms, so everyone was at least comfortable for the time being.

The next day when the aluminum box arrived at the federal building, the Feds weren't going to open it without letting the bomb squad get a look in the inside of it first; the bomb squad cleared the whole building out. Everyone had to come out of the building; they weren't taking any chances. The bomb squad sent for one of their robots called TARD stands for tactical action retrieve and destroy. Once the robot took pictures with the mini-camera, it sent the pictures straight to the bomb squad. When they saw it was a head of a human being, they went ballistic because they had seen just about everything but to find a human head. It was sending one hell of a message.

Olivia's superior was heated. He couldn't believe Olivia was gone; he took one look at her head in that aluminum box and lost his breakfast. He ordered an all-points bulletin. He wanted the Columbian mafia at any cost; they took one of his federal agents, and if they killed one, they might as well had killed them all because now it was on like a pot of neck bones. Everybody who was affiliated with the Columbia mafia was going down. Angel woke up the next morning wondering if the Feds had got her surprise she had delivered. She only wished that she was a fly on the wall when they opened up that box.

Olivia's superior couldn't sleep after he viewed her head in that box. Angel had even pinned back Olivia's eyes so that they would remain open as if she was staring at the person who sent her to info trade the Columbia mafia. Olivia's superior had to call Olivia's parents to tell them that their daughter was dead and that they wouldn't be having a proper burial for their daughter because she didn't have a body, just a head that had been decapitated from the rest of her body. He didn't know if he could handle telling them that because he put Olivia in dangerous situation, knowing that she wasn't ready to be out in the field with notorious people like the Columbia mafia.

Chapter 17
Sophia and Michelle on the Run

SOPHIA AND MICHELLE had been in the intensive care unit at north side hospital in Atlanta for two months; they were finally going to be released. They both were doing fine physically, but mentally they were a nervous wreck. They knew they had to get the hell out of Atlanta and fast. They got discharged from the hospital and went straight and got a rental. They didn't want anything that connected them to Atlanta or the dream team; they were going to start their life over somewhere else. They both had their four million dollars transferred to a bank in South Dakota; they had plans on seeing a plastic surgeon when they arrived in South Dakota. They knew it was going to cost them a great deal of money, but they didn't care because the way they looked now was like something out of monster scene. Sophia and Michelle cried every time they would look at each other; both of them were bitter with hatred. The thought of what Angel did to them hunted them; they wanted her to suffer just as bad as she made them suffer and to think that she was their aunt was devastating. They had to find a way to get justice for their mothers and themselves. She had turned Sophia and Michelle to bitter people just like her.

Michelle had drove all night; their faces was so disfigured that they didn't want anyone staring at them like they had a role in a Freddie Kruger movie, so they just drove nonstop to south Dakota. When they had to stop for gas, Michelle had to put on a mask that she bought from a costume store. She felt like the ugly duckling. They knew that they would be too embarrassed to even stop at a fast food restaurant to get them something to eat, so they got all the snacks they thought they would need from the snack machine at the hospital when they were released.

When Michelle stopped at a rest stop off the highway, she took a Yellow

Pages while no one was looking. She wanted to look up every plastic surgeon she could find before they got to South Dakota. She was worried about Sophia because she was so messed up that she stopped speaking the whole time. Michelle was driving; the only sounds she heard coming from her sister was sniffling, coming from Sophia crying. Michelle told Sophia not to worry. She was going to fix everything. They were going to get Angel one way or the other. "She will pay I promise you she will." When Sophia heard her sister say those words to her she was thinking the same thing, but she just couldn't form her mouth to say so. It was getting dark fast, and Michelle was feeling a little bit at ease. She had passed a couple of cars on the highway that had caught a glimpse of her disfigured face, and it made her feel very uncomfortable, but she just sped up to get out of their view. She knew she was burnt badly, and she was missing a beautiful head of hair. She didn't know if her hair would ever grow back, but she was sure going to find out if anything could be done for her scalp.

Two days later, they had made it to South Dakota; they had went to a real state agency to purchase them a condo, but the office was closed so they rented them a hotel room at the regency hotel for a couple of weeks until they could get their business in order. Michelle ordered room service because her sister hadn't ate anything the whole time they were on their way to South Dakota. She knew she had to eat something to keep up her strength. She wasn't about to lose the only family she had left. Room service brought up enough food for the two of them to last a couple of days. Sophia still didn't want to eat until Michelle told her that they had to be strong for one another. We have to gain back what Angel took from us. We can't let her win. She has to pay if we don't see to it that she reap what she sow who will. Sophia understood what her sister was saying to her. She just felt like her soul had been drained. She still was beautiful, but her bodied had made her feel like a stitched up mannequin. Sophia was afraid to pull off her clothes because all the marks that the stitches left on her body, it looked like a road map.

Michelle made two phone calls to two different plastic surgeons that specialize in the type of plastic surgery they need. She set up appointments for both of them for the next morning at ten. They also had to go back to the real state office again; they wanted some place they could finally call home for a change. That night while Michelle was sleeping she had a dream about her mother. She told Michelle she was sorry about what happened to her. She also told her that she loved her very much. Her mother also told her to use what she left her to bring Angel down. Sometimes you have to think before you move too fast on revenge, you will be the one laying on cold steel with a tag on your toe.

The next morning came quick; that was the first time that Michelle was able to sleep all night without jumping in her sleep, thinking that Angel found them and was trying to finish the job. She looked over in the other bed to see if Sophia was still asleep, but she wasn't in the bed at all. She also had a dream about her mother also. She told Michelle, "Life brings changes and challenges, but don't let the challenges change your life. Make it worth living." Even though her mother opened her mind to what she knew she should be doing. She also opened her heart. Sophia looked at her sister.

She said, "You know we are going to be all right. All we need to do is get our bodies reconstructed, and the rest will be history."

That same morning, the girls went in to talk with the plastic surgeon. They were proud of what he said because he looked at them and told them he could make them look the same way they did before. They had pictures of themselves which they showed the surgeon. The only thing about their surgery was that they didn't want to look like they did before. They wanted to look totally different; they were beautiful before, but they wanted their whole appearance to be changed on the outside. They knew he couldn't do anything about the inside. As long as they didn't look like Sophia and Michelle, they were going to be hell on wheels. They even came up with new names for themselves as well. Sophia's name was going to be Olympia Strong, so Michelle said, "You know you're right if we are changing the way we look why not change our names as well, so I think my name should be Darcy Cobs." They both had their first laugh together since Angel disfigured them. Now that they were going to get their lives back, they were happy for a change.

Chapter 18
The Abduction and Rape of Baby Girl

GLORIA A.K.A. BABY Girl, Denise, and Ava had gotten board. They started bar hopping every other night; they found another new club that had opened up on the east side of Atlanta. They wanted to see what it was like; they heard from other girls that this club was off the chain. It had three floors with wraparound bars; each floor accommodated their own dance floors. The club called the underground spoke volume. It had high ceilings; each floor was decorated differently, and the atmosphere was something that made you feel relaxed and at home. The people that frequent the club was high-profile people that carried a lot of weight in Atlanta like attorneys, undercover cops, and niggas with big drug dealers status; those big-time drug dealers felt right at home because they paid a substantial amount of money to the undercover cop's to socialize in the same setting with people of power. Baby Girl and the remaining crew got dressed to go to the underground to check it out. When Denise, Ava, and Baby Girl arrived at the underground, they were in an awe. The underground was just what everyone said it was. It had people of all races there, spread throughout all three floors.

When Baby Girl walked in, she immediately got spotted by this big-time drug dealer named Jose. He had only been in Atlanta for a few months. He and his two bodyguards Bumper and Dick Tracey were peeping Baby Girl and her friends out when they entered the door. He had heard from his cousin Lemon that Baby Girl and her crew were the ones who killed their cousin Crazy Red a.k.a. Patrick Willis. When Jose thought about how Baby Girl and her crew got down with robbing dope boys. He thought to himself, *I might as well get to know my arch enemy a little better. Maybe if I let her get to know my drug status, she might think about trying to rob a nigga. That way I won't feel bad about what I'm going to do to that bitch.*

Baby Girl was standing at the bar, admiring the hell out of Jose. He was dark with smooth chocolate skin; he had a low fade haircut with enough jewelry on to give at least five people in the bar. He stood 5'11; he was drape in a cream-colored Armani linen suit with a pair of Armani cream-colored loafers trimmed in dark brown stitches. When Jose smiled, he had pearl white teeth. When Baby Girl saw that Jose was admiring her, she was hoping that the handsome specimen of a man would come over to her and sweep her off her feet. As soon as she thought it, Jose went straight over to the bar and offered to buy her a drink. She accepted, and it was on from there. He asked Baby Girl was she there by herself.

She said, "Why? Are you here by yourself."

Jose said, "Hold up, ma. I'm sorry. Let's start over. My name is Jose, and your name is—"

She said, "Toni." Right then and there, he knew she was lying because he knew for sure her name was Gloria Carter because he saw the news when they were arrested, and he followed the trial.

Jose's two right-hand men earned their name titles from high jacking people for their cars. Bumper was the one who used to cause accidents with his victims by bumping the back of their cars, just to get their attention, while Dick Tracey came up behind them with his 9 mm and surprise them with the element of surprise. Jose had plans for Baby Girl; he didn't want to kill her just yet. He wanted her to suffer first; he could tell from the way she carried herself that she thought she had balls as big as any man. Jose carried his self with pride and confidence; he carried a lot of power in Atlanta being a drug lord. He had at least four corrupted police officers on his team as well. He paid them a substantial amount of money; they did everything from murder to drug trafficking for Jose so to abduct Baby Girl would be a walk in the park for them. Baby Girl was sitting in VIP with Jose and his right-hand men, enjoying herself when Denise came upstairs to tell her that they were ready to leave. She asked Baby Girl was she staying or was she leaving with them. Before she could answer Denise, Jose told her that she could stay with him. He would see to her getting back home when she was ready to go. She told Denise that she and Ava could go on home, and she would see them as soon as she got there. They said their good-byes, and Denise and Ava bounced.

Jose excused himself from Baby Girl to go holler at his boy's in private; he told them to tell two of his corrupted police officers, Duncan and Freddrick that he wanted them to intercept them when they got ready to take Baby Girl home. He wanted them to pull them over and kidnap Baby Girl, and Jose would call them later with instructions on where he wanted them to take her. Bumper delivered the message to Duncan, and they agreed. They didn't like Baby Girl anyway because she had the mentality of a man, but in reality they didn't like Baby Girl because she got off with murder charges of two people that they knew. She committed those murders, and she had killer Murdock for her attorney; they were out for blood, so kidnapping Baby Girl would be an honor for them.

Club underground was getting ready to close for the night, and Jose told Baby Girl that Bumper and Dick Tracey were going to take her home because he had some important business he had to take care of before he turned in for the night. She said all right and kissed Jose on the cheek and left. What Baby Girl didn't know was this was going to be a nightmare she would never forget because right after she left the club, the two officers pulled Bumper over three blocks from the club. They said he had just rolled through a stop sign. He said, "Fuck you pigs, y'all just see a nigga in a fifty thousand dollar ride, and he's black that's some bull shit, and you know it." The officer told Bumper to shut the fuck up and get out of the car. As soon as Bumper stepped out of the car, Officer Fredrick told Baby Girl and Dick Tracey to step out the car too.

Dick Tracey told Officer Fredrick, "Why are you harassing us? We didn't do shit y'all punk ass police just profiling a nigga that's all." Dick Tracey told the officers that they were some damn renter cops with a little authority that gave them the power to push up on black people.

Duncan told Bumper and Dick Tracey to shut the hell up before they take them somewhere and beat the hell out of them. Both Bumper and Dick Tracey shut the hell up; they played their part perfectly into the kidnapping. Right when they shut up, Officer Duncan pulled out his 9 mm shot up in the air, and Bumper and Dick Tracey took off running, leaving Baby Girl to fend for herself. Before Baby Girl could scream, Officer Duncan hit her with the butt end of his 9 mm, knocking her unconscious. Officer Fredrick picked her up and laid her in the backseat of their crown Victorian. Jose called Officer Duncan right on time because Baby Girl was still unconscious; he gave both officers instructions to bring Baby Girl to one of his dope house.

When Jose got to his dope house, Baby Girl was already tied up with duct tape to a bed that they had in one of the bedrooms. Jose dismissed the officers, and he went over to the bed to undress Baby Girl. He wanted to rape her. When he was finished with her, he wanted Bumper and Dick Tracey to have a turn in raping Baby Girl too. The whole time Baby Girl was being raped, she didn't move. She thought that she was in a bad dream until she opened her eyes to see Dick Tracey humping on her like a dog in heat. She couldn't believe she got setup by the police who are the ones that suppose to serve and protect you, but nothing was like it seemed to be these days. She just thought, *it was payback time for what she had done to so many other people.*

After Jose and his right-hand men finished raping Baby Girl, he bought a picture of his cousin Crazy Red a.k.a. Patrick Willis and shoved it in Baby Girl's face. He told her I know for a fact that you and your little crew robbed and killed my cousin. Baby Girl was looking at Jose with a death stare because she knew if they didn't kill her, she was going to most definitely kill him and his men and those two dirty corrupted cops. Jose had a black bag with everything he needed to torture Baby Girl. He pulled out a pair of brass knuckles; he had Bumper to sit her up in a chair.

He told Baby Girl, "Bitch, since you want to act like a dude, I'm going to treat you like one."

Jose started hitting Baby Girl in the face with those brass knuckles like she was a nigga; he broke both her jaws and her nose. He knocked out four of her front teeth. Baby Girl passed out from the brutal beating Jose was putting on her. When Jose got done beating Baby Girl, she was unrecognizable. She was so bloody until she looked like a pig that had just got gutted for a Summer Bar-BQ. Jose told Bumper and Dick Tracey to get rid of her. He told them to take that bitch and put her in the trash can dumpster where she belong, but don't put her in no can near his dope house.

They did what Jose told them; they dropped Baby Girl in a dumpster near the underground club. She had been raped and beaten to a bloody pulp; the bartender of the underground was taking out the trash when he spotted this naked figure of a female that was bloody from head to toe; he ran back in the club to call the police. When they arrived on the scene, she was still unconscious. The ambulance arrived five minutes after the police. The EMS lifted Baby Girl up out of the dumpster and put her on the gurney. She had lost so much blood that she barely had a pulse, so they gave her some oxygen and rushed her straight to mercy general hospital. Baby Girl didn't have any identification on her so they had to call her Jane Doe.

Denise woke up the next morning wondering why Baby Girl hadn't come home so she started calling Baby Girl's cell phone, and it kept going straight to voice mail. Denise felt that something was terribly wrong because Baby Girl never turned her phone off. Denise woke up Ava to let her know that something was not right.

"I knew we shouldn't have left Baby Girl at the club by herself. Now she's missing." Ava told Denise to calm down because they didn't know for sure if Baby Girl was missing or was she just laid up with that drug dealer Jose. Denise told Ava that, "If she doesn't show up in the next four hours, we're going looking for her all right because I'm getting this sick feeling in my stomach, and I only get that feeling when something is wrong. I'm telling you, Ava. Our girl is in trouble." While Baby Girl was having surgery done on her face at mercy general hospital, Denise and Ava were on their way to club underground to see if anyone saw her leaving last night with anyone. The bartender remembered them from the night before, but he couldn't tell that Baby Girl was the one that was with Denise and Ava because she was so bloody lying in that dumpster.

When Denise asked the bartender about Jose, he pretended that he didn't know who she was talking about, but in reality he knew Denise was referring to Jose, and he wasn't trying to get caught up in nobody's mess. Denise was worried to death, and she needed a drink to calm her nervous stomach so she ordered her a shot of Crown Royal on the rocks. When she dropped her purse on the floor next to the bar stool, she noticed Baby Girl's purse caught up under the bar stool. She picked it up and showed it to Ava that's when they knew something was going on because Baby Girl wouldn't have left her twelve hundred dollar designer clutch purse anywhere. She was right. When they were going to ask the bartender another question, the detectives came in to ask him about the woman he found in the trash dumpster this morning.

The bartender saw the look that Denise and Ava were giving him, when the detectives said something about a female being found in the dumpster. Before the bartender could answer the detectives question, he was turning the sound up on the television he had on, only to notice that the news reporters were at the hospital, trying to get an interview with the doctor who was doing surgery on the female who they found in the trash dumpster outside of the club the underground. Denise told Ava that they needed to go over to the hospital because she had a funny feeling that it could be Baby Girl, and the only way they could be sure if they went over there and checked it out.

When Denise and Ava made it over to the hospital, they went up to the receptionist desk and asked the nurse about the young lady they found in the trash dumpster outside of the club underground. The nurse asked them were they related to the young lady because if they weren't any kin to her, she couldn't give them any information. Denise told the nurse that they were cousins. She even told the nurse Baby Girl's government name. Once the nurse heard her say Jane Doe's real name, she was happy because now they could put a name to their Jane Doe. The nurse told them that it would be another hour before she came out of surgery because whoever beat her broke both of her jaws and her nose; she was even missing four teeth. Ava and Denise started to cry because they felt it was their fault because they knew they shouldn't have left her in a club they only visited once and with a drug lord that they were planning on robbing in two days.

Baby Girl came out of surgery in a coma; her jaws had been wired together, and her nose had to be reset. She was in bad shape, and Denise didn't know if they should contact Angel to let her know that Baby Girl needed her. Denise knew that the Feds were hot on Angel's trail, and she didn't want it to be on her conscious if Angel came to the hospital and got picked up by the Feds, but she knew for sure that she would die by the hands of Angel if her daughter Baby Girl died and she didn't get the chance to see her one last time. Denise thought she was in a sticky situation, but she couldn't deny that if it was her, she would want her mother right there by her side, so she decided to give Angel a call on a pay phone away from the hospital.

When Angel received the call from Denise stating that Baby Girl had been beaten and was in a coma, she didn't care about getting caught. Her daughter needed her, and she was going to be by her side. Angel was preparing to leave Columbia to get to Atlanta as soon as Uncle Leo got the jet fueled and ready to go. Ramon wasn't letting her leave without him to keep Angel from getting busted by the Feds; he was going to rent a hotel room and make her stay locked up in the room until he came back from the hospital, checking things out first. When Ramon and Angel arrived in Atlanta, he got them a room at the Ramada inn. Angel was historical. She wanted to know what the hell happened to her baby. Somebody was going to pay for beating her baby, and Denise and Ava better have a damn good explanation.

Ramon arrived at mercy general hospital and called Denise to let her know that he was downstairs in the lobby; he wanted to know what floor that they were on. Denise told Ramon they were on the second floor in room 232. They had Baby Girl in the intensive care unit; she was just laying there like she was asleep. Ramon saw Baby Girl, and he broke down crying because she didn't look like herself at all. Her skin was black and purple; she looked fragile. He couldn't believe that they left her behind. She should have left with them when they went back to Columbia.

Angel was going to see to it that Baby Girl went back to Columbia this time, plus she wanted Denise and Ava to fix what happened because if they didn't, she was going to make them look worse than her daughter did.

Chapter 19
Bad Move

BABY GIRL WAS still in the hospital in a coma. She was getting around the clock treatment from the doctors and the nurses on staff. She even had an admirer name Chico that she knew nothing about; he took one look at Baby Girl and knew she was the one for him. Even though she was covered with all those bandages, he could see her beauty. He made sure every day that he checked in on her; he would sneak in her room at night and read books to her. He was told by his grandmother that comatose patients could still hear your voice when you spoke to them; it just meant that they were in a deep coma like sleep. Chico was black and Puerto Rican with a head full of black wavy curls; he had skin as smooth as a baby ass. He also had swagger something Baby Girl always looked for in the guys she chose to hang out with. When Jose heard that Baby Girl was hanging on by a thread; he was smiling because he wanted her soul to be badly beaten down to the point where it would change her lifestyle of trying to do a grown man's Job.

What Jose didn't know was he had opened up a can of worms; he was going to be six feet deep fucking around in Angel's backyard. He would soon find out that he made a bad move because now him and his right-hand men will meet a mast of destructions that will make him afraid to close his eyes at night. Denise and Ava stayed camped outside club underground for days, trying to catch up with Jose and his men. While they sat there waiting, they found out that undercover cops, politicians, attorneys, and the mayor were frequent visitors of club underground; they took pictures of everyone who visited club underground for the past two days. Jose had called ahead to club underground to reserve the third floor VIP section for an important meeting that he had with his drug connect from Kansas city.

The connect wanted to meet with Jose in a public place; he was bringing over a quarter of a million dollars worth of product to Jose, so he had to bring two of the biggest brothers he could find to the meeting with him; each one of these guys stood 6'7 inches, weight in at three hundred pounds of nothing but muscles. That night was going to be something that Denise and Ava had been waiting for they slept in their car at night waiting on Jose to arrive but was ordered by Angel to call her as soon as they found out anything.

Denise knew that Jose had something to do with what happened to Baby Girl because his cousin Lemon told his girlfriend Connie everything that took place with Baby Girl and Jose. Connie was a girlfriend of Denise's who attended Spellman as well. She didn't know she was about to get Jose killed. She just thought that she was making girl talk.

Ava told Denise, "Girl, don't you know pillow talk is a motherfucker. Word of mouth will get your ass wiped the hell out." She said the funny thing is if it wasn't for Lemon running his damn mouth to Jose, he wouldn't be on the shit list with his cousin so that makes him a liability as well, so instead of three niggas dying, it's going to be four because once Jose gets what's coming to him, we are going to personally fuck Lemon up for talking like a bitch.

Mercy general hospital was crawling with the media; they were trying to see if the police found out who Jane Doe was, the female they found outside in a dumpster behind club underground a week ago. They had found out who she was; they just weren't ready to leak it to the press just yet. They were trying to keep everything hush-hush for now; they had bigger fish to fry, and telling the media that Baby Girl was the daughter of Angel Carter wasn't an option right now, especially since she was wanted by the Feds. This case had to be on high alert but on a low profile on a need-to-know basis; the FBI had shit on lock wasn't nothing moving Unless they knew about everything and everybody, the case they had built up on Angel was top priority. Angel knew that if she showed up at the hospital, it would most definitely be a shoot out at the hospital between her and the Feds so she kept her distance for now.

Jose arrived at club underground at eight that night. His connect Diego was there waiting. When he arrived, the meeting began soon. As Jose sat down, Diego's two bodyguards, Jesus and Alex, stood attention at Diego's side. They were waiting on something to pop off, but Jose had everything under control. He didn't want to lose this connect with Diego; his shit was potent, and Jose loved the quality of its potency. While the meeting was taking place, Denise had put a call to Angel to let her know that Jose and his two men were at the club and that they were going to need some reinforcements.

Angel told Denise don't worry reinforcement was closer than she thought, and she would let them know when to move. The owner of club underground had his own meeting taking place in his underground office; he had a sliding door down there that if something happened, it would lead him safely out into a tunnel coming up into his home office two blocks away. While the owner was down in his office, all hell broke loose upstairs. Angel, Ramon, Denise, and Ava came in firing shit up; everyone of them was carrying Glock 27. The power of the Glock 27 was unmatched. It had great unstopping power. They also carried Beretta px4 storm subcompact semipistols; they used them as their side arms. When the shooting started on the first floor, Diego and his men thought that Jose had set them up. Diego's men started firing at Jose and his men; they had the third floor flooded with smoke-exchanging fire at each other before Angel and her crew even made it to the third floor.

When Angel and her crew finally made it to third level of the club, Diego and his men were already dead from Jose's men firing. Their 9 mm's striking them in the chest, dropping them instantly to the floor. Jose had been hit twice: once in the leg and in his arm. He was trying to stand up when Angel and Ramon came in through the smoke like a floating cloud of smoke. When Jose looked up, it was too late Angel fire a shot hitting Jose in his other leg, and he dropped to the floor like a ton of bricks. Jose didn't have Bumper and Dick Tracey to come to his rescue because when they came running down the steps, Ava and Denise started firing their Glock 22 with the military grips; they put so many holes in Dick Tracey and Bumpers's face that they wouldn't be recognized by no one.

Angel heard police sirens coming from a distance; she told Ramon to grab the bartender. I know he knows another way to get out of here, but before Ramon could grab the bartender, he volunteered to help them. He wanted Jose to pay for what he did to that young girl because she could have easily been his daughter, and he would have done the same thing that they were going to do to his ass. Angel had Ramon to drag Jose to the back where the tunnel was located in the back of the club. The bartender made sure he showed them where they would end up in the office of the owner, two blocks away. When Angel, Ramon, Denise, and Ava were traveling through the tunnel, Jose tried to put up a fight with Ramon until Ramon hit him in the mouth with the butt end of his Glock 27, knocking out the same four teeth he knocked out of Baby Girl's mouth.

When they made it to the owner's office of club underground, he had already left to take his wife out to dinner so he hadn't heard what went down at his club while he was gone. Angel had Denise and Ava to check the whole house out to make sure they were alone before she started administering pain to Jose.

Jose looked at Angel and said, "Bitch, you might as well kill me because if you don't, you won't be able to hide nowhere because I'm going to track you down and kill you my damn self."

Angel told, "Jose, baby boy, you don't have to worry because you're not going to leave this room alive, before Jose could utter another word." Angel took a pair of brass knuckles out of her pants' pocket, and Jose knew she was going to beat him like he did Baby Girl. Angel started punching Jose until her own knuckles started bleeding. She even went as far as sticking a mop handle up his ass to let him see how it feels when something is forced up your ass without permission. Once Angel was through torturing Jose, she shot him twice in the head right between his eyes. She leaned over him and spit right in his face. She said to everyone in the room let this be a lesson to anyone who messed with my children will die by the hands of Angel Carter.

Chapter 20
Sophia and Michelle with New Faces

SOPHIA AND MICHELLE who are now Olympia Strong and Darcy Cobs are living in the cosmetic clinic until it was time for them to reveal their new looks, which will be in two months; they are still wrapped in bandages, waiting for the doctor to unveil them when their two months were over. Sophia had over a thousand stitches over her entire body. She had the most intense surgery because her body was like a road map; the doctor had to give her evasive skin grafts. She was in a great deal of pain, so she stayed sedated all the time so she wouldn't have to feel anything. Michelle was burned real bad. The doctor had to replace her ears; she too had to have skin grafts. She also had to have a whole head of hair plants; her head had to be scrapped to the second and third skin before the doctor could put in any hair plants into her scalp. She had to be under constant sedation because she would cry out in the most horrible pain that no human could handle. She told the doctor that every time she closed her eyes, she relived the torture all over again. Sophia and Michelle had the best cosmetic surgeon money could buy; he even stayed with them day in and day out. He was closer to them than he should have been because he was feeling things for Sophia that he haven't felt in years. He would visit her while she slept like an Angel to him; he was going to make sure both girls had their lives back because they had their whole lives ahead of them, and they deserved a chance to enjoy their lives.

Dr. Murray thought to himself who ever had it out for these two young ladies was serious about destroying them for life; whoever this person was should be committed to a crazy institution for some heavy therapy because God knows this person truly tried to destroy their ambition to live. Dr. Murray was in the hall at the clinic when he heard a loud scream coming from Sophia's room. She was having another bad dream he thought until he heard her say mommy. She was repeating what her mother was saying to her in her sleep; her mother was warning her that she was having a bad dream. She told her to turn her pillow over because good dreams are on the other side. Dr. Murray heard what Sophia said so he did just that. He lifted her head and turned her pillow over; that calmed Sophia down, and she went back into a deep sleep.

When the doctor went into Michelle's room, she was tossing and turning like she was fighting someone. She was moaning saying don't please don't. He couldn't imagine what happened to the two young women when they were being tortured because they were going to need intensive mental therapy as well. He prayed that their mind would be healed of all the pain that their bodies had endured. It was going to be their fourth skin grafts. Dr. Murray hated to put them through so much pain over and over again, but their bodies were beginning to look good. It was going to be well worth the pain they were going through. Michelle had to be treated for infection; the doctor had to get it under control. She had started leaking; she was losing large amounts of fluids from her tissues in her face and everywhere else. She was burned. He was trying to keep her from going into hypovolemic shock.

Two weeks later

Michelle and Sophia were in the process of learning their new names; both of them had been progressing very well since their last skin graft. Dr. Murray thought that they were healing very well. It had been a couple of weeks now; there were no more nightmares, and both girls didn't need round the clock care anymore. They showed Dr. Murray that they were winning the battle of getting their lives back on track. He was proud to see that they didn't need to be heavy sedated to sleep so they wouldn't feel pain; they took the pain like troopers now, and Dr. Murray was very pleased to see that they were stronger than he gave them credit for. Michelle and Sophia had a will to live; they had unfinished business they had to take care of, and nothing was going to keep them from it.

Olympia a.k.a. Sophia was feeling great. She wanted her bandages to be removed; she only had a couple of days left before Dr. Murray removed her bandages, but she couldn't wait. The nurse entered her room to check her vitals. When she requested to see Dr. Murray, the nurse told her he was with another patient, but he would come to visit her as soon as he was done. Olympia told the nurse she would be all right with waiting on the doctor. When Dr. Murray entered Olympia's room, she sat up in her bed to let the doctor know that she wanted her bandages to be removed. He asked her why she couldn't wait one more day. She said I could, but I really don't want to. Will another day make a difference? Dr. Murray said not really, but if you want to see the beautiful woman you have become, then let's remove your bandages. Sophia a. k. a. Olympia was ecstatic; she couldn't hardly control her excitement. She was wrapped like a mummy so it took Dr. Murray about an hour trying carefully to unwrap the bandages.

When Dr. Murray was done unwrapping all of the bandages, he had Olympia to standup so he could walk her over to the long-length mirror. He asked her to close her eyes and do not open them until I tell you to all right. When they made it up to the view of the mirror, Dr. Murray said open your eyes. Olympia could be heard all over the clinic's second floor. She was crying so loud; her body was flawless. She had very thin visible scars which would be gone in the next week or so. She couldn't believe that she had been reborn again; only this time she was perfect. Her face didn't even look the same; he gave her a full-body reconstruction job. In her mind, she thought to herself, *she could walk up face-to-face with Angel and snatch her heart out and she would deserve it for what she did to her and her sister Michelle a.k.a. Darcy.*

Dr. Murray let Sophia a.k.a. Olympia and Michelle a.k.a. Darcy know that their bodies were improving wonderfully and that they would be free to leave the clinic in six weeks, but mentally they needed to talk with a therapist about the torture their bodies went through physically; they looked at each other and told Dr. Murray they were fine. They didn't need to talk with any quack that was going to tell them that they needed more therapy. Darcy told the doctor they were fine, and they would be signing themselves out of the clinic in three weeks instead of six; they felt it was time to get out of there and start their lives over. Darcy a.k.a. Michelle's face, neck, and ears had been reconstructed perfectly; she looked just like Jennifer Lopez. She was hot to this male nurse name Romeo.

Romeo would go in the room to take Darcy's vitals in the evenings, and he would daydream about her all night. He thought she was beautiful beyond words; he would tell himself that he would do anything just to have a date with her. Romeo said thinking out loud I could at least throw caution into the wind don't nothing beat a failure but a try I won't know unless I try. That evening Romeo had to go into Darcy's room to take her vitals again; he was sweating bullets just thinking about introducing himself to Darcy. He didn't want to get rejected by her; he just wanted her to be a part of his life. He wanted to make sure no one ever hurt her again. He wanted to vow to her that he would always be there to protect her. When Darcy a.k.a. Michelle noticed that Romeo was taking her vital and looking at her like he had true feeling for her, she thought that was special because he didn't really know her so why was he lusting after someone that came to the clinic looking like Freddie Kruger. What she failed to see was the signs he looked past how she appeared to be on the outside; he fell for what she had on the inside. Romeo told Darcy that she was a beautiful person; she just needed to let go of all the bitterness she harbored inside.

When it was time for Sophia and Michelle to leave the clinic, they told everyone on staff that their names would be Darcy and Olympia for now on. Dr. Murray had plans on making a couple of house calls to make sure the girls were making more progress in their eating habits since they were signing themselves out of the clinic early. Both Darcy and Olympia had lost about twenty pounds because they wouldn't eat what the clinic had prepared for them to eat. What Dr. Murray didn't know was they couldn't wait to get out of there and go to the outback steak house; all Darcy thought about was a nice juicy steak with a baked potato with Texas toast.

Romeo wanted to be with Darcy; he just couldn't let her get away without him telling her how much he cared for her. He just didn't want her to think that he was some kind of stalker; he just had it bad for her. He was like a love-sick puppy; he made sure that Darcy gave him her cell phone number before she left the clinic. That right there gave him a little hope that she was at least interested in talking to him over the phone. Dr. Murray was more than love sick over Olympia; he wanted to wife her. He thought that she was the apple of his eye, and he was going to make sure she knew how he felt he was going over to their condo to confess his love for her in person. He just hoped that she returned the love she had for him. He knew she had and was too scared to admit it.

Olympia and Darcy were living the life. They both had men in their lives who loved them, and they finally decided to have a relationship with someone who wasn't doing illegal things, but they couldn't shake the feeling of getting revenge on Angel and Baby Girl. They had to make them pay for everything that they went through; neither one of them wanted to tell their boyfriends the different turns of events that they had hovering over their heads, but if they really loved them like they said they did, they wouldn't look at them like they had two heads when they told them their stories. When Darcy told Romeo about her mother being killed by Angel and her daughter, he wasn't shocked at all because his mother had been killed by the hands of his father. His father killed his mother right in front of him when he was seven years old; he even remembered his uncle killing his father, so they pretty much carried the same burdens.

Olympia was in her bedroom with Dr. Murray, now Olympia's boyfriend. They were sitting there watching a movie "The Imitation of Life" staring Lana Turner and Sandra Dee. When they started playing that song "I'm going home to live with my lord" by Mahalia Jackson, Olympia broke down crying because she didn't get the chance to tell her mother that she loved her. She didn't even get the chance to give her mother a proper burial.

She told Dr. Murray she knew her mother was dead because Angel told them so, but she never mentioned where their bodies were. She just told her and Darcy that their mothers were never going to be found. Olympia cried hysterically because she knew deep down inside that she would never have the opportunity to hear her mother voice or would she ever be able to wrap her arms around her mother again. Angel took their mothers away from them, and they weren't going to rest until she is buried six feet deep.

Chapter 21
Baby Girl's Pregnancy

GLORIA A.K.A. BABY Girl was still in the hospital. The good news is, she's out of her coma and she doesn't remember too much of what happened to her, but she soon realized that her jaws had screws in them. When she looked up and saw Ramon, she knew her mother is there somewhere. Just as she was about to ask Ramon about her mother, the Dr. came into the room to tell her the news of her being a mother. She had been unconscious for two months. The Dr. asked Ramon, Denise, and Ava to leave the room so he could examine Baby Girl and talk with her in private about her condition. She really couldn't talk with both of her jaws wired shut, but she could write on a wipe off board the doctor gave her to write on. Dr. John Parker told Baby Girl that she was healing faster than he thought; he let her know while she was in a coma for seven weeks, her body was healing itself. He also told her she was in her first stage of pregnancy due to the rape that she had endured, and if she wanted to keep the child or abort, it would have to be her decision, but she had very little time to give him a decision because even though her body was healing, he didn't want to put her body through too much more friction that he thought she could handle.

Baby Girl was devastated that she was pregnant by Jose and his boys due to them raping her, but now that she knew the facts about what really happened to her, she cried because she was beaten furiously and left to die in an alley trash dumpster. She wanted them dead, but she didn't know that they were already dead because when Ramon was going to tell her, the doctor came into the room. Once the doctor had finished talking with Baby Girl, he told her visitors they could return to the room, but he didn't want them to stay too long because Baby Girl was still weak.

When Ramon, Denise, and Ava came in the room and saw Baby Girl crying, they wanted to know what had her so upset. She told them that the doctor informed her that she was pregnant; they all looked at her in a devastated stare. Baby Girl told Ramon she needed to talk to her mother; he asked her was the doctor sure because they should have found out she was pregnant before now. She told Ramon that the doctor said when she was first bought into the hospital she had lost a lot of blood, and they had to rush her straight to surgery. They couldn't tell if she was pregnant then because the rape has just happened but they drew more blood two weeks ago, and it was positive, but the doctor held the information until he thought that I was strong enough to hear it. Now I don't know what to do because I got raped by all three of them. It's not the baby's fault, but I don't want to make a decision without talking to my mother.

Ramon knew how Baby Girl felt; he felt sorry for her because he could feel the pain that she was going through, and he knew that her mother could advise her in what she needed. Ramon told Baby Girl that he was going to talk to her mother for her; he also told her he met this guy who had burned out cell phones. He told Baby Girl he had to leave, but he would be back up to the hospital later on that day to bring her the burned out cell phone so she could talk to her mother since she couldn't come to the hospital to see her. When Ramon made it back to the hotel where he and Angel had been staying, he looked at Angel with compassion in his eyes. Angel asked Ramon what was wrong? She asked was anything wrong with her daughter, he told Angel that Baby Girl was pregnant due to the rape. Angel said don't say that because as ruthless as I am, I don't agree with boarding my grandchild, but if she wants to have the baby and put it up for adoption is a choice we can make together because of the way the baby was conceived.

Angel really didn't know how to handle her baby being pregnant; she was throwing a fit because that shouldn't have happened to her daughter, but she did know what goes around comes around. While Angel was throwing a tantrum at the hotel, Ramon was on his way back up to the hospital to take Baby Girl the cell phone so she could talk with her mother. Once he arrived and he was about to go into Baby Girl's room, Denise came out and told him that the detectives were in the room, questioning Baby Girl now, and it would be best if he waited in the waiting room until they left. He told Denise thanks for looking out, so he went down the hall to the waiting area and had a seat until Denise came to get him after the detectives left.

The two detectives were questioning Baby Girl about what happened to her. She told them she wasn't going to tell them shit because they had dirty cops and detectives in their precinct, and she didn't trust none of them, because she remember being in the car with Detective Duncan and his partner Detective

Fredrick so for her to trust any official of law would be no time soon in her book. When the detectives left Baby Girl room, they were heated because they were truly the good guys; they knew they had bad cops and detectives working in their precinct, but they weren't on their squad, but Baby Girl didn't see it that way because she was taught that one bad apple could spoil the whole bunch if you don't take the rotten ones out. As soon as the detectives left the room, Denise went and got Ramon out of the waiting area. He came in the room to see Baby Girl angry; she wasn't crying anymore, so he took it as she was past the crying stage. When Ramon handed Baby Girl the phone to call her mother, she was happy even though she couldn't talk. She wrote down everything on her pad. that She wanted Ramon to say to her mother. When Angel spoke, he would put the phone up to Baby Girl's ear so she could hear her mother's voice and that cheer her up a little. She wrote down that she wasn't happy being pregnant by some guys who tried to kill her even though it's not the baby's fault. She decided to carry the baby full term and put it up for adoption, and she needed to know how her mother felt about her decision. Angel told Baby Girl that's what she wanted her to do because the baby would have a chance to grow up with someone who could show him or her how to live in a productive world. Angel hadn't realized what she said to her daughter because Baby Girl started crying again because it finally hit home for her that she was never shown how to be a productive product of life—she only knew how to kill or be killed.

Baby Girl had a lot of time to think she didn't want to just kill people anymore, even though she liked the rush it gave her. She wanted to go back to college. She wanted to get some credentials under her belt so she wanted to apply at a different college. When she was able to leave the hospital, Angel had already decided to take her daughter back to Columbia. As soon as the doctor gave her discharging papers to leave, she would be well taken care of in Columbia with Angel. Baby Girl could carry her baby to full term and deliver it there in Columbia, but Angel and Baby Girl both knew that once they saw the baby for the first time, they weren't going to be able to hand it over to an adoption agency. Baby Girl was feeling better day by day; she had even started trying to talk a little between her teeth. She was ready to leave the hospital, but Dr. Parker wanted her to stay another week before he discharged her.

Angel and Ramon left going back to Columbia three days later. She wanted everything ready when her daughter arrived in Columbia. She had even got to know a couple of mid-wives to deliver the baby when the time came. It had been a short trip for Angel and an agonizing one as well. She really couldn't go to the hospital to visit her daughter like she wanted to, but she saw the picture of what Jose and his right-hand men did to her daughter from Ramon's cell phone, and that had took its toll on her. Shit was beginning to hit close to home, and it was making Angel a little bit more cautious, plus Angel had been talking to Ramon about letting Baby Girl take her place. She felt that with a little more training Baby Girl could handle being her replacement.

A week and two days later, Baby Girl was being released from the hospital, and Ramon was going to fly down to Atlanta and pick her up. He found out from a friend that the Feds will be waiting on his arrival, but with the help of his friend from the inside of the Feds office helping him, he would be able to fly under the radar to pick Baby Girl up and get her back to Columbia. His friend called him and told him that Baby Girl would be at the airfield. Once he gets there, she would be waiting there with Ava and Denise; they were going to Columbia as well, but what Ramon and his inside connect didn't know was that the call was traced. It was going to be two units of FBI officers waiting in the shadows. Ramon wasn't worried about the Feds because he had the best shooters money could buy traveling in a decoy jet just like the one he was flying just in case something jumped off. Denise let Ramon know that they were on a landing strip not too far from the original one that he usually land on. He knew exactly where she was talking about so he sent his men to land at the original landing strip.

Once the men landed, the Feds immediately got their bull horns and asked whoever was flying the jet to shut it down and step off the jet with their hands in the air, but the guys who were flying the jet weren't going easy; they started shooting out the jet door like Tony Montana in the movie "Scare face." They had some fire power for the Feds; they had some smith & Wesson model 10, colt models 1902 sporting models, and colt model 1903 pocket hammerless; they had nice fire power, but they were still defeated. The Feds had more firing power and shooters; they had hit the jets fuel tank and blew the jet up. It went up in flames like it was hit with C4. It was over as fast as it started. Ramon was in the air when the shooting started, he got a way Scott free again, but he knew one day he was going to cut it to close, and he was either going to be captured and go to prison or get killed, but he knew one day his day was coming.

Baby Girl made it to Columbia safe and sound, and her mother was more than happy to hold her daughter once again in her arms. Angel knew sooner or later she was going to have to pay the piper, but right now wasn't an option. She needed to be around for her son who was growing up pretty quick; he was in school now going on his fifteenth birthday, and Ramon wanted to teach him the family trades. She was happy that his father and uncles were going to be the ones to teach him the ropes. Meanwhile Baby Girl was sitting around glowing; she was getting as big as a house, and the baby was growing her hair down her back. An old lady told them one day at the super market that Baby Girl was having a boy and that he was going to bring joy to her life. Didn't know if anyone believe the old lady, but Angel did. That was the same little woman that gave Angel that piousness plant she used to kill the Sanchez brothers, so she knew the old lady spoke the truth.

Nine months later Baby Girl went into labor with her baby boy the midwives stayed in the house with Angel so that when Baby Girl went into labor, they would be close by. It was two thirty in the morning when Baby Girl was woke up out of her sleep from her water busting at first. She thought she peed on herself because the water was very warm when it came out, but right after that she started having pains, hitting her in her abdomen like something was trying to come out. Baby Girl started screaming so loud until she woke everybody in the house up. Angel started running toward her room when she ran straight into the mid-wives going into Baby Girls room. She had been in labor for two hours before she delivered an eight pound twenty-one inches long baby boy; he was dark and had a head full of curly hair. She fell in love with him as soon as the mid-wives laid him on her stomach. Angel knew then that she and Baby Girl would be raising her baby together, but Baby Girl was going back to college to get her a degree in criminologist. Angel had pulled a few strings to get her into Columbia State University College. She would be attending school in the fall. Denise and Ava agreed to go to Columbia College as well. They were going to be criminal lawyers; they all started school in the fall. Baby Girl didn't have to think about who was going to take care of her baby while she way at school. Angel had that covered, but she did have to come up with a name for her son. She looked at Angel and asked her what do you think about me naming my son after my grandfather Cane? Angel smiled because she did think of the name herself, but she gave Baby Girl the choice to name her child what she thought was right for him. Cane Cantrell carter was reborn inside Baby Girl's son. Angel was happy that Baby Girl thought enough of her to give her son her father's name; she will always remember the day her grandson was born.

Chapter 22
The Marriage of Sophia (Olympia) and Michelle (Darcy)

DARCY AND OLYMPIA had been dating their boyfriends for over a couple of months; they treated them like the queens they were. They hadn't told them they were rich; they just thought that the timing wasn't right, even though they were about to marry them. It was funny how Olympia's boyfriend asked her to marry him; they were in bed getting their groove on when she used her pussy muscles to clamped down on him. He asked her to marry him right then; she started laughing because she knew the power of the p. o. t. p. which stands for the power of the pussy. She accepted his proposal, and they were laying in bed, planning their engagement party. When the phone ranged, it was Darcy calling to tell her sister Olympia that Romeo just asked her to marry him and she said yes. They started screaming because both of them were happy to have someone in their lives who loved them for who they were and didn't judge them for what they did in their past, but truth be told Darcy or Olympia didn't want their fiancées to know that they had money that their mothers had left them just in case their marriages didn't work out.

The next morning, the girls were supposed to meet up with each other for breakfast to arrange their wedding plans. The guys were going to meet up at Tiffany's to purchase the girls engagement rings. Dr. Douglas Murray had money he wanted to buy Olympia the biggest diamond he could find. Romeo on the other hand didn't make that kind of money being a male nurse, but he still wanted to purchase Darcy an engagement ring worth twenty thousand. He thought that if he paid for her ring in installments he would be paying installments until they had their first child and their child went off to college.

They all agreed to have their vows said in a Baptist church; they really didn't have any family to acuminate them in their wedding nuptials. The guys could tell that they weren't all right with it, but neither one of them showed it, so to make things easier on them, Dr. Murray and Romeo decided to pay someone in the marriage licenses office to stand up and be a witness for them. After the judge signed their marriage licenses, they got married that day. They all went out to celebrate together, then all of a sudden it hit Olympia like a ton of bricks that her mother wasn't there to see her get married for the first time. She realized that her mother wasn't going to be a part of anything that happened in her life anymore because Angel made sure of that. Darcy asked their husbands to excuse them for a minute while she took her sister to the bathroom to calm her down because she knew how she was feeling she felt the same way; she missed her mother to.

Two months into the marriage of Romeo and Darcy, he started spending a lot of time in the streets away from home. He would come in the house at unusual times of the night, giving Darcy every excuse in the world. He didn't want her to know the truth about him stealing drugs from the clinic that he worked for to pay off the expensive wedding ring he had bought her. He had even purchased a big amount of cocaine from a drug connect he met named Big Tommy. He cut a deal with big Tommy on a sixty forty split; he didn't know that he was digging a hole for himself that would create a big problem for him and Darcy. One night Romeo came in the house at one thirty in the morning, and to his surprise, Darcy was waiting in the living room drinking a glass of wine. She had been sitting there for hours, thinking about what to say to Romeo. She did know she was about to take some drastic measures. If he didn't come clean about what he was doing in the streets into wee hours of the morning, she knew all too well what could be going on either it was dope dealing or it was a female, and Darcy wasn't having any of it that part of her life was over.

Romeo was walking softly in the living room when the light came on. When he saw Darcy, his facial expression completely change he knew one thing for sure he had to come up with a quick lie before she started her chain of questions. Romeo was definitely caught off guard. He didn't know what to say, but once Darcy asked one question, she wanted to know is there another woman in the picture. He knew he had his shit in the bag because in Romeo's mind Darcy was the only female that had his heart beside his mother. Romeo tried to plead his case to Darcy; he told her she has to have faith in him that he would never cheat on her with anyone. Darcy told Romeo that right now her faith was in the gutter; he told her baby even with your faith in the gutter, you still have to hear with your heart.

Romeo told Darcy that life doesn't promise you anything you have to go out and make things happen to get what you want. Darcy told Romeo that she thought that once they got married, he would leave the life, he once lived, but she saw now that you can't teach an old dog new tricks. She also told her husband that you learn to stay away from people who have the same problem you have and you get around people who have the solution, do you understand what I'm saying? I've been there I know it takes a strong-minded person to give up things that come into your life by doing illegal things. For now I just want to establish a quite life because I don't know where I might wind up later on in life. Romeo didn't know what the hell Darcy was talking about where she was going to wind up later; they were married, and she wasn't going anywhere without him. If it ever came a day where he thought Darcy would leave him, he would take a gun and blow his own brains out because he loved her that much.

Olympia and Dr. Murray a. k. a. Douglas was enjoying being married; they had even planned on having a child. Together they had already started on making their child. Olympia was having problems producing fertile eggs. She had a doctor's appointment with her gynecologist the following morning; she couldn't sleep the night before because she had a dream warning her that she wasn't going to be able to carry a baby full term. She thought that maybe it was a sign or maybe it was just a bad omen either way she was going to find out as soon as the doctor's office opened for her nine thirty appointment. Olympia was in the shower getting ready for her doctor's appointment when she heard Douglas praying very loud. He was asking God to forgive us for our sins; he asked the lord if he could heal our bodies and to take any problem that I might have to just be healed in the name of God, Amen.

When Olympia and Douglas arrived at the doctor's office, she had her vitals' and her blood work done. She began to get very scared because she felt something was very wrong but didn't know actually what it was. Once her test results came back, the doctor walked in the room, and she immediately started sweating. She knew it wasn't good news. The doctor started off with, "Mrs. Murray, your test results came back with the stipulation of preeclampsia." Olympia didn't know what preeclampsia was and how she got it. The doctor asked Olympia did she know of anyone in her family that had preeclampsia. She explained to the doctor that she didn't know; her mother is deceased, and she has a sister, but she doesn't know her sister's health information. The doctor told her that she probably inherited from a female family member; he also explained to her that preeclampsia can be treated. Preeclampsia is a medical condition in which hypertension arises in pregnancy; he gave Olympia the risk factors as well, with first time pregnancy, obesity, being older than age thirty-five, and a history of diabetes. The doctor wanted to perform a physical exam for blood pressure, usually higher than 140/90 mn. The doctor told Olympia the only way to cure preeclampsia is to get bed rest lying on your left side most of the time, drinking extra glasses of water a day, eating less salt, and frequent doctor visits to make sure you and your baby are doing well.

Olympia asked the doctor will preeclampsia prevent her from conceiving a child. The doctor let her know that preeclampsia will not prevent her from conceiving. Olympia was happy that she and her husband could conceive their child, so they decided to keep on trying and keep up with updated doctor's appointments when they finally conceive.

Darcy had to decided to give Romeo the benefit of doubt; he said he wasn't having an affair so she had to trust him until she found out what really was going on until then, she was just going to enjoy her life with her husband. Darcy called to check in on her sister Olympia; she hadn't talk to her sister in a couple of days, and she weighted heavy on her mind. The phone only rang twice before Olympia picked up the phone saying, "Hello sister, what's up with you?" She felt real good, hearing Darcy's voice. She missed staying in the house together with her sister. She missed the late night talks they used to have. They had a very good sister relationship that bonded them together. Olympia wanted to tell her sister about her preeclampsia situation, but she wanted to wait until they did their lunch date. She really couldn't believe what was going on with that preeclampsia scare she had earlier, but as long as it could be treated, she was fine with it.

Chapter 23
Baby Girl Going Back to School

GLORIA A.K.A. BABY Girl had got accepted at Columbia University College; her baby was now four months old. He was beginning to look more and more like her grandfather Cane. Angel and little Ramon loved baby Cane. He had the most beautiful dimples that Angel had ever seen. Angel knew her son and grandson were going to be two of the most notorious criminals that the world had to offer, plus her son little Ramon was already getting groomed by his father and uncle who was the head of the Columbian mafia. Baby Girl really didn't want her son to be a criminal. She wanted better opportunities for her son. She didn't want him growing up the way she did, but she just didn't have the guts to tell her mother Angel. Baby Girl was getting ready for her first day of college classes. her, Ava, and Denise. When she heard her baby crying, he was taking his morning bath the one she usually gave him, but now that she started school, his whole schedule had changed. She went into the bathroom to give him reassurance that she wasn't leaving him she was just going to school. He looked up and grinned at his mother because she would always talk to him in baby talk because he was only four months old. He didn't understand anything she was saying; she just made him laugh a lot, when she was making horrible baby sounds to him.

Baby Girl only signed up for four years of college; she didn't want to spend more time away from her son than she had to. Motherhood to Baby Girl was different than it was for her mother; she had opportunities for her son. Angel didn't give her any opportunities; she put her right into training mode to kill or be killed. She knew how to snap a man's neck into in twenty seconds or less. She could handle any kind of artillery that Angel put in her hand. Baby Girl could seduce a man into just about anything she wanted him to do. Angel taught her well. She even learned how to break down weapons of any sort and clean them and put them back together piece by piece. Baby Girl decided that she was going to finish school and open up a small business. She wanted to become a lawyer. Once she talked to the administrator at the university, he told her she had to go to school for at least four years to become a high-profile attorney. She told the administrator if that's what I have to do, then I might as well get started because I'm on a mission because I need this opportunity to start my own business. Baby Girl also knew that with her lawyer credentials under her belt, she could become her family's secret weapon and still remain her mother's sidekick. Baby Girl took her studying very seriously. She made sure that Ava and Denise were following suit. She didn't want them around being a liability to her so they had to get their shit on the ball as well.

Baby Girl got home from class early one day when she heard a lot of shooting going on behind the house. She didn't know what was going on so she decided to go take a peep out the backdoor. When she saw Ramon standing there watching her brother shooting a 9 mm at beer cans that he had lined up on the fence, she shook her head, because she knew her brother would be joining the family business at the age of fifteen like she did he was just getting his training earlier than she did. Baby Girl had six different classes that she went to faithfully every day. She didn't miss, not even one day. She fought hard to keep her grade average up, and she made sure that Ava and Denise were on top of theirs as well. Baby Girl was a fighter from the heart, no matter what situation presented itself she was going to fight until she just couldn't fight anymore. She was never the type to give up. She was taught by her mother that only the strong survives.

Baby Girl would come in from class and play with her son a little while, and she would go straight to studying. She was very adamant about finishing school; she wanted that lawyer's degree so bad she could almost taste it. She would often think about how her attorney Murdock stood out in court when he took their case and got them off on murder charges. She liked his style and the respect that he got from the police and the prosecuting attorney when he walked up in the courtroom. She also like his persona and personality, and the brother had swagger about himself that gave him confidence enough to get the job done. He gave her the push she needed, and she didn't even realize it she watched killer Murdock in action in the courtroom. He carried a lot of power, and she wanted to have that same power and respect that killer Murdock carried. She didn't know if she could get his swan shay affect, but she was sure going to try.

Baby Girl's mental health had started taking its toll on her; she would be so tired after studying half of the night that she would fall asleep in the chair at night. One night in particular she fell asleep; she had a dream about Jose. He was trying to get her to come into the light that he was standing in. He said, "Come on, I'm not going to hurt you. I just need you to be here with me." She was never the type of person to be scared, but this time she was afraid because he looked like he had been burned very bad, and that scared the living shit out of Baby Girl because she knew her mother killed Jose but how that part she didn't know and she wasn't concern about it either. He told Baby Girl since she didn't want to come with him that she should take real good care of their son because he was going to be just like him, and she wasn't going to be able to stop him. When she heard the last part of what Jose told her, she jumped up out of bed and ran to her son's room and picked him up. She kept him in the bed with her all night because she didn't want Jose to visit her son in his sleep like he just did her. She held her baby in her arms all night. She was afraid that if she closed her eyes, she would be visited by Jose again, and she didn't want to be alone if he showed back up again.

The next day was Saturday, and she wanted to spend her day with her son when she took him downstairs for breakfast, her mother Angel and her little brother were sitting at the table laughing. She asked them what were they laughing about? They both said in unison, "You, you look like you seen a ghost." Baby Girl broke down and told her mother about her dream. She told her that Jose said that baby Cane was his son and that she better take care of him because he was going to be just like his father. Baby Girl went on to tell her mother that Jose's body was badly burned, and he was standing in a bright light. Angel told her daughter what the old folks saying used to be, don't ever follow the dead in your sleep. If they reach their hand out for you to take it, please say no every time they come to visit you because you could be signing a death certificate in your sleep that you would never wake up.

Baby Girl took to heart what her mother told her and she hoped that Jose wouldn't ever come to visit her again; she had a lot of things on her plate, and he definitely wasn't one of them. The next day, Baby Girl was in class when she felt a cold breeze come by her and sat next to her. She was told by her Aunt Marie when she stayed with her for that short time when her mother Angel left her there. Her aunt told her that when dead people would be in your presence, you would know it because a cold breeze would come and let you know they are there. She got frighten because she felt someone was there, but she didn't know who it really was she just hope it wasn't Jose again. This time the visit was different she could smell a sweet fragrance of perfume; she remembered the smell. When she was a little girl, it was her Aunt Marie. She could feel her rubbing on the side of her face. She wasn't frightened anymore. She felt safe she was always told by her aunt that dead people can't hurt you. The people who were still living were the ones that could hurt you.

Baby Girl was handling her business in school. She was getting good grades. She was taking care of her son; she was being a mother and a father to her son. She didn't know being a single parent could be so hard, especially raising a boy. She didn't think she had the skills she needed to raise her son, but she was going to give it her best shot. Baby Girl's son was growing up very quick. She happened to look up one day, and he was already going on a year old. She had to slow down long enough to get things ready for little Cane's birthday party. She didn't know that her mother had already planned a birthday party for Cane's first birthday. She even had little ponies for him to ride on. The party was going to be amazing. Cane's first birthday party will be one that Baby Girl would never forget.

Chapter 24
Angel in Virginia Beach

ANGEL WAS GETTING her groove on with Ramon when they heard a knock at the door. It was the maid letting Angel know that she was wanted in Uncle Leo's quarters. She hadn't been on any hit in a while, and her time had come for her to take a trip to Virginia Beach. Uncle Leo was having problems with this African guy name Galba Saar. He was sent to Virginia Beach to control the east and the west side of Virginia; he had decided on his own that Uncle Leo and his brothers were some chumps. Even though they were heads of the mafia, they didn't scare him. He had just as much power under his belt as they did. He thought that it was stupid of them to front him a million dollars worth of cocaine and pure uncut heroine. Once he got out of their sight, he didn't think that they would come looking for him, knowing they were hiding out from the Feds. What Galba didn't know was Uncle Leo and his brothers had a beautiful secret weapon.

Angel was preparing to leave the next morning. Ramon was going with her on this trip because he wanted to be close by if she needed him. Angel and Ramon flew out that morning arriving in Virginia Beach in five hours; they rented a car from enterprise at the airport. Angel had already called ahead to make reservations at the comfort inn. Once they arrived at their hotel room, Angel had to go check out the neighborhood where Galba had three dopes house on the same block. Once she got there and saw that he had his shit on lock, she knew she had to come up with an in-and-out strategy. Angel noticed he had at least six or seven soldiers at each house so she decided to stay camped out for a while to see if Galba was going to show up so she could follow him back to where he laid his head at night. Angel didn't want to stay in Virginia Beach too long; she wanted to stick and move, but Galba wasn't going to make it easy for her. It was going on two days, and he still hadn't showed up yet.

Angel came up with a strategy to bring Galba out in the open. She followed a couple of his soldiers to a restaurant; they were sitting there eating and talking shit when Angel walked through the door, wearing a short sequins skirt with a sequins bra with six inch stilettos. It was like time had stop; each one of Galba soldiers was drooling so hard they didn't even notice that Galba had came in and sat down at their booth right beside them. Angel knew she had all eyes on her just the attention she was trying to get, but she didn't think that they were waiting on Galba to show up. Now that he was there, her job was going to be completed quicker than she thought, but first she had to get his attention focused on her so she decided to get up and go to the restroom. She had to pass their table to get to the restroom which was a plus for Angel because she seen how Galba was watching her when Angel got up to their table, Galba reached out and grabbed Angel's hand. She said excuse me. He told Angel she was sexy. He asked her would she like to have some lunch with him. Angel said, "Why would I want to have lunch with someone I don't even know."

Galba said, "I'm trying to get to know you, baby. You don't live around here, do you?"

Angel said, "I'm here visiting my sister."

Galba said, "If you have lunch with me, I can change your visiting status from visiting to moving to Virginia."

Angel said, "Oh really."

He said, "Yes, I'm that kind of guy. Trust me one night with me, you would be following me around like a love-sick puppy. You don't know anything about African men, do you?"

Angel said, "Not really, I never dated an African guy before." Galba told Angel first time for everything let me be your first how about it princess.

Angel told Galba, "First of all, you didn't tell me your name, and I defiantly did tell you mine, all right."

"I get where you coming from sexy lady. Let me introduce myself. I'm Galba but my associates call me Beast."

Angel told Galba her name was Lynn, "But can I ask you why your associates call you Beast." He told Angel that because when it comes to having sex I'm a beast in the sheets so in other words y'all exchange stories about y'all sex lives "huh"? Galba was infatuated with Angel; he had lust in his eyes. He was sitting there looking Angel's body over like a dog in heat. His dick was jumping, letting him know he had to do something quick to get this woman.

Angel was in the restaurant a little longer than she expected. Ramon was sitting outside the restaurant in a stolen impala that he stole to follow Angel in. Angel told Galba that she had to go meet up with her sister, but if he wanted to meet up with her later, she would be available in a couple of hours. Galba said, "That's cool. Here is my cell number. Call me when you are ready, and I'll come by and pick you up."

Angel said, "I tell you what give me your address, and I'll come by your house because my sister don't like strange men coming to her house. She has a jealous husband."

He told Angel, "Okay, I can dig that." Galba was so into Angel that he gave her the address to his house and his cell number. It was like Angel hypnotized Galba, only thing he was seeing was Angel naked spread wide eagle in his bed. Angel said her good-byes until later leaving. Galba was sitting at the table with his boys drooling. When Angel came out the restaurant, it was a relief for Ramon. He thought something had happened, but he didn't hear any shooting so it was all good.

Two hours later, Angel was parked outside Galba house. She called his cell, and he answered on the first ring; he had been thinking about Angel since she walked out of the restaurant. She had left her mark on Galba. Galba had rushed home to put some wine on chill and to make them a small snack of crackers, cheese, strawberries, and grapes. He had lit some vanilla candles throughout the house. He had the lights dim and soft music playing in the background; he was getting ready for a romantic night, but Angel had other plans. Angel was getting ready to get out of her car when Ramon told her don't forget to unlock the backdoor. Angel was upset with Ramon about the statement he just made to her like she was an armature. Once Angel made it up to the door, Galba was in awe because Angel steep to the door wearing a sheer red dress with the matching red stilettos; she had her long black hair flowing down her back laying down smooth around her face. She had just enough makeup on to minimize her sexiness. Galba invited Angel into his living room to have a seat, while he went to get the wine and glasses out of the kitchen. When he came back into the living room, Angel was standing there in her Victoria's Secret plum-colored lace tong and bra. Galba almost dropped the bottle of wine; his mouth flew wide open. He never had a female to come on so strong, but he was down for whatever Angel had planned he thought. Angel took Galba by the hand and lead him down the hall; he told Angel to turn right. His bedroom was the first door to the right. When Angel opened the bedroom door, Galba had a king-size round bed that spin around in circles in the middle of the floor. She told Galba, "Oh, we're about to have some fun in this bed." Angel asked Galba did he know how to talk in tongue.

He told her, "No, but I damn sure can learn."

Angel said, "Before we get started, can I use your bathroom first."

He said, "Sure it's down the hall third door to your left." While Angel was going down the hall, she ran to the kitchen and unlocked the backdoor for Ramon. Angel ran to the bathroom real quick and flushed the toilet so Galba would think she was really in the bathroom. She got her purse out in the living room to get her 9 mm to put the silencer on it. Right when she was getting ready to go back in the bedroom with Galba, Ramon entered the backdoor. Angel was a freak for real if Ramon hadn't came in the backdoor right then, Angel would have been in the bedroom with Galba trying to sex him up. Once Angel walked back in the bedroom with Galba, he was buck naked lying across the bed smoking a blunt. The weed's smell was so loud you could smell it over the vanilla candles.

Galba told Angel to come lay down with him and take a hit of this blunt.

"Its some good hydro. I got this from my country. My brother bought me a pound of this shit last week." Angel took the blunt out of Galba hand. She put it in her mouth and took a long drag, and she handed it back to Galba.

He looked at Angel and said, "Do you like this?"

She said, "What are you talking about?" When Galba rolled over on his back, his dick was standing right up. Galba was hung like a horse. Angel had seen something like that before, but this time was different. Galba had the balls to go along with his twelve-inch dick. Ramon was standing outside the door. When he heard Galba say something containing to the side of his dick, that got Ramon heated. He kicked open the door, and Galba jumped up grabbed Angel around the neck.

He told Ramon, "Drop your gun. If you don't drop it, I'm break this bitch neck. I knew this fine ass bitch was too good to be true. You set me up huh bitch." Angel was trying to focus on breathing when she felt Galba's long ass dick sticking her in her back. Angel pretended like she had passed out when Galba crazy ass dropped her to the floor. That's when Angel came back up with her 9 mm, hitting Galba right in the dick with her 9 mm. Ramon was firing shots into Galba's body; also his body was jerking and going down to the floor in slow motion. When Galba hit the floor, his eyes were wide open; blood was running out of his body like a fire hydrant. Once Angel and Ramon check his vitals to make sure he was dead. They started searching the house for the drug shipment that Galba had received from Uncle Leo; they tore the house up inside out, and it wasn't there.

Angel knew killing him before they found out where the money or drugs where was a big mistake. She knew letting Ramon jealous ass come with her would cause a problem, and it did. He couldn't stand the fact of Angel getting sexually close to her targets. The way that she did it made him feel like he wasn't man enough for her. When Angel and Ramon finished searching the house, they sat down in the living room thinking about what to do with the dead body. When Ramon reach over and started caressing Angel's clit, she asked Ramon was he crazy they had just killed Galba, and he wanted to have sex in the man's house. Ramon told Angel he wasn't crazy. He was horney; he wanted to have sex with her, and he didn't care about Galba being dead. He wanted to make love to Angel in the spinning bed in the middle of the floor. Angel told Ramon the man is dead in the middle of his floor, and you want to have sex in his bed.

Ramon said, "Hell, yeah, he wanted to have sex with my woman in his bed so why can't I accommodate his wishes, the only thing different is it's me making love to my woman. It will be me making you scream." Angel and Ramon made love in Galba's bed for two hours; they had semen all over his sheets. After they were done, Angel snatched the sheets off the bed and put them in a plastic bag to take with them when they left Galba's house. Ramon was still heated at the fact that Galba thought that he was going to stick twelve inches of dick in his woman; he looked at Galba laying on the floor and pissed in his face. Angel thought that she was crazy; her man was just as much as a nut case as she was. They decided to cut the stove gas on and let the house blow up. Ramon rigged up a lighter so it could ignite when the gas fumes spread it throughout the house.

Angel and Ramon went back to Galba's three dope houses to find the money, but they had to kill his soldiers first. Angel didn't care about taking down Galba's soldiers. She just wanted to get out of Virginia Beach so they waited until it got dark before they entered the dope houses. It was two thirty in the morning, when they decided to enter the house. Galba didn't know that his soldiers were scamming off the top. They had been stealing from him for a while, but he was too much of a sex fend to pay attention to his product. Angel caught one of the soldiers coming out the house to go make a drop when she hit him in the back of the head with the butt end of her 9 mm. He grabbed his head because the blow to the head busted his head instantly. She made the soldier take her back inside the house; it was only one person there. He was in the kitchen cooking up the product when Angel told him to get down on the floor. Butter got down on the floor like Angel requested. She asked butter was anyone else in the house?

He said, "Bitch, I'm not telling you shit."

Angel said, "Big mistake" and shot butter right between the eyes; the young guy whom she hit in the head with her 9 mm was so scared he pissed on himself; he had just got pulled into the drug game by Butter.

Angel asked the young boy if he knew who was in the other two houses, he started telling Angel that there were two guys in each one of the houses.

She said, "All right, you want to live or do you want to die."

He told Angel, "I'm fifteen, of course, I want to live."

"All right, this is what I want you to do. I need you to go over there and tell them that its two armed men over here holding Butter hostage. If you try to play me, my partner outside is going to put two in your head you understand. Before Angel let the young boy go next door, she made him put on some more pants. He told Angel he didn't have clothes there, but she noticed him, and the dead guy on the floor was about the same size, so Angel had the young boy to take off Butter's pants and put them on right. When the boy was about to put the pants on, they heard a loud knock at the door. It was shocker—one of the soldiers from the dope house next door. Angel told the boy to open the door and step back. When he opened the door, Shocker started going off.

He asked, "Beanie, what the fuck took you so long to open the door." When Ramon seen Shocker step inside; he jumped out of the bushes and ran up to the door just in time to kick him in his leg to trip him that's when Angel sprung into action. She put her 9 mm to Shocker's head and said, "Don't move."

Angel and Ramon had two hostages so far, and they were about to have more company. All of a sudden the front door came flying off the hinges; three more of the soldiers came in shooting. They saw Angel when she hit Beanie in the head and took him back in the house; they had been watching things unfold before they made their entrance. Angel and Ramon were returning fire. When they heard somebody's gun jam, they stood up from behind the turned over sofa. Everyone was dead but Beanie, the young boy, had jumped in a closet in the hall so he wouldn't get hit by a stray bullet. Angel didn't know Beanie was in the closet; they thought that he just ran out of the house until they heard movement in the closet. Angel told Ramon to hold his gun up to the closet while she opened it.

When the door was opened, Beanie started screaming, "Don't shoot. Please don't shoot. I'm coming out." Angel, Ramon, and Beanie went through all three houses before Angel found what she was looking for. She just couldn't leave Beanie alive; he would be a liability, and she couldn't have him identifying her in a police lineup. Angel strangled Beanie with a rope she found in the closet. Beanie tried to fight, but his lungs gave out on him. He closed his eyes, and he was gone just like that. Angel and Ramon left the car at the airport and headed back to Columbia with Uncle Leo's money and drugs.

Chapter 25
The Hunting of Baby Girl

BABY **GIRL HAD** been doing very well in school; her grade average was a 4.0. She was two weeks away from her gradation when her nightmares started back. She had been staying up late at nights, studying her tests; she would be so tired until she would fall to sleep anywhere she would be sitting. She had been feeling like she had a dark shadow following her around. For a while, she couldn't shake the feeling that someone wanted to tell her something because when she would be in her bedroom at night, she could swear that a dark figure would be standing in the corner of her room, watching her. This particular night, she was lying in bed, almost asleep, when she saw this dark-skinned gentleman standing there, looking at her. Baby Girl thought maybe she was just seeing something when the dark figure came closer enough to her so she could see his face. When she saw that it was Raymond, Cash's brother, she wasn't scared because she really did believe that Raymond cared about her.

When she looked at Raymond, it was like he was trying to say something to her, but before he could speak, another shadow came from behind Raymond; she closed her eyes because she thought that her mind was playing tricks on her. She kept shaking her head from side to side to try to shake what she saw out of her head, but that didn't happen; it seemed like everybody that she killed in Atlanta was coming to pay her a visit. Crazy Red, Raymond, and Cash were hunting for her; they wanted her to admit to their murders. She didn't kill Raymond, so she didn't even know why he was even there.

Raymond started floating toward her like he was on a skateboard, moving in slow motion. Baby Girl started moving backward. She didn't want him to touch her; she told them that they couldn't hurt her, and she wasn't afraid, so whatever their reason was for being there, that they needed to move on. Right when she dropped to her knees to pray for God to remove those bad spirits out of her room, Cool and Candy showed up, burned to a crisp.

Cool told Baby Girl that it was time for her to go straight to hell where he would be spending eternity; he also said that she needed to be right where she sent him and Candy. She told Cool, "If you went to hell, it wasn't me that sent you there. You better check with Satin. He's the one that has the power to send you to hell, not me."

Before Baby Girl could say anything else to Cool, she woke up with someone standing over her, trying to wake her up out of her sleep. It was her little brother; he was on his way to the kitchen when he heard her talking and moaning in her sleep. She was glad little Ramon woke her up because she was just about to get dragged to hell by the ghost of Baby Girl's past.

When Ramon woke his sister up, she didn't go back to sleep that night; she had been having nightmares for the last two weeks. She didn't know why all of a sudden she was being hunted by the people she had killed. It was getting worse for Baby Girl because she was afraid to even close her eyes even in the day time; she was in class, falling asleep when her teacher asked her if everything was fine at home. Baby Girl told her teacher that everything was fine. She told her teacher her son wasn't feeling well, and she had been up all night, taking care of him. Baby Girl's teacher looked at her and told her she really needed to get some rest and that she looked restless and worried about something. She didn't respond to her teacher's last comment because she didn't want to tell him that she was being haunted by people she had killed.

Baby Girl wanted the demons that hunted her to leave her alone so she could sleep at night. So she went to Uncle Leo to ask him for help. He told her he knew a few people that could burn some sage that would run the demons out of her room. She told Uncle Leo that would be fine if he could get them right away. She couldn't afford to lose anymore sleep.

Uncle Leo called in a few favors to get Baby Girl the help that she needed; the old woman that came to cleanse the room found out once she walked into Baby Girl's room that she was haunted by spirits with great power. They weren't going to stop hunting for her until she gave into their desires: their desire was for her to feel the pain she put them through.

Baby Girl didn't want to hear that. She wanted them to move on so she could do the same. She knew what she did was wrong, but she wasn't going to admit to anything. Right when the old lady started to move into light, the sage she was burning and the language she was speaking made her sound like she was speaking in tounge. The smoke from the sage was real, the old lady. She stopped right in the middle of the floor when she noticed a dark shadow appear right before her; it was three male figures. Baby Girl knew who they were right away; she noticed Jose, Bumper, and Dick Tracey. As strange as it may seem, they came to apologize to her for what they did to her. That wasn't going to change the fact that they were dead and wouldn't be coming back physically, but spiritually their soul couldn't move on. Baby Girl didn't want to forgive them because she couldn't forget herself that she did a lot of things in her life that she wasn't proud of but nevertheless she wasn't giving in to their demands; they just had to find another way to repent.

Baby Girl decided to keep a positive mind. With all the people hunting for her, she wasn't going to let them interrupt her sleep any longer; she was going to finish what she started. She was going to get her attorney's degree and open up a small law firm; she still did hits for her mother when she needed them done. That to her wasn't an option because she learned early to protect the family at all cost. The spirits had stopped visiting Baby Girl; she hadn't seen any shadows in about three weeks. So she went on doing what she did on a normal basis: she would still stay up, studying half of the night. Baby Girl happened to be asleep again at the kitchen table when a big, beautiful bright light, with a floating angel appeared. She had the most beautiful wings Baby Girl had ever seen; the angel told her she was there to watch over her. Baby Girl was happy that she was there, but she was also scared because she knew the life that she was living was dangerous. She was doing things that she didn't want the angel to see. Baby Girl was tormented by all the mixed emotions that were going on in her head. She didn't know how to accept the thoughts she was experiencing, but she knew she had to keep a level head, especially for the sake of her son.

Baby Girl was graduating in two days. She was finally getting her degree! She was happy to achieve what she sat out to do, and she had plans on having the biggest party money could buy. She only wished that her father could be there to see her walk across that stage. Baby Girl and her sidekicks, Ava and Denise, were going to do big things for themselves. They had already set the stage; only thing left for them to do was to pick a State, find a building, and open up an ass-kicking law firm.

.

Chapter 26
The FBI Hunting down Angel

THE FBI HAD put together a special team. They had a hard-on for Angel; they wanted her bad. She was committing too many crimes around the world, and they were out for blood; she was slipping through their fingers like she had some kind of vanishing power. Every time Angel would commit a crime, they would always be two steps behind. She made their job hard for them, and they weren't liking that one bit. She had to be found and stopped; they couldn't even find a picture of her in their database. They didn't even know what she looked like to be hunting her down. The picture that they had was an old picture. Angel had got a whole new look. Her plastic surgeon worked wonders on her; he even changed the color of her eyes. What they didn't know was that she could walk up inside their office and set off a block of C4 and kill them all.

Angel had an inside man working with the FBI; he would use his burned-out cell phone to let Angel know when the feds was moving in on her; she paid him a substantial amount of cash to keep her wired up on the moves the feds was making. What Angel didn't tell her inside man was that she had someone watching him as well. She hired two thugs to watch him at work and at home so if he ever played her, she would make sure that when he closed his eyes at night, it would be a permanent sleep. The feds couldn't believe they were slipping because they were one of the most prominent ones in law enforcements; they started to think someone was helping her stay two steps ahead of them. It had to be someone working from the inside; so everyone came under suspicion. Angel's inside man started to get a little jumpy. He thought everyone in his office was looking at him funny; his mind had begun to play tricks on him. He didn't want to get caught, because if he did, he would lose his job and go to jail, and so when he found out from his superiors what they thought was going on, he was sweating bullets.

The feds thought they found out where Angel and the mafia were staying, but when they rushed up to the house, it was empty. There wasn't even a chair left in the house; it looked like they had left days ago because it didn't look like they rushed to move. That made the feds even madder because she was costing the government money, trying to locate her. She was moving faster than they anticipated. Angel and the mafia had moved up higher on the mountains of Columbia and didn't let anyone know that they were there, but the people who needed to know and the ones that did know wouldn't dare cross the mafia unless they wanted their tongues cut out of their mouths.

Angel's inside man, Derrick, was feeling like his every move was being watched; he had got so caught up on being greedy that he put his life and his family in jeopardy. Before Angel hired him, she ran a series of tests on Derrick. She knew he was weak to a pretty face and a smile, but she also knew he needed the money, having a sick child with a heart disease. Angel knew all Derrick's information because she ran a background check on him; she even knew where his parents stayed in Atlanta, so to cross her would be a big mistake. Derrick was so angry with himself for selling his soul to the devil because in reality that's exactly what he had done by dealing with Angel. He felt that he was damned if he did and damned if he didn't, so he was tossing with himself about what he should do because if he went to his superior and told that he was the weakest link in their chain, he would take a chance on losing his family because he knew for sure Angel would kill them all. The superior came into Derrick's office to talk about the turn of events that took place when they went to raid Angel's and the mafia's houses. He told Derrick it was like they knew they were coming. Derrick couldn't respond to what the superior had said because he was afraid he might give him a sign that he warned Angel that they were coming, and he didn't want to put any doubts that he was the culprit that was giving out information to Angel, the Columbian assassin; just like Angel did a background check on Derrick, he checked Angel out also, but they only had the file on Angel when she did her killing spree in Chicago before she had reconstructive surgery done; Derrick himself couldn't tell you how she really looked because when she met him, she had him to meet her at the movies where she knew it wouldn't be lit up with bright lights, plus she had on a pair of sunglasses. She handed him pictures of his wife and children and his parents so he knew she wasn't about playing games with him. Every time Derrick would think about disclosing her whereabouts, he would get jilted back to reality; he just had to keep up with the charade of deceiving the feds. He did have choices, but he couldn't rely on the feds keeping his family safe if he was to tell them he was the one giving Angel details of everything that was taking place concerning her.

The feds thought Angel was too good, and she was moving just like a ninja and that she was killing her victims without batting an eye; she didn't show any remorse in how she killed them. It was like she didn't have any conscience; they never had to track down a female with the heart of a man. She was definitely awarded the most wanted poster; they couldn't wait to meet up with a female that was as heartless as Angel; the feds had just got a call about a gruesome murder that had taken place in Virginia Beach. When they heard it was dead bodies stacked up all over Virginia Beach, they knew it was the job of Angel because she didn't spare anyone. If it ever was a wittiness the feds didn't know anything about it, Angel was a force to be reckoned with, and they knew it, so to capture her, they too had to come up with a foolproof plan because people were popping up dead in every state. From St. Louis to Delaware, Angel was traveling under the radar, and it was getting tough for them to keep up with her. What they didn't know was Angel had so many different identifications. She was using that, she felt like she was stepping out of her body into the role of all these different other people she had to portrait.

The feds came up with a plan to keep Baby Girl under surveillance. She had moved from Columbia to Chicago to open up shop; she had one of her mother's dummy corporation buildings that was big enough for her, Denise and Ava to conduct their business. She couldn't wait to get the ball rolling; when she happened to spot the feds sitting down the street from her office building, one day on her way from lunch, she went up to the window and asked them to roll their window down. When the feds saw her coming up to their car, they knew they were busted; she told them that they were harassing her. She then went on to tell them that they didn't have a reason to be investigating her, and if they didn't stop harassing her, she would be hauling their assess into court on harassment charges.

The feds knew she was right, but they were running out of patience, trying to catch Angel. She had been making their job hard for them, plus they were wasting a lot of funds, trying to catch a ghost, so they thought that if they sit on Baby Girl, eventually she would lead them to her mother, Angel. Baby Girl knew what they were trying to do, and she wasn't going to make it easy for them to catch her mother; She was ready for whatever the feds threw at her; she had her credentials under her belt now, and she wasn't going to let them stop her from being the best kick-ass attorney she planned on being.

Chapter 27
Ava and Denise

AVA AND DENISE were busy, being partners in Baby Girl's law office. They were so busy they forgot about their love lives until they were sitting in the restaurant, having lunch when these two handsome gentlemen in Italian suits walked in. Denise shoved Ava and said, "Damn, girl, do you see what I see?"

Ava said, "Hell, yes. Those are two fine brothers right there."

Before they could say another word, the guys came over to their table to introduce themselves. Jason Apprentice was a tall black guy with a bald head and very sexy hazel brown eyes. He approached the table looking directly at Ava; he had her pegged from the time he entered the restaurant, and his partner that was with him was a tall, handsome Italian guy, with beautiful dimples and muscles that wouldn't stop. He looked like he lived in the gym. When Denise looked at him, she noticed he had hazel green eyes, actually like her's. He introduced himself to Denise. He said, "Hi, my name is Irvin Martenez."

Denise couldn't talk. She was staring at him like he was her last supper.

Denise finally found her voice to speak. When Irvin took her hand and kissed it, she acted like she had been hit by a bolt of lightning because Irvin had the deepest and sexiest voice she had ever heard, and Denise introduced herself to Irvin. She also apologized for not being able to speak at that time. She told Irvin that he was sexy as hell to her. He thanked her and asked her if he and his friend, Jason, could join them at their table for lunch. She said yes without even asking Ava because she knew they were on the same page.

Ava and Denise were an hour late coming back from lunch because they were entertaining Jason and Irvin. Before they left the company of Irvin and Jason, they made sure to exchange numbers on their way back to the office. They couldn't stop talking about their two handsome gentlemen callers. When they made it back to the office, they were like two little school girls. Baby Girl wanted to know what had her partners so giddy. When Denise told Baby Girl that they met two handsome brothers wearing Italian suits, an alarm went off in her head, but she didn't say anything just yet because she wanted to meet these guys first to make sure they weren't feds. She didn't want to rain on her friend's parade, but she wasn't going to have the feds hanging around harassing them either. Baby Girl came up with the idea for them to have a dinner party to celebrate opening up their new law firm; she went on her e-mail and put out invitation for her law-firm-opening dinner party. She invited everyone; she even left the office early for her and her partners to go shopping at the mall. She had already called the catering service; she set up a menu that was set for a king. She had preserved shrimp, lobster, crab, and veggie trays with cheese and cracker platters with steamed asparagus. She went online to find a decorator to decorate their office; she gave them a time to meet her there so she could let them in while she went home to get dressed for the party.

When Ava and Denise and Baby Girl made it to the mall, they were walking to Sax's when Ava decided to call and invite Irvin and Jason to their party. That's exactly what Baby Girl wanted her to do because she wanted to check these two gentlemen out for herself; something just didn't sit well with what Ava and Denise were saying about them. She wanted them to have a man in their lives; hell, she wanted companionship, but she wasn't taking chances with the feds trying to tap into her life to bring her mother out of hiding. Baby Girl wanted to call her mother real bad to check on her son since Angel decided to keep him with her until she got her business off the ground; she didn't want her grandchild around anyone that wasn't family; she just wanted her daughter to get her life started without any interruptions.

Denise was falling fast for Irvin. She didn't know if he was married or gay; she just fell straight over heels for him. She was so messed up until she would find herself calling his phone and hanging up before he would answer. She didn't want to seem desperate. She was desperate because she hadn't had sex in months, so Mr. Irvin was looking very good to Denise right about now. Ava was a mover and a shaker; she knew what she wanted. She was damn sure she wanted Jason. He had swaggered something that made Ava drunk with silliness; she wanted to try out a piece of that smooth hunk of chocolate he wanted to melt Ava's strong interior. She would break out with hot flashes every time Jason would say her name. She wanted that man like peanut butter needed jelly. She and Denise were about to walk out of their door when a van pulled up to deliver them some roses. They were so twisted for Jason and Irvin that they didn't notice that. They knew where they stayed.

Denise was riding in the car with Ava when her phone rang; it was Baby Girl letting them know she was already at the party and that their gentlemen friends had just walked in. They said all right and asked her if she would keep them company until they arrived. She assured them that they would be well taken care of until they arrived.

Baby Girl sashayed her way over to Jason and Irvin to introduce herself to them. When she walked up to them in that little black dress, they almost choked. She said hello to both gentlemen and told them that her name was Gloria and that she was Ava and Denise's business partner. She asked them if they wanted a glass of champagne. They said yes, and she had her waiter to bring three glasses. Jason asked her how she found the building her office was in because it had good bones. It was large and beautiful. She said she went through a real estate and purchased it. She didn't want to spend too much time talking to Irvin and Jason because she felt like he was trying to stick his nose in her business.

The party was in full swing when someone started getting loud. Baby Girl went toward the loud noise and was shocked to see that it was Jason pulling Ava, drunk-ass, off the dance floor. She was bumping and grinding with a number of guys she didn't even know. Baby Girl grabbed Jason by the hand and told him, "I'm going to handle it from here. I'm sorry you had to see her getting ignorant. She doesn't drink and when she does, this is the result."

When Baby Girl took Ava in the back office to talk to her she didn't say anything because she knew she had fucked up literally. She knew not to get belligerent with Baby Girl unless she wanted to get her teeth pushed down her throat. Ava knew she wasn't supposed to drink anything because she knew alcohol had a crazy effect on her; it made her do things she wouldn't normally do and for her to show her ass of all nights was beyond Baby Girl. She had clients that stopped by for someone on one consultation about Baby Girl's firm handling their cases. They loved the name of her firm, which was KAWA, which stood for Kicking Ass with Attitudes? The party had begun to slow down; everyone was leaving to go home. Baby Girl sent Ava home with her driver; she didn't want her going back up front, making a fool out of herself again, and she wasn't about to make them lose the clients that she had just signed on.

After everyone had left, Denise stayed to help Baby Girl clean up. She told Irvin that she would give him a call once she made it home. He said all right and gave her a kiss and left. Irvin and Jason rode together to the party so they were able to talk about what had taken place with Ava. Jason told Irvin that Ava was a little too loose for him. He told him that he was going to give her a call the next day to let her know that she doesn't need to drink period, and if she continued to drink, she had to move on because he can't put up with a woman that can't control her behavior when she drinks.

That night when Denise made it home, she gave Irvin a call as she promised. He immediately asked her what was wrong with her friend. He told Denise, "I think she straight up disrespected my boy."

He also asked Denise if she had problems with drinking. Denise told him that she had never been able to drink.

"Every time she had it, it made her do stupid shit like what you saw tonight. Gloria and I normally watch her, but tonight was different. We had a lot riding on tonight. We had potential clients that was at the party, but we got the chance to talk with them after the party and everything is fine. Tell Jason I'm very sorry that he had to see my friend in rare form, but I promise you after tonight, he won't see her act like that again because she really likes him."

Denise told Irvin , "I'll tell him what you said, but I really don't think he would be interested in Ava anymore. She really put my boy on front street tonight."

Irvin said, "I hope her apology will soften the blow a little because all that she talks about is Jason I believe he can straighten her out."

Irvin asked Denise, "So what's your story? You don't have no hidden boyfriend or husband or anything, do you?"

Denise started laughing. She thought that Irvin was so funny. She said, "Look, I'm going to be honest with you. I haven't had a serious relationship with a man in over two years."

He said, "That sounds good to me. I would love to take you on another date where we could be alone, if you don't mind."

Denise said, "I won't mind at all, but I have to check my schedule tomorrow when I get to work because we just took on four new cases. So how about we do lunch tomorrow, and I would be able to tell you what my schedule is by then?"

Irvin agreed to meet Denise for lunch. She was happy too because he didn't know that every time he got close to her, she would sweat bullets. She didn't know why this man had so much of an emotional connection with her.

Ava came in to work the next morning with one of the most terrible hangovers ever. She had to put on sunglasses because the sun hurt her eyes. Ava asked Baby Girl what happened at the party and how did she get home.

Baby Girl told Ava how she embarrassed herself and the law firm in front of all their guests. She also told Ava that Jason was pretty upset with her and that he even went as far as snatching her ass off the dance floor. Ava didn't remember what happened. She knew that every time she would drink alcohol, she would have blackouts to the point where she didn't remember anything.

Irvin met Denise for lunch; they had a nice conversation going when Irvin's phone rang, and he excused himself to go outside to take his call. That made Denise suspicious; she wanted to know who could be calling him that made him go all the way outside to talk in private. She was most definitely going to find out once he came back in. When Irvin came back inside the restaurant, Denise couldn't hold her temper. She asked him if she could ask him a question. He said, "Shoot."

Denise asked him who he was talking to that had him to take his phone call all the way outside the restaurant. Irvin said, "Please don't tell me you're jealous already."

She said, "No, I just thought it was disrespectful for you to leave me sitting here for thirty minutes while you're outside talking on your cell phone. That's all."

Irvin told Denise he was sorry, but his phone call was an important one concerning to his job.

Denise asked, "By the way, what do you do for a living?"

Irvin told Denise that he and Jason owned their own corporate pharmaceutical company that went worldwide. Denise was very impressed. She said to herself that she hit a jackpot because he had money just like she did.

Ava called Jason to apologize to him for her behavior last night at the party, but Jason wasn't answering his phone. He wasn't ready to talk to Ava at the time, so she stopped calling. Later that day, Ava, Denise, and Baby Girl were in a meeting with a man that had killed his wife and left her lying dead in a hotel room. It brought back thoughts of Baby Girl being left in a trash-can dumpster. She was left there to bleed to death. She got so upset that she started shaking, and she had to excuse herself from the meeting until she could get her nerves under control. When Baby Girl got herself together, she was able to handle the man's case; they took his case in consideration that they had to first find out what happened that spun this man out of control. When he told them that his wife had an affair with his brother and that when he had followed them to a hotel not far from their house, he didn't only kill his wife, but he killed his brother also, Denise, Ava, and Baby Girl's mouth flew wide open because he was telling them the events that took place, and he wasn't showing any remorse. He just didn't want to spend the rest of his life in jail. He wanted to cop an insanity plea; he was out of jail on a half million dollar's bond.

Jason decided to give Ava a call; he had been dodging her for two days. He just wanted her to sweat a little bit; he knew how much she liked him because he would literally see her break out in a sweat anytime he got close to her. When Ava noticed Jason's number pop up on her cell phone screen, she hurried up and answered. She wasn't expecting him to ever call her again. Jason invited Ava over to his house after work. He wanted to set her straight on a few things; he wasn't going to dismiss her just yet because he saw true potential in Ava. She just needed someone to show her that they cared for her.

Baby Girl didn't know if she wanted to take on the case where the man killed his wife and brother. She didn't like how the man looked; he had the appearance of someone crazy for real. Then again, she thought why not because Marcus Green could be as fruity as a fruit cake. In December maybe she could get him sent straight to an insane asylum because you can definitely see that the man was crazy for cocoa puffs.

Baby Girl was doing her own private investigation on Jason and Irvin; something just wasn't right with them. She could feel bad vibes from them every time they came around. It stuck out like a sore thumb, and it bothered her that her girl's couldn't feel what she was feeling, but she still wasn't going to say anything yet to Ava and Denise about it until she found out about who they really were. Baby Girl was on her way into the coffee shop when she spotted Jason sitting across the street with a female in a black Victorian. She knew that was the type of cars that the feds drove. She said to herself, "oh." Now the shit was about to hit the fan. Baby Girl sat at the window at the coffee shop, watching Jason for twenty minutes before he got out of the car, but what he did next fucked Baby Girl up; he bent over inside the car and kissed the woman he had been sitting in the car with. Baby Girl said to herself, "Maybe she's not a federal agent. She could be his wife or his mistress, or maybe they've seen me coming in to the coffee shop and trying to play it off. Either way, I have to go finish my investigation on Jason Apprentice and Irvin Martenez."

Chapter 28
The Murder of Detectives Duncan and Fredrick

ANGEL HAD FINALLY got a call from Baby Girl. She hadn't talked to her daughter in over a month. She was so busy getting her business off the ground that she hadn't even called to check on her son. That was the first thing she asked her mother that how was her son. Angel knew it was something on her mind because she was saying words in code, so Angel knew what and how to answer her daughter. Baby Girl was letting Angel know about the feds sitting outside her firm, harassing her until she told them that she would sue them for harassment. She also told her mother about the case she took on with Marcus Green that brought back the nightmares of being beaten and raped by Jose and his men. She told her mother that she remembered now, but she wouldn't have remembered that part of it; if it wasn't for the case she took on for Marcus, she had blocked that part out of her mind. The two dirty detectives that Jose had on as his retainer were the ones who knocked her out and took her to one of Jose's drug houses.

She told Angel, "I don't want to have to relive that scene again, but now that I know them two dirty-ass detectives were just as responsible as Jose and his men, they have to be rocked to sleep."

Angel told Baby Girl, "It can happen but not without me by your side. Let's take them down together."

Baby Girl wanted it done that following weekend; she didn't want them to get away with what they'd done to her, so she told her mother that she would meet up with her Saturday morning in Atlanta. Angel asked her daughter if she wanted her to bring anything special. She told Angel to bring her baby Suzie; she knew actually who Suzie was. It was her own personal Glock 27. Baby Girl loved the power of the Glock how it felt in her hand. With the Glock, she felt unstoppable. Baby Girl was willing to stop the nightmares of Detectives Duncan and Fredrick. She was going to send them to hell with Jose and his men. She knew what she was about to do was wrong being an attorney now and all, but she said to herself she didn't give a damn because she was a leopard that wasn't going to change her spots. Angel was excited to be doing a hit again with her daughter. It's been a while since they teamed up to take someone out. She went into the artillery shed to pick out some heavy artillery. She wanted to make another statement with those so-called dirty detectives; they were out of bounds, messing around with Angel Carter's daughter.

It was early Saturday morning when Angel flew in under the radar to meet her daughter in Atlanta. She didn't even rent a hotel room this time; she was going to be in and out. She met a guy on his way to his car at the landing strip; he looked toward Angel, and he cracked a smile because he thought that she was sexy. Angel went up to the guy and said, "Excuse me, Do you happen to be going into town? My ride hasn't showed up, and I don't like waiting around by myself."

The man told Angel, "If you want, I would love to give you a ride." The heel of Angel's shoe broke off while she was walking up to the man's car. She was switching so hard until her hips started hurting. When the man bent down to assist her with the heel of her shoe, she snapped his neck like a twig; the man didn't even see it coming. Angel jumped in the man's Expedition and pulled off; she was running a little late. She met up with Baby Girl in front of Cash's old apartment.

Angel told Baby Girl that they had to disguise themselves and that she knew actually what outfits they needed; they went to the wig store first to purchase some blonde wigs. Angel had picked up the lace wigs because they looked more natural to their own hair. When they tried on the wigs, they did look very different. So she decided they needed to change their eye colors as well. When they were done in the wig store, they left there and went to get fitted for their disguises. Baby Girl was dressed in a gold sequins dress. She could pass for Beyoncé's twin sister; she was wearing the hell out of that dress with her blonde wig flowing in the wind. Angel was dressed like the show stopper that she was. Her attire was sexy, and she stepped out wearing a long silk red dress that dropped down her back; it was so far down her back that you could see where her ass split began.

Baby Girl told her mother that the two detectives hung out in the club underground. She really didn't want to go back in Club Underground; it carried too many bad memories for her, but she knew that this was going to be the only way that she could forget about what happened to her if she faced her problem head-on. Baby Girl and Angel walked in Club Underground like they were the head bitches in charge. And you better believe that they stopped the show. Every man in the club was running up to the bar, trying to buy them drinks; they accepted one drink. They waited in Club Underground two hours before both detectives Duncan and Fredrick showed up. When Baby Girl saw them walk in the door, her blood started boiling; she felt pressure all in her chest. She knew if she didn't stop what she was feeling about them two dirty-ass detectives, she was going to burst her heart wide open. Detective Duncan was enjoying the show. He was sitting back, drooling like a dog that had rabies. He wasn't the type of man to get unnoticed by any female. He thought that all women should bow down to him. He thought that women were the worst kind of human beings there was only because his wife left him for a female. So he was very bitter when it came to women. Detective Fredrick fell for the female charm. He was over at the bar with Angel and Baby Girl buying drinks like he had money to burn, but what he wasn't paying attention to was that Angel and Baby Girl weren't drinking shit because every time he would turn his head, they were pouring their drinks into his glass.

Angel pretended that she and Baby Girl were a little tipsy; she wanted the detectives to offer them a ride to wherever they were going. Detective Fredrick went over to his partner, Duncan, and told him, "Let's go, partner. I think we have a couple of freaks there, drunk as shit, and I bet you we can get them to do just about anything we want them to."

Detective Duncan was as drunk as his partner; he would get liquored up every chance he got because he still wasn't able to get over the fact that his wife left a stud like him to get with another female. When they escorted Angel and Baby Girl to their police car, they didn't even ask them where they wanted to go. Detective Duncan just kept driving to his apartment. He knew they were going to get freaked down.

When detective Duncan made it to his apartment, he got out and grabbed Angel by the arm; his partner followed suit and grabbed Baby Girl by her arm; they walked them inside Detective Duncan's apartment. When Angel and Baby Girl thought the coast was clear, they asked if they could use the restroom. Detective Fredrick said, "Sure, it's down the hall to your right. The other one is in the bedroom to your left."

While Angel and Baby Girl were in the restroom, Duncan and Fredrick were in the living room, sitting on the couch, nodding; they didn't even notice Angel and Baby Girl had come back into the room. Baby Girl noticed they were nodding, so she went back in the bedroom to get Angel. She told her mother that they had passed out. Angel told Baby Girl, "All right! Let's get this over with. Go and look in the kitchen to see if he has any duct tape."

Duncan had two rolls of duct tape in his kitchen draw. Baby Girl went in the living room where her mother was. She was standing over them with her 9 mm Luger.

Angel and Baby Girl taped Duncan and Fredrick up; they were so drunk until they thought Angel and Baby Girl were getting freaky with them by tying them up. Baby Girl smacked the shit out of Duncan with her Glock. She said, "Wake your punk ass up!" She had pulled off her wig so they could see who she really was. Fredrick was already woke because Angel threw ice water in his face; She told him, "Wake the hell up! Don't worry. You're going to sleep permanently in a minute." Duncan couldn't believe his eyes. This was the same little bitch they kidnapped for Jose; they thought that she had died the way Jose had beaten her and left her in the trash dumpster to die. Angel pulled out two pairs of brass knuckles. She told Duncan and Fredrick, "Now, you two trifling motherfuckers are going to see how it feels to be beaten damn near to death and thrown in a trash dumpster."

Duncan screamed out at Angel and said, "Bitch, do you know that we are the god damn law? We are detectives. We don't give a damn about dying, bitch. That comes along with the job."

Angel said, "Good, now you would know how it would feel to be found in the trash dumpster by your peers. Oh shit, my bad! You won't know how it feels, will you? Because you will be dead, but don't worry. I'll make sure to leave a note explaining how you two dirty mother fuckers were serving a drug dealer."

Angel and Baby Girl started beating the hell out of Duncan and Fredrick with the brass knuckles; they were hitting them so hard until Baby Girl's knuckles swelled up on impact. She took off the brass knuckles and started beating Duncan with his own black jack he had hidden behind a shoe box in his closet. Angel had beaten Fredrick until he was as bloody as a piece of beef beaten with a meat tenderizer. His eyes were completely closed; he was leaning over like he was dead, but he wasn't; he had just passed out from the beating Angel put on him. Baby Girl and Angel decided to blow torch their bodies first and then put them in some plastic bags and take them back up to Club Underground and put their know-good-assess in the trash dumpster. But before they put them in the trash bags, Angel wanted to cut off their fingers to send to the feds. She wanted them to know she had been right there in their town right up under their noses without them ever knowing she was there. She was letting them know not to fuck with her and her family because there were going to be consequences. She also told the feds they should up their pay grade to keep their officers on the job so they wouldn't be turning dirty to support their living status.

Angel and Baby Girl took Duncan and Fredrick and dropped them off in the dumpster at Club Underground. Once they were done with them they headed back to their separate destinations. Baby Girl really didn't want to see her mother go back to Columbia without her, especially since her son was still there. She missed her son a lot, and she couldn't wait to get him home with her where he belonged. She was rushing to get back to Chicago. She forgot to tell her mother about Jason and Irvin, but it's fine because she learned from the best, her mother, Angel.

Chapter 29
Jason and Irvin Working Undercover

IRVIN AND JASON had been going hot and heavy with Denise and Ava. They had been happy couples for about two months now; they were dining and romancing each other like crazy. Baby Girl still thought that it was some shit in the game somewhere because out of nowhere these two guys happened to show up right after she peeped the feds sitting outside her office one night watching her. Baby Girl couldn't shake the feeling that Irvin and Jason were not who they said they were, and she will soon prove it without a shadow of doubt. Irvin had been watching Baby Girl all day. He and his partner Jason would take turns, keeping a watchful eye on her, but they weren't watching close enough because Baby Girl slipped off their radar when she went to Atlanta to meet her mother to kill Detective Duncan and his partner in crime, Detective Fredrick. When their superior called Irvin to see if Baby Girl left town at all, he answered with a no, knowing all the time he didn't know because he and Jason had been too busy chasing ass. Jason and Irvin were glued to Denise and Ava like they were forbidden fruit; they just couldn't get enough of them. It was like they had been hypnotized by them. Truth be told, Ava and Denise felt the same way about them; it was basically a tit-for-tat situation brewing among the four of them. Jason knew that they needed to get back at the job at hand, so he met up with his partner that day to tell him about his concerns only to find out that his partner was on the same page, especially since their superior called to wake up their damn senses.

Jason's day had come for him to sit and watch Gloria a.k.a. Baby Girl. He really found her to be intriguing to him; he loved everything about her when she walked sashaying her hips from side to side like Mae West. Jason started feeling things for Baby Girl the first night he met her at their office party; he thought that she was sexy with a capital S. He knew he would never be able to have her because her mother was a stone killer, and what he had been hearing was that she was as dangerous as her mother, but that wasn't keeping Jason from wanting her. Jason liked Ava, but his heart strings were pulling at him for Baby Girl. She had that whip-appeal effect going on that had Jason's mind on lock; he didn't know sometimes if he was going or coming, but he knew one thing for sure that he had to get his mind right. Irvin was getting ready to take Denise out for lunch; he hadn't found out any information on Baby Girl from Denise like he had supposed to have done. He was trying to gain her trust first; he didn't want to seem too pushy, but time wasn't on his side. He had to get some answers fast. When Denise walked into the restaurant, she took Irvin's breath away. He really did care for Denise, but she came secondary to his job. He knew that if he didn't have any information to report back to his superiors, he was going to have his nuts in a sling.

Irvin started off with the conversation by telling Denise how beautiful she was. He thought that if he broke the ice a little bit, that will soften her up a little. Denise asked Irvin wasn't they supposed to have dinner that night, why did he want to have lunch. Was it because he wasn't going to be able to have dinner with her or what. Irvin told Denise that he wasn't going to be able to have dinner because he had to work late that night, so he arranged for them to have lunch together, and he hoped that she wasn't upset about him making lunch plans without letting her know ahead of time. Denise let Irvin know that he was good at what he'd done and so she excused his behavior for now. She did think it was odd, though, but she wasn't going to tell him. Irvin ordered them a glass of white wine before lunch; he wanted to start asking questions early. He wanted to make sure Denise was comfortable first. He asked her how long she and Baby Girl had been friends and how did they meet? Denise told Irvin the truth; she told him that her and Baby Girl went to Spellman together. She told him that how some girls were stomping the shit out of her and Baby Girl jumped in and saved her ass; they had become friends after that, but she also let him know that their friendship was way beyond friends; they're more like sisters now. They all were so close now that if you came after one of them, that meant you were taking them all down. Irvin knew that already.

He knew they were close knit; he was just hoping that he could sweet talk Denise into changing sides. He wanted her to flip on Baby Girl. Irvin started firing question after question to Denise, and that's when she noticed that his ass was up to something. She hadn't been trained to be stupid. She felt right away that Irvin was using her and trying to set her up.

Denise finally decided to stop answering any more of Irvin's questions.

She was beginning to get very upset, and he noticed it right away, so he took the conversation another way to keep her from getting suspicious. Denise was so upset that when the waiter came over with their orders, she didn't have an appetite to eat. She excused herself from the table and went straight out the door, leaving Irvin sitting at the table alone, wondering if he'd blown his cover. Denise went back to the office to talk to Baby Girl about what had just happened with her and Irvin, but she wasn't in the office.

Baby Girl had left to get a checkup; she had been feeling a little bit under the weather, so she decided to nip it in the bud before whatever it was got any worst. Denise was still steaming when Baby Girl came in from the doctor. She looked at Baby Girl and started crying. Baby Girl asked Denise what in the world had happened to her to make her so upset.

Denise told Baby Girl, "All this time, I've been dating Irvin. I thought that he was the man for me. I really thought that he cared about me. All the time he's been using me to get information about you. At first, I thought he wanted to get with you, but it's not even about you. He wants to know about your mother, Angel. He wants to know her whereabouts." Baby Girl said out loud, "I knew them tight-eyed motherfuckers' plan. I've been knowing since the first time I laid eyes on them. I just didn't want to burst your's and Ava's bubble." Denise asked Baby Girl, "All right, now that we know, I think it's time we told Ava."

"She might not believe us, but she will soon find out that Jason is not only a federal agent, but he also has a wife and two kids."

Denise couldn't believe what Baby Girl just said.

She told Baby Girl, "Hold up! What did you just say?"

Baby Girl said, "Yes, I investigated them two clowns because as soon as I saw them, my antennas went up, told me something, Denise. You and Ava had been dating them two guys for a couple of months, right? Have they ever taken you guys to their home? I'm not talking about an apartment. I'm talking about a real house."

Before Denise could answer Baby Girl's question, Ava came walking in the door with this look in her eyes like she could kill somebody. They both asked Ava in unison. "What's up with you, girl?"

She told them that Jason had just broke up with her for no reason at all. That's when Baby Girl said to both of her girls that she knew both of them were federal agents. "They had been sent in to spy on us, hoping they could get their hands on my mother and the mafia. But we know that's not going to happen. They are going to have to come harder than that to trip us up. Now that they showed their hand, let's make them work for what they want," said baby girl, .

Baby Girl told Ava and Denise, "Since they are spying on us, we are going to reverse the shit. We're going to see if the federal agents want to follow the leader." She further said, "I suggest we give Irvin and Jason a run for their money since they want to play games. They don't know they just stepped in some shit. We're about to show these assholes how we get down first. We're going to set them up for the fall of their lives." Baby Girl explained to Ava and Denise that she did a background check on Jason and Irvin. They both worked for the feds for over ten years. They should have known not to get their cover blown, plus they both were married with children. Ava didn't know Jason had children; neither did she know he had a wife, but Denise had just found out about Irvin's family, so she wasn't shocked by it. When Baby Girl just delivered the blow to Ava and said that Jason was married and had children, the room started spinning out of control for Ava. She couldn't say anything about that lying son of a bitch.

Baby Girl said, "I know you both were feeling something for them, but it's time to face the fact that they were using both of you for their own personal gain. It's time to put some fire under their assess. Meet me tonight at my house and together we are going to come up with a strategy to make them regret ever messing around in our backyard."

Ava and Denise agreed to meet up with Baby Girl after work to work out their strategy. Ava told the girls that she would bring the wine. So that left them open to bring the food. This was going to be an all nighter, so Ava and Denise agreed to bring their night clothes.

Denise came up with the demonstration they used on the Sanchez brothers when they murdered them in Columbia; they had used a poison wine that Angel had concocted for them that rendered a man paralyzed of his smooth muscles. They did like that conception, but Baby Girl wanted something that would bring a whole lot of pain; she wanted something that the coroners couldn't detect in their blood streams.

Ava came up with a perfect idea. She told them, "This may sound strange to y'all, but I think we should go down on a hoe stroll and find a hooker who has the HIV disease and get some of their blood and transmit it into Jason's and Irvin's blood through one of their veins, deep under their skin; it will be easy to inject them. It only takes a booty call invite."

Baby Girl and Denise said in unison, "That's a good idea!"

"Them bitches on the hoe stroll will sell their souls to the devil, so if we get a couple of them and pay them to get tested, I'm telling you they will go for it. I say we offer five thousand dollars. I think that's the least we could offer them for their time and affected blood. What you guys think?"

Baby Girl told Ava that's a grand idea. They were so juiced up on the wine that they decided to go sit down on the hoe stroll to find a couple of girls they thought were good for the job. Then it hit them that they didn't have their identities covered up; they couldn't be caught sitting down on a hoe stroll. They were attorneys. What would that look like for them three well-known attorneys caught on a hoe-stroll raid? They were so tipsy until they couldn't do anything but laugh. When they finally decided to stop laughing, Baby Girl pulled off and headed back to her house.

The next morning, the girls woke up with hangovers; they were trying to find aspirins to stop their headaches. Baby Girl and Denise remembered what happened the night before, but Ava didn't have a clue because every time she would drink, she would have blackouts. So to bring Ava up to speed about what happened the night before, they told her about her idea to pay a couple of hookers and get them tested for their HIV-infected blood. Ava couldn't believe she came up with the idea, but she was definitely down with the idea. Now it was time to put the idea in effect. Baby Girl was tipsy last night, but she did notice two cars behind, someone was following them last night. She told Ava and Denise about it at breakfast this morning. Now that Irvin and Jason knew that they were down on the hoe stroll last night, she wondered if they thought that they were going down there to comp something. Baby Girl told Denise and Ava that since they were being followed, she's going to leave out first before the two of them. So that way, Irvin and Jason would follow her instead of them.

Once Baby Girl left the house—she was right—Irvin and Jason pulled off right behind her. She took them two idiots on a joy ride; she didn't have anywhere to go in particular. She just wanted her girls to get past them to go take care of what they had planned the night before. Baby Girl wanted them to know that she saw them; she walked up to their car window, like she did the other feds, and asked them if they wanted to join her for a cup of coffee. They just laughed in her face. Irvin told her, "Oh, you have jokes?"

"Huh," Baby Girl told both of them. She said to herself, "Laugh now, but I guarantee you that I will have the last laugh."

Jason said to himself, "I like the fire in that woman. She is very sexy and intelligent. She has a lot of spunk."

Jason told his partner Irvin that if it was under different circumstances, he would have been on Baby Girl like snakeskin on a pair snakeskin shoes. Irvin knew his partner wasn't lying about how he felt about Baby Girl because he was having the same feelings, but he wouldn't dare tell his partner that he was competing with him in his mind over a woman that neither one them was ever going to get a chance to be with. Baby Girl was on her way out of the coffee shop when her cell rang. Ava told her to meet them back at her house. She told her that they had completed the task at hand, and everything was a go. When Baby

Girl stepped into her house, Ava and Denise had brought a girl named Katie. She had been on the hoe stroll since she was fifteen. She told them she had run away from home because her mother didn't believe her when she told her that her boyfriend would molest her every time she would leave for work. Katie was now twenty-two years old. She found out she had HIV last year. So she really needed the money for her medication. Baby Girl looked at Katie. She felt sorry for her, but it was nothing she could do for her. She did tell Katie that she was sorry her mother didn't trust her enough to believe that her no-good man was molesting her young daughter.

Denise and Ava went to the doctor with Katie, so they knew that Katie was definitely diagnosed with the HIV virus. All they had to do was inject a syringe in her arm to get some of her blood to put in a valve for safe keeping, Katie asked Denise for her money as soon as she finished taking her blood. Denise gave Katie the five thousand dollars as planned. Katie hadn't seen that kind of money ever because her pimp at the time was taking every dime she made. Katie's pimp treated her worse than her mother's boyfriend ever treated her. He stomped out all of Katie's teeth; she looked way older than she really was. Baby Girl felt that they should help Katie in some way. She could tell that the young girl was hurting real bad. She could see Katie needed medical assistance immediately.

Jason and Irvin were sitting outside Baby Girl's house, wondering what the hell was going on because Ava and Denise still hadn't left Baby Girl's house. Irvin really missed Denise's company; he wanted to climb back between Denise's legs one more time for the road. Jason was thinking the same thing about Ava, but only this time, it would cost them their life in a slow and agonizing death—one that they wouldn't find out about until they have infected their wives with the HIV virus. Jason wanted to call Ava to see if he could spend some time with her; he really didn't want to spend any time with Ava—he just wanted to get a quick fix for the growing pains he had in his pants. When he called Ava, she agreed to meet with Jason for another roll in the hay, but this time was going to cost Jason more than just getting his dick wet.

Denise was sitting in the kitchen, loading up the syringes when her cell started vibrating; she looked at the screen to see who was calling. It was Irvin. She answered it right away. Irvin started to apologize to Denise about how he treated her on their last lunch date. She pretended to accept his apology so that she could get close enough to his lying ass to inject him with the HIV disease. Denise and Ava met with Irvin and Jason that night; they all went out to dinner together first, and then they went back to Irvin's apartment for their last roll in the hay. Jason knew Ava couldn't drink, but he wanted her to have one with him. Irvin had purchased a bottle of Cristal; he wanted their last night to be the one that he will always remember, not knowing that his last night will be the one he will never forget.

Ava and Denise rode Irvin and Jason like they were invited to a cowboy's rodeo show; they wanted to make sure that once they were done with Jason and Irvin, they would never pull that bull shit on another female. Irvin and Jason were worn-out; they both laid back on their beds and fell off to sleep. Denise and Ava met up in the kitchen to retrieve their syringes. When they returned back into the bedrooms where Jason and Irvin were sleeping, they took their syringes and stuck them up under their foot with the syringes. Baby Girl told them to stick them under their foot. That will be a good spot because they will never think to look up under their foot. Ava and Denise did what they went there to do, and they succeeded in their mission to inject the HIV into Jason and Irvin; only thing they had to do now was to sit back and let nature take its course.

Chapter 30
Baby Girl's Father St. Louis

GLORIA, A.K.A. BABY Girl, had a dream about this man that kind of favored her grandfather Cane, the Hawaiian Kingpin. She didn't think much about it at first until this guy smiled at her in her dream. She woke up, thinking about a picture her mother Angel had shown her when she was about ten years old, but she never, not once, mentioned to Baby Girl about her father. Baby Girl thought that her mother never said anything because she never spoke of her father, but she decided that it was time to confront her mother about her father. Baby Girl wasn't going to take any chances calling her mother on her personal phone due to the fact that the feds was still hanging around, trying to locate her mother. Baby Girl thought about this guy named Chiller who hung out on the west side of Chicago. He would be standing on the corner, selling burnt-out cell phone. You could use them phone and the authorities had no way of tracing the calls. Baby Girl paid Chiller a hundred dollars for the cell phone. She called her mother, Angel. Baby Girl asked about her son. Then she asked her mother about her own father. Angel wasn't expecting to hear her daughter speak of her father because she never said anything to her about who her father was. She knew that one day she would ask about him. Angel told her daughter she rather not talk about her father to her over the phone. She told her she rather talk to her face-to-face about her father.

Angel asked her daughter to meet her at her condo on the outskirts of Chicago. Baby Girl knew where her mother was asking her to meet her. She stayed there herself before she went off to college. Baby Girl made sure to tell her mother to bring her son so she could see him. Angel said all right and said good-bye. When Angel hung up the phone, she was stunned. She couldn't believe the time had come for her to tell Baby Girl about her father, St. Louis.

Angel knew how to explain the situation; she just didn't know how her daughter was going to handle her father being her uncle as well. Angel thought the only thing could save her from reliving the past was to tell her daughter the truth; she wasn't going to sugarcoat it by lying. She had to tell Baby Girl that she found out later on, down the line, that St. Louis was her brother; they had the same father and that she killed him because he set her up to go to jail, him alone with the prosecuting attorney Isabella Stallone, who happened to be her sister also, with a different mother. She just hoped her daughter could handle hearing all the madness that Angel went through to get where she is now. Angel knew she was going to have to get her a stiff drink behind all this shit. She was about to relive all over again but to clear things up with her daughter so she could understand that what happened to her father was his own choice, not hers. He made his own bed; she just made sure he slept in it. Baby Girl was dying to know who her father was; she didn't know if he was dead or alive. She didn't know where he stayed or anything. She just wanted to find out once and for all what her mother was hiding from her and why she never even mentioned her father.

Baby Girl arrived at her mother's condo that Friday night. She drove around in circles for a while to make sure she wasn't being followed by Jason and his sidekick, Irvin. When she realized she wasn't being followed, she hurried up and jumped on the freeway, and she made it to her mother's condo in record time. When she made it up to the front door, she heard her son calling Angel mommy. She felt sick inside. What did she expect? She left him with her mother for almost two years. When Baby Girl stuck her key in the door, her son came running to the door, screaming mommy; she just dropped to her knees and took her son in her arms. How she had dreamed of holding her son again! Angel looked on as Baby Girl and her son gave each other hugs and kisses. She said to herself that she could clearly see that her daughter loved her son as much as she loved her daughter. That's why she came with all his clothes so Baby Girl could raise her own son. She thought it was time because he would cry at night for her; he missed seeing his mother, and she missed him.

Angel cooked dinner for her and her daughter; she wanted them to sit down to a cooked meal before she told her everything. She had to tell her about her father. She had a bottle of white wine, chilling in a bucket of ice. Angel was really nervous because she didn't want her to think that she had sexual relations with her brother; it wasn't like that she wanted her daughter to understand that she found out about her father being her brother after she got arrested. After Baby Girl fed her son, she gave him a bath, and she put him to bed so she and her mother could talk. Baby Girl could tell that her mother was a little jittery. When Baby Girl finally finished with putting her son to bed, she went in the den to talk with her mother. She asked Angel to tell her the truth. She said she could handle it and she wasn't a child anymore. Angel told her daughter that she loved her father before she found out that he was setting her up. She told her that her father, St. Louis, was known in the community as a big-time drug dealer; she also told her that she and her soldiers were going to rob him of his fortune, but somehow he found out by putting a snake in her camp.

"The girl he put in my camp was his sister Mia. She reported back to me when he would be away from home, and me and my soldiers happened to be there when he came home. Long story short, we didn't rob him. He let me know that if I would have robbed him, it would of have been a big mistake. After that we started dating. He even helped me kill the Russian Mafia. I had no idea he hadn't forgiven me like he said. He had pictures of the killings that took place with the Russian Mafia. He was working hand in hand with the prosecuting attorney who turned out to be our sister as well from our father, Cane. So you see it wasn't that I knew firsthand that he was my brother. I found out the day I got arrested. He played his part very well. He was even killing people that was assigned to my case to keep me out of jail, long enough for me to give birth to you, Baby Girl. Shit! It was so stressful for me back then. To make matters worse, the attorney that he hired to take my case St. Louis told me that he was my brother too, but I found out later, after I spent a year in jail, that his mother used to just have sex with my father. He wasn't my father's son. He was the police commissioner's son. The police commissioner had raped his mother one night when he picked her up for solicitation because his mother was a crackhead just like my mother was."

Baby Girl could see the pain in her mother's eyes as she was telling her about what she went through with her father, St. Louis. She told her mother that she didn't want to hear any more. She had heard enough. She looked at her mother and told her she was sorry for what she had been through. She could only imagine how she must have felt loving someone only for them to turn around and set you up to go to prison for the rest of your life. One thing Baby Girl did want to know was how her mother escaped the prison turn of twenty years. Angel told her it was really a piece of cake.

"My attorney, Steven Blake, was a ruthless person and didn't have a conscience. He helped me to get out by blackmailing judges, the commissioners, and a few other people. We had them dead to right. We even had evidence to back up our complaints about them being caught with their pants down."

Baby Girl thought that she had been through a lot in her young life. Her mother had been to hell and back, so it didn't seem as bad for her. She only wished she could change time so that she wouldn't have St. Louis as her father.

She wanted to see a picture of him. Angel knew her daughter might want to see a picture of her father, so she pulled the picture out of her purse. She showed it to her. Baby Girl looked at the picture. She immediately tore it up; she told Angel that her father was just a sperm donor, that's it. She told her mother that it's over now, and they can go on with their lives.

Angel and her daughter enjoyed the rest of the night together because Angel had to leave, going back to Columbia the next morning. She told her daughter that she needed to find a daycare to put her son in while she worked, but if she ever wanted him to come back to Columbia, all she had to do was call, and she would be there to pick him up in a heartbeat. Baby Girl smiled because she knew her mother meant every word. The next morning, they were up, fixing breakfast when Baby Girl let Angel know how they set Irvin and Jason up. She told her mother that men were always suckers for a female with big assess and a pretty face. She told Angel that Irvin and Jason wanted to have their last piece of ass from Ava and Denise, so they paid a hooker with the HIV virus, retrieved some blood from her, put it in a syringe, and shot the virus into Irvin and Jason. Angel was proud of her daughter because she had taught her well. She knew if she died today or tomorrow, her daughter could most definitely handle herself.

Chapter 31
Fifteen Years Later

ANGEL'S SON, LITTLE Ramon, had grown up. He was now graduating from high school. He was anxious to move forward in his father's footsteps. Ever since he was ten years old, he was trained by his father and great uncles to handle heavy artillery; he was so good with the weapon as far as shooting them, he could hit an ant on cotton! The day he graduated, he asked his mother Angel if he could talk to her and his father in person. He wanted to let his parents know that he was ready to spread his wings, that he didn't want to go to college, and that he wanted to go live with his sister, Baby Girl, in Chicago. What his parents didn't know was little Ramon had been a drug dealer in Columbia for two years. He was known as King Raj; he was selling big time quality heroine. He had even stepped his game up to cocaine and crystal meth. He was never caught without his weapon of choice. King Raj kept a 9 mm or a Mac 10 in his possession. Angel made sure he was strapped just in case anything occurred. When King Raj finished talking to his parents, they thought it was time. He was eighteen years old now. Killing was what their family did and that's all they knew, so they weren't going to stop their son from doing what they did best.

Two weeks later, King Raj was on his way to Chicago to take over where his mother Angel left off. He was going to take Chicago by storm. He was going to be the next Chicago drug lord; he had already set up his drug connects in Columbia with his uncles Leo, Ben, and Joe, so he was set. His father Ramon knew what was going on, but he kept that part from Angel. She didn't know her son was going to Chicago to be a drug dealer. Baby Girl hadn't seen her brother in ten years. When she left Columbia, he was only eight years old. When he arrived in Chicago and showed up at his sister's law firm, she thought that he was a new client. He asked Baby Girl what was her fee for a murder charge. She told him it depends on if he'd done the murder or not. He broke out laughing because his sister didn't even recognize him. When she heard him laugh, she knew it was her little brother. They hugged each other for about two minutes. They were so glad to see each other. She told little Ramon he'd grown into a very handsome young man. He said, "Hold up, Sis, I need you to call me King Raj." Baby Girl said, "Excuse me, what?"

He said, "No disrespect, but I'm a man now, and I want to be treated like a man. All right, Sis, we need to talk for real. Are you busy right now because I don't want to take you away from your job?"

Baby Girl told her brother, "Give me twenty minutes. Then we can go for lunch."

King Raj said, "Cool, I'm going to be sitting out there in your waiting area. Is that cool?"

Baby Girl was finished with her client. She went into her waiting area and got her brother and they went for lunch.

Baby Girl was so excited to see her brother. He was sexy to her, and she knew the females in Chicago were going to eat him up literally. King Raj asked Baby Girl about the property buildings their mother owned under the dummy corporations. She asked him why? He said, "Look, Sis, I didn't come to Chicago to play games. I'm here to take this city by storm in the drug game. Now I want to know how much you will charge your little brother to have you on retainer, to be my personal attorney." Baby Girl said, "First of all, we are family. There's no charge, and second, if you really want to get in the drug business, we're going to run this shit together. Our mother is the most notorious female we know, so why can't we be better than she is? She always said to be better than her. So let's do the damn thing. Let's put Chicago on the map. We were born to notorious people that did nothing but illegal shit, so why should we be any different? That's all we know."

The next day, Baby Girl set her brother up in her mother's condo on the outskirts of Chicago. When they walked into the condo, King Raj was very amazed that his mother had good taste. He thought to himself, "This shit it set up for a king."

King Raj had a shipment being delivered in two days. He was going to need a warehouse to put his shipment in. Baby Girl told King she had just the spot their mother owned—a warehouse not too far from Club Sexy, which would be perfect. King Raj was now looking for guys to recruit. He wanted at least five guys to start with his army of soldiers. He needed guys with backbone; he wasn't worried about the muscle because he had been trained in all areas of karate, plus he was trained with artillery experience, so he had a lot up under his belt. He went to his sister to talk about hiring some of her rough-neck clients. She told her brother she had four clients that she had on drug charges and trafficking. King Raj told his sister, "Let's set up a meeting with them to see if they will travel on this side of the fence."

Baby Girl set the meeting up with the four men for that evening. They agreed to meet up with her at the Red Lobster. Blue, Bow Legs, Frank Nettie, and Dinky came to the meeting on time. When they saw Baby Girl sitting there with this young nigga, they couldn't believe it because all of them tried to holler at her, but she dismissed them all. So they knew this nigga here didn't have a chance. The meeting started with the introduction of King Raj being the biggest drug lord of Chicago. He told the guys what he wanted them to do and who was the head nigga in charge, and if they didn't accept his rule, then they could step off. Blue was the first to ask what they were going to get paid to hold him down. King told them fifteen hundred a week. Before King could say anything else, Bow Legs said, "Hold up, man! Let me talk to the rest of the guys in private." Bow Legs pulled the guys to the side and told them, "I know what y'all cats tripping off. This young nigga coming on the set, trying to recruit old niggas like us to hold him down while he come into our town and take it over making big time cash and shutting our shit down."

Bow legs told the guys, "The way I see it is we all could run this shit if we band together with young blood. We all could get to eat and rise to fame at the same damn time." They all agreed to follow King Raj but before they went any farther with the meeting, Frank Nettie wanted to know how old King Raj was because everyone of them was in their late twenties.

King asked Frank Nettie, "What my age has to do with us stacking paper? Nigga, you either be with it or you'er not, so what's it's going to be?" They were impressed with King's power of authority; he didn't back down from neither one of them. He let them know he wasn't no punk in any form or fashion. When Baby Girl saw the look in her brother's eyes, it frightened her just a little bit. She knew they had an assassin bloodline, but King was more advanced in the drug business than she was. Before the meeting ended, King Raj had all four men on board. They agreed that King might have been young, but as far as the drug status he had, shit on lock, he had one hundred keys of pure uncut cocaine.

King Raj had his sister to run background checks on each one of his soldiers to make sure it wasn't anything in their background check to come back to bite him in the ass later. Baby Girl retrieved their files from her office that night and took them home with her so she could start her investigations. She felt what her brother was saying because she already had Irvin and Jason buzzing around like flies on shit. Baby Girl turned on her computer and went to work. King wanted to know the guys' life history and so did Baby Girl! They had a substantial amount of money they were going to be investing in, so every move they were going to make had to be precise. Jacob Jones, a.k.a. Blue, was the first one on the list. He was born in Columbus, Ohio, to Mary and Donald Jones. He had two sisters and three brothers. He had been in trouble for drug trafficking since the age of eighteen; he also served ten years for an arm robbery with a concealed weapon. His parents still live in Columbus, Ohio. All his siblings live there as well. He has two children: a son, named Javari, and a daughter named Aaliyah, that reside in Columbus, Ohio, as well. Baby Girl took down the addresses to make sure that if anything went wrong, she and King would know where to find Blue's parent's residence.

Baby Girl had the computer warmed up; her next client was Caden Welsh, a.k.a. Bow Legs. He was raised right in the heart of Chicago; he was born to Clarita and Anthony Welsh. They still reside in the projects of Country Side Court. Bow Legs has two twin sisters named Aiden and Jayden. They go to Chicago public school. She found out that his mother Clarita worked as a nurse at Chicago general hospital and his father was a construction worker. She also found out that Bow Legs had just got out of jail, doing a five-year bid for burglary. Now she has been hired to defend him on a trafficking drug charge of cocaine. Bow Legs got that name from his mother. When he was born, she had his legs broken and reset, and he still was bow legged. Bow Legs has a daughter named Stephanie. She stays with her mother Toni who lives in Chicago as well.

Next, Baby Girl pulls up Dashawn Jackson, a. k. a. Frank Nettie. He inherited that name from his uncle T. top because he had an old car like the one Frank Nettie used to drive on the old movie, *The Untouchables*. Frank Nettie learned how to shoot guns from his uncles as well. His mother died of cancer when he turned thirteen years old. Frank never knew his father. His grandmother raised him; she died last year. Frank Nettie had been in and out of jail since he was thirteen; he started stealing cars on his thirteenth birthday. Then it manifested from there; then he went on to bigger things. He served time in the juvenile system for two years. Frank got out of juvenile and started up his own drug business; he was selling dime bags of weed first and then he upgraded to selling cocaine with his uncles. He got busted distributing cocaine to an undercover cop when he hired Gloria, a. k. a. Baby Girl, to defend him in court.

Baby Girl was getting ready to pull up Devon Cain, a. k. a. Dinky, when her phone rang. It was her brother King Raj calling; he wanted to know if she had any details on the four guys yet. She told her brother to give her thirty minutes and she would have all the information they needed, plus pictures. He said cool and hung up. Dinky was from New York. His mother was a dope fiend. She put Devon up for adoption after he was born. Soon after that, she died from a drug overdose; he ran away from his adopted parents and never looked back. He grew up on the streets, living from pillow to post, until he ran into an older gentleman named Big Papa. He took him in and showed him the tricks of the trade, and Dinky had been moving weight every since. That's all Dinky knew was drugs. Big Papa was the only family he had. He loved Big Papa.

Chapter 32
Angel Going Underground

ANGEL WAS SLEEPING when she had a dream about her mother. She was warning her that she had to leave the country. She told her that she had to run for her life; she couldn't escape the long arm of the law but for so long before they caught up with her, Angel hadn't ever had a dream about her mother but to see the vision of her mother with suitcases in her hand made Angel rethink her strategy of events that took place in her life. Angel couldn't go back to sleep after she received that visit from her mother. She went in the kitchen to make some coffee when it hit her like a ton of bricks: she had to go underground for a while because she knew one day that the feds was going to catch up with her. While angel was sitting in the kitchen, contemplating her move to going underground, the feds was teaming up with the CIA and Homeland Security. They were getting close; they had already had people calling in to report Angel being spotted in the mountains in Columbia. They were getting ready to make their move in two days; Angel's mother gave her warning in just the nick of time, and now Angel was ready to move. Uncle Joe had made reservations for Angel to pack up and leave. Before her mother put that thought in her head, he could tell that Angel was restless; she meant the world to him, and he didn't want to see her locked away for the rest of her life.

Angel packed her bags r and her and Ramon left. Before she disappeared, she called Baby Girl to tell her that she would be retiring for a couple of years; she really wasn't sure if it was a couple of years or it might be longer than that, but she did know for sure that she would be out of commission for a while. Baby Girl and King Raj told their mother to do what she needed to do, and they would be there if she needed them. Angel told her children she loved them and to be safe because going underground, she wouldn't be able to be in touch with anyone; right when Angel and Ramon were on their way to meet the people to go underground, the feds and the CIA and the homeland security were kicking in the doors of their house. Uncle Joe and his brothers were ghost, and they had moved to another area. Angel didn't want to leave her children out there alone, but she taught them everything they needed to survive; she just hoped King Raj didn't get caught up tripping with a big head, thinking he ruled the world because even with all the killings she did, she knew she didn't rule the world. She sacrificed her life, and now she was running for her life. Angel knew she had to lie low because once again, she was wanted on the most-wanted list; her face was flashed all over the news. She had to wait until the heat died down again for her to go back under the knife to get plastic surgery again. She didn't care about getting butchered up; she just wanted to get her life back on track to continue what she started. She still was a Columbian assassin.

An assassin is what she was going to be until the day she died. She was going to be what she was trained to be from the time she was old enough to tie her own shoes. Angel started to reminisce about what she accomplished in her life. She killed so many people, and she didn't regret any of it. Her biggest regret was that she couldn't be there for her children and grandson. She knew she was going to be worried about them, but she had to make sure that she would be around if they needed her. She couldn't help them from behind bars. Angel was so worried about her children that she thought about coming back to kill every law enforcement that came after her. Angel and Ramon drove all the way to Pennsylvania to the Amish country; they would be dressed like the Amish to hide their identities. What Angel wasn't going to like was living in their community without any connections to the real world. She didn't know that they were going to be without a television, and radio cars didn't exist in their community; they had horses with carriages, and everything they ate was home grown. Angel had to get used to a lot of things different from her element if she was planning on staying in the Amish community.

When Angel and Ramon arrived at the Amish community, Angel told Ramon, "I don't know if I could wear their clothing. My whole body will be covered up." Angel hadn't seen anything yet. They didn't have electricity or running water from a faucet, plus they made their own clothing. Their bathrooms were outside, which they called the outhouse. Angel told Ramon, "Baby, I don't think this is going to work."

They had to get up before daybreak in the morning, washing clothes by hand on washing boards, and cooking everything from scratch. The older women had to teach Angel how to make homemade bread, kneading the bread by hand that wasn't Angel partake. She had never seen anyone cook anything from scratch, nor was she trying to learn, but staying in the Amish community, she had to learn a lot of things she wasn't used to doing. The ladies were all gathered around in the kitchen, talking when one of the ladies asked Angel what she was running from. Angel didn't say anything because she didn't discuss her personal life with anyone outside of her family. The older lady told Angel that the best way to alter the mind is by telling the truth. Angel looked at the women like she had just bumped her head because she wasn't the one to be telling these Amish people her business or anything else as far as that matters. The lady told Angel that mistakes are meant to be learnt from and not to repeat them. She also told Angel, "Live your life in the manner you want to make good reflections of you."

The wise old lady was dropping some knowledge on Angel; she never had a woman to teach her what she needed to know. To become real with herself, she'd foreseen what the lady was talking about, but it wasn't enough for her to go turn herself into the feds. When the lady told Angel that life is a trial and error and let's not make it a trial you will regret. Angel thought to herself, "Lady, you just don't know. It will be a trial for real if the feds caught up with my ass." Angel wanted to tell the old lady to mind her own business, but something prevented her from speaking because in Angel's heart, she knew the old lady spoke the truth to her. Before the old lady left the kitchen, she told Angel one last thing: she told her not to spend too much of her time wasted because there was no chance of her getting it back.

Chapter 33
Baby Girl's New Man

GLORIA, A.K.A. BABY Girl, had been spending a lot of time in court these days. She had more clients on her plate than she thought she would ever have. She and the prosecuting Attorney Brad Davies were working long hours together. Brad had feelings for Baby Girl, but he didn't want to make any advances toward her until he felt she was ready to receive what he had to offer. Every time she would walk in the court room with Brad, his adrenaline would be pumping anxiousness; he would be pouring sweat like he had just been hit by a rain storm. Brad Davies was a flawless man; he didn't have a hair out of place. He was clean cut, with a Jamaican accent, and he had a beautiful dark complexion with the broadest shoulders. Baby Girl thought in the back of her head that yes, Brad Davies was one hell of a specimen of a man, but she just wasn't ready to be back out in the dating field unless Brad gave her a good reason to do so. They were leaving the court room for lunch when she bumped into Brad on purpose; he told her, "Why the rush? Is something on fire that you have to run into a brother?"

Baby Girl grinned at the fact that Brad was still holding on to her arm; she could feel the warmth coming from his hand up her arm. She said to herself, "Damn, this brother is sending electricity all through my body. I don't know if I should pass this brother up or not, but with the time I'm spending around him, I will definitely find out what's up."

Brad wanted to invite Baby Girl on a date; he wasn't the type to get rejected by females, and he wasn't going to break his stride now. He just knew he had to find a way to get close to this attractive woman that captured his soul; she would look at Brad with her hazel green eyes, and his inside would turn into jelly. Every evening, when Brad would go home to his big, beautiful four-bedroom ranch-style home, he would sit on his balcony with a glass of wine, thinking about how Baby Girl would creep into his mind and burn his soul like an unsuspected Chicago snowstorm. Brad was so caught up on thinking about Baby Girl that he temporally lost track of time; he was supposed to go over to his mother's house for a fish fry. She was going to welcome his baby brother back from being overseas. He had been in the military for four years and he reenlisted for another four years and this would be the first time he would be seeing his brother Reginald in four years. When Brad finished drinking his wine, he jumped in the shower and headed to his mother's house. When he arrived, his brother had already made his entrance. Brad rang the door bell, and his brother opened the door. They hugged each other for at least two minutes. They were very close before Reginald left to go serve their country. Now that he was back for two weeks, maybe they can pick up where they left off.

Brad was a dresser. He had a fetish for designer clothes. He told his brother they should hook up the next day and go shopping; he wanted his brother to have the same fetish he had with designer clothes. Their mother, Mae, was a heavy-set Jamaican woman, with a beautiful smile. She had the sweetest personality. She loved everyone that they would bring to meet her. She loved to cook and spend time with her two sons. She was hoping that Brad should hurry up and get married so she could have her some grandbabies. Brad had talked to his mother about Baby Girl; he even told her that she was an attorney, and he also told his mother that he cared a lot about her, but he just couldn't get enough nerve to ask her out on a regular basis. He didn't want to get shot down.

Mae told her son, "Brad, that doesn't beat a failure but a try. How would you know, Son, if you don't try?" Brad's soul hardly agreed with his mother, but he decided to give it a shot. What could he lose but his pride if she said no? Brad went to work on Monday morning, glowing like the sun. He was just about to call Baby Girl when she walked into his office, dressed in a dark blue pinstripe navy blue Armani skirt suit, she was looking like the dime piece she was, and Brad took it all in; he was smiling like he had just won the lottery. Baby Girl asked him if he was ready for court. Brad jumped up from his chair and said, "Yes, I'm ready. Let's do this." The only thing Brad hated about their job positions was that he was the one to always prosecute the case, and Baby Girl was the one fighting for her client's life. To Brad, she was a damn good attorney. She had won four cases so far, fighting against him, and he was very proud that she didn't back down from a fight.

After court, Brad thought he would try his hand by sending Baby Girl two dozens of red roses; he had them delivered to her office before she made it in from court. He paid extra for a twenty-minute delivery, before she could get to her office. Denise said, "I see someone has a secret admirer."

Baby Girl said, "Please, girl, who are you talking about?"

Denise said, "I'm talking to you. Someone has their eyes on the kick-ass attorney Gloria Carter."

Baby Girl started laughing because she knew Brad had it bad for her, but she wasn't going to be the one to make the first move. Brad had placed a card inside the roses that read, "How would you like to have dinner with me tonight at seven at my house?—Brad." He had also put his cell number inside the card so she could call him to confirm if she would make his dinner invitation or not. When Baby Girl picked up the phone to call Brad to let him know that she would love to have dinner with him, Brad was very excited that she accepted his invitation. He called his maid to put in his menu for the evening; he knew he didn't have any more wine, so he had to stop at the store on the way home to purchase another bottle or two. Brad made sure when he arrived home, he would have vanilla candles throughout the house. He had freshly cut roses sitting in vases in every room; he was rushing to get ready like Glady's knight and the pimps were having a concert in his living room. When Brad realized it was almost seven, he started tripping over his own foot; he had to slow himself down before he caused an unwanted train wreck with himself. Brad had to laugh because he had never been this nervous for a woman before, but to him, Baby Girl was well worth everything he was going through to get her attention.

Baby Girl arrived at Brad's house at six fifty-six; she was taught that it's better to be punctual than late. Her mother would always tell her that women take enough time getting pretty as it is, but when you're already beautiful, it only takes ten minutes to add to your beauty. Baby Girl decided that she would surprise Brad with what she wore: she had on a royal blue Donna Karen dress that dipped down the middle of her back. She had on a pair of silver stilettos with the bag to match; she had her hair flowing down her back with soft curls coming down around her face as well. When Brad answered the door, he was in awe; he had seen Baby Girl every day at work, but to see her dressed like she was made him see her in a different light. He would be lucky to have her on his arm.

Brad invited Baby Girl into the living room while he went into the kitchen to get them a glass of wine. She made Brad weak in the knees. Brad came back with the wine and gave Baby Girl her glass of wine. He sat across from her on the sofa, staring at her like she had just stepped off *Essence* magazine. She looked gorgeous to Brad; he was feeling things for Baby Girl that he thought didn't even exist. He wanted to wife her; he saw Baby Girl definitely as wife material. Once the maid was done, setting the table for the two of them, Brad escorted Baby Girl into the dining area; he pulled her chair out for her. She sat down. Brad said grace, and they started eating dinner. Brad's menu was superb; he had smothered lamb chops with stemmed broccoli and roasted small potatoes with lemon meringue pie for dessert. He didn't know at the time that Baby Girl's favorite pie was lemon meringue. When she saw Brad's maid come in the room with the lemon meringue pie, she almost jumped out her chair because she hadn't had lemon meringue pie since she was fifteen.

After dinner was over, Brad invited Baby Girl to sit on the balcony to have an after-dinner drink before she went home for the evening. Baby Girl was so in tune with Brad that she really wasn't feeling like going home; she wanted to enjoy being in his presence, away from the job and her two nosey friends. She was sitting beside Brad, taking in the aroma; he was smelling good enough to eat. She had to ask Brad what he was wearing, and he told her that he was wearing Kenneth Cole Black. She loved the way the cologne went along with Brad's chemistry. She was about to lose all control of her body functions, and the two glasses of wine she had consumed wasn't helping. Baby Girl and Brad sat on the balcony until they had consumed two bottles of wine. They were looking into each other's eyes like if they didn't go with what they felt right, then they may never have this chance again. So they both went with the flow. Brad leaned over and kissed Baby Girl seductively with passion; they were so in tune with kissing each other. When she let a light moan escape her mouth, that's when Brad knew he had to pick her up and carry her into his bedroom.

Baby Girl was second-guessing herself with Brad. She had been used to running background checks on anyone she came in contact with, and Brad wasn't any different; even though she worked with Brad, she still wanted to know more before she fully accepted him in her life. That night was special to Baby Girl. She hadn't been with a man since her abduction; she didn't think she could fathom being with a man again. She held all men responsible for what she went through with Jose and his men, but being in Brad's company eased her mind a lot; he made her feel comfortable and at peace, so she thought that she will keep him around for the time being. They made love in ways Baby Girl only dreamed about. Brad massaged Baby Girl's clit with his tongue in a very slow and sinuous movement; she was squirming and moved with the motion of Brad's tongue. Brad knew he was about his business with the head game; he wasn't in a hurry to demonstrate with his dick game just yet, and he didn't want to scare her with the size of his penis; home boy was working with twelve inches of hard steel. His mother used to call him bigram when he was little because she knew one day some woman was going to be in trouble with what her son was working with. Brad started to work his way up Baby Girl's stomach. He opened her legs wider to accept his dick with ease; he entered her slow, and he had problems putting the tip of his dick in because she was so tight from not having sex in two years. Brad couldn't believe that after all the licking he had done, she still wasn't lubricated enough for him to enter her without ripping her vaginal walls. Once Brad started whispering nasty words in her ear, she was spitting juice from her vagina like a porn star. She wanted Brad to crack her back, and she was hollering so loud. When Brad finally put all twelve inches inside her, she said shit so loud, he was going to pull out, but she clamped her legs around him, pulling him deep into her pussy like she was never letting him out, but he enjoyed the ride.

The next morning, Baby Girl left Brad's house, smiling. He put some shit on that ass, and she couldn't wait to tell Denise and Ava that she finally got her back cracked. Brad hit her g—spot just the way she liked it. Brad was amused himself; he just knew she was going to say, "Hell, no! You're not going to stick all that in me!" What Brad didn't know was Baby Girl was on cloud nine. She didn't care if Brad was hung like a horse because it had been so long since she had a man that close to her. Baby Girl had run her background check on Brad. His stats came back, and Brad came back clean as a whistle. Baby Girl said to herself that she still was going to take her time because she still wasn't sure if she wanted a long-term relationship. She had another secret admirer; he had been watching her every move lately. He even sent her a stuffed teddy bear to her office without a note; she just thought it came from Brad. Baby Girl's secret admirer was a white guy named Steven. He worked at the law firm down the street from Baby Girl's law firm; he was partners with Dominic and Lucas, the firm's name was LDS, which stands for Lucas, Dominic, and Steven. Steven was flashy. He was rich; his parents were doctors, and he went to Harvard to get his degree to be a lawyer. Steven wanted Baby Girl and wasn't going to let anything come in between what he wanted. Steven knew she was dating Brad, but he also knew Brad wasn't in his league. He knew everything about Brad. He was knee-deep in Brad shit; he even knew when Brad got up in the morning to take a shit. Baby Girl was sitting at her desk when this white guy walked in; she just knew he was the feds from the way he was dressed. He had on a smoke-gray Italian suit, with some smoke-gray Italian-stitched smoke-gray loafers. He had hazel grey eyes. Steven said, "Excuse me! I'm here to see Gloria Carter."

Baby Girl was in a daze. She was saying to herself, "Damn! This man is sexy as hell."

She told Steven she was sorry for staring. She said, "How can I help you, sir?"

Steven told her that he was attorney that worked down the street from her. He also told her that he was interested in her. He told Baby Girl, "I don't mean to come on too strong, but I like your style. You peaked my interest. I'm here personally to ask you out on a date."

Before she could answer Stevens question, Ava and Denise came busting in the door from lunch, smiling at the fact that it was this fine-ass man standing up in Baby Girl's face like he was ready to leap over her desk and kiss her or something. Baby Girl asked Steven for one of his business cards so she could call him later with her decision. She didn't want to cheat on Brad, but in reality, Brad wasn't really her man. Yes, they slept together, but she didn't agree to be his woman yet.

Baby Girl gave Brad a call to let him know that she was going out with her girls, so he wouldn't be calling her while she was out with Steven. She just wanted to know what her options were before she made her mind up to settle in with Brad. Before she could hang up with Brad, he was shooting twenty questions at her, trying to find out what club will she be at just in case he wanted to show up there. Baby Girl had only slept with Brad once, and she couldn't understand why he was acting all brand-new and shit. She said to herself, "I have to put a stop to this shit before he started stalking me. I'm not going to deal with a guy that's aggressive. The next thing you know he will be abusive, and she is not going to let anyone control her. She hung up with Brad and called Steven; she met up with Steven at a club called the Hot Spot.

Chapter 34
The King Tower's

KING RAJ HAD established his drug business status. He was going to be the youngest kingpin in history. He was going to take Chicago by storm. Cane, the Hawaiian kingpin, wasn't going to have shit on King. King thought about his name long and hard before he dropped his middle name Raj. He wanted to be known only as King; he liked the way it rolled off his tongue, plus he liked the power king carried. King had opened up all six of his mother's apartment buildings; he had each one of them designed to have hidden doors so that if the police kicked in, they wouldn't have a clue to what was really going on. He had mini micro cameras set up in every room; he also had alarm systems throughout every building, and if anything went down in one of his buildings, he would be the first to know about it because they would be hooked up to his wristwatch that he had custom-made to be in tune with all of his systems and mini micro cameras. He even met a few undercover cops. Once when they pulled him over for running a stop light, King ran down his plan to those two dirty cops. They were on King's team because he was offering them more than they made in their entire life. King's next stage was to recruit his army of soldiers; he had already come up with the name for all six buildings, calling them the King Towers. He had bought cooking utensils, big pots, weighing scales, valves, bottles, and a lot of baking soda: he had everything known to man to bring his business full circle.

Bow Legs knew of four brothers that stayed in Michigan that were gunmen that will rock a nigga to sleep if they blinked twice. He asked King if he wanted to bring them down from Michigan for a trial run. King told Bow Legs, "I don't do nothing before I investigate a nigga first homey." Bow Legs knew that young King had a right to be cautious because the drug business wasn't a joke. A nigga would kill you out there in the street just on general principle. It amazed Bow Legs about how strong King was to be so young. He knew in his heart that if you came wrong with King, he would fuck you up. There was no doubt in his mind that whoever schooled young blood, he had his shit on lock. King had purchased two more dope house in the projects. He met this girl two weeks ago named Precious; he could tell she was hot in the ass, so he made the first move; the only thing she saw was King driving a brand-new candy apple red 2012 Maserati Granturismo. She couldn't believe someone as young as King would be driving a 123,000-dollar car; he either had to come from money or this nigga was a drug dealer.

King found out three days after fucking Precious that she was just a squirrel, trying to get a nut, so he told himself that he was going to use her to his advantage. King asked Precious if she had any brothers. She told him that she had two brothers that just got out of county jail. She asked "Why?"

King said, "I thought that I could hook them up with some work." Precious said, "I don't know, King, because my brother would think that you are weak and try and rob you."

King grabbed Precious's face and told her, "Baby Girl, don't worry! I can handle your knuckle-head brothers. Trust me! King got this." Precious agreed to set a meeting up with her brothers to meet King, but she told him she wasn't going to do it if she couldn't be there. He told her, "If you want to be around some grown niggas discussing man business, that's on you, but I'm not responsible for you if some shit kicks off."

Precious gave her brothers a call because she knew they needed the money, but she also knew firsthand her brothers were known as the stickup guys of Chicago. Precious's brothers, Face and Dirty Red were anxious to meet this little nigga their sister was talking about; they both knew that their sister was the project hoe. They heard when they were on lock down that she was fucking niggas just to get a pair of name-brand tennis shoes. Now that they were back on the set, she wasn't doing that shit no more; they took care of their sister because their mother was a crackhead. She was never at home, so Precious had to take care of herself by any means necessary. Face and Dirty Red told her to tell King to meet them in Countryside Park at twelve. She said cool, and they hung up. King told Precious he would see her at twelve if she was going to be at the park. He didn't feel right about meeting her brothers by himself, so he had Frank Nettie, Bow Legs, and his two hired undercover cops, Williamson and Johnson, to meet him in the park at twelve. He didn't want to tell Precious that if her brothers tried to rob him, then she was going to be kissing the babies good-bye with her brothers. He couldn't afford to leave any witness. When King finally

178

arrived at the park, Face and Dirty Red were sitting on the bench, smoking a black and mild; they looked at each other when they saw King walking their way because to them, this little nigga didn't look old enough to them to blow his own fucking nose. Face and Dirty Red were twins; they were identical and had just turned twenty-five years. Every time they went to jail, they got sent up the river together.

King walked up to them with hard swagger; he let them know that his heart didn't pump no Kool-Aid, and he wasn't a pussy by a long shot. He started his conversation by introducing himself as King. Before he could say anything else, Precious came running up the hill, screaming, "King, it's a setup. They're going to rob you." She heard her brothers' conversation when she walked in the house; they didn't hear her come in the house because they were too busy loading up their thirty-eights and planning how they were going to beat the shit out of King and take his shit. When King heard Precious say that, he turned just in time. He caught Face trying to pull out his gun; he was too slow. King pulled up his two 9 mm, hitting both Face and Dirty Red in the chest and head. They dropped to the ground like a sack of rotten potatoes. Precious tried to run back up the hill when Bow Legs hit her with his desert eagle; she was split like a chicken, straight down the middle. When King and his soldiers left the park, it looked like St. Valentine's Day massacre. There was blood everywhere; King even had some on his clothes and face.

King sent word to Uncle Leo that he needed some hired guns. Uncle Leo called King and told him not to worry and that he had three brothers up in Dallas that would kill a crawling roach. He told King that he would be in touch with him in a few days. Uncle Leo called Diego in Dallas to let him know that King needed their help; he was more than happy to help King because all three of them were King's godfathers, but they haven't seen him since he was eleven because they were away, serving time on a drug case. When Diego told his brothers Dallas and Detroit that King was running a drug empire in Chicago, they got their shit together and was en route to go help their godson; they were known as the triple threat. They found out while they were locked up that they got busted because a nigga they knew named Bubblehead was a police informant. When they got released, they found Bubblehead standing on the corner. Dallas walked up behind Bubblehead, grabbed him from the back, and threw him to the ground. That's when his two brothers Diego and Detroit snatched him up and dragged him into the alley. Bubblehead knew his days were numbered as being a street-corner drug dealer. Dallas told Bubblehead, he was a snitching ass nigga, and he broke the street rules running his damn mouth to the wrong people. "Now you're about to get dealt with. Street justice is a bitch, isn't it?" Before Bubblehead could say anything, Detroit told him to open his mouth, but Bubblehead refused. That's when Diego grabbed his jaws, and his mouth popped open. Once Bubblehead's mouth flew open, Dallas pulled the pin out the hand grenade, put it in his mouth. Bubblehead's body popped like a helium balloon; his shit was scattered all over the alley. Right after the brothers killed snitching-ass Bubblehead, they gassed up their Gran prix and headed to Chicago. The brothers' mother gave them their names because each one of them was conceived in the states that they were named after. While the brothers were on their way to Chicago, King was spending a substantial amount of money, securing the King Tower; he had an underground tunnel going up under each building that stretched out at least five blocks long.

King wanted a bank vault installed in the floor with an elevator that took him down inside of the vault. But first, he had the floor in one of the buildings made of steel with a whole sliding floor that was up under the hardwood floors; he had the switch connected to his wristwatch and to his sister, Baby Girl's matching watch, which could only be activated with both watches at the same time, but they were also connected to their eye-heat senses. King had his shit hooked up; he was a multimillion-dollar drug lord in a very short time. He was stacking paper, hand over fist; the young drug lord was pulling in a million dollars a week. He even upstaged a nigga that though he was running the block with his little drug connect until King showed up on the set, King made Styles feel like he was selling now and later compared to the shit King put on the streets. King's shit talked volumes. Word of mouth spread through the streets of Chicago like wild flowers. King's shit was pure uncut dope; his young ass had a franchise hotter than Popeye's chicken. He even had a courtyard where his dope clients could smoke in peace. He also had one room set up with glass coke pipes, weed pipes, weed rolling paper, cigarillos, and all King was about was stacking his paper by any means necessary.

Dallas and his two brothers were fifty miles out from Chicago; they would be meeting up with their godson King in a few hours. They couldn't believe he grew up to be a drug lord, but they didn't mind because they were going to be there to watch his back no matter what. Uncle Leo told them about Baby Girl. He told them that Baby Girl would be their attorney on retainer if they needed her assistance. The brothers were glad to hear that because they would be bringing some heavier artillery with them; they had their car customized to carry whatever artillery they needed. King was glad to hear that he had some known reinforcements coming to watch his back. He had ten soldiers that he recruited already, but he only had six that he knew for sure were loyal to him;

the other ones he wasn't so sure, but he did let them know if they ever crossed him that they would be in body bags delivered to their mothers' front doors.

Dallas and his brothers arrived in Chicago as planned; when they touched down, they called King to let him know where to meet them. When King got to his destination and stepped out of his 2012 Lincoln Navigator silver with butter-cream leather seats and interior with custom-made rims sitting on twenty-eight-inch spinners, Dallas told his brothers that he thought that was King right there.

His brother said, "I don't think so." Dallas said, "Young blood has more swagger going on than we do." Dallas said hold up I know how we can tell, Dallas said young blood who's the baddest nigga you know was something they used to tease King about when he was small. King said right away, "Me, nigga? That's who?" They all started laughing because they didn't think that King would remember them, but he did. They were much older, but King never forgot their faces.

King had Dallas and his brothers to follow him back to King Tower's so he could introduce them to his other soldiers. When Bow Legs saw King had hired some other niggas to be his right-hand men, he started feeling left out, plus Bow Legs didn't trust any of them; he was pissed that King didn't take his advice to bring the niggas he chose for him from Michigan. It wasn't that Bow Legs didn't trust Dallas and his brothers. He had a heavy debt that he owned to them niggas in Michigan; he knew if he didn't pay up pretty soon, his ass was going to be floating in the river. Dallas was amazed at how King had set the towers up; he had soldiers on top of the building as well as around it; he had a hundred-foot security gate wrapped around the whole perimeter. He had it locked down like Fort Knox. King even had his soldiers wearing wrist bands that had electricity in them; if they were somewhere they weren't supposed to be, he would shock the shit out of them and bring their ass back to reality quick. He wasn't to be fucked with at all; he wanted them to know he ruled his kingdom, and if they wanted to eat, they weren't going to bite the hand that fed them.

Chapter 35
Olympia and Darcy

OLYMPIA (**SOPHIA**) **AND** Darcy (Michelle) were living the married life; Olympia was still having problems, trying to get pregnant. Her husband wasn't rushing her to have a baby, but she wanted one sooner because she didn't want her biological clock to start ticking before she was too old to have one. Her husband understood where she was coming from, but he didn't want to have any children if it meant losing the love of his life in the process of Olympia giving birth to their child. Olympia knew her husband Douglas's loved her; he would give his right arm if it meant that his wife will carry and deliver their child without any complications. Olympia had another doctor's appointment coming up in a few days, but when she woke up this morning, she immediately started to feel nauseated; she started vomiting everywhere. Douglas jumped out of bed to hurry to the bathroom to get the trash can because Olympia couldn't make it to the bathroom. When she finally stopped feeling nauseated, she got out of bed to go take a shower when she started vomiting again; she told her husband she needed to see the doctor right then. Douglas called the doctor's office to get an early appointment. Then he heard his wife Olympia scream out in pain; she had started bleeding from her vagina that frightened Olympia. Douglas told her that they needed to go to the hospital; she couldn't wait to see the doctor. Douglas helped her get dressed, and they headed out to the hospital. When they arrived at the hospital, Douglas told the emergency doctor in charge what he thought was wrong, and the doctor rushed Olympia to the back to examine her. What the doctor found out was actually what Douglas had prescribe to Olympia that she was pregnant with a tabulation pregnancy; she would have died if Douglas hadn't moved as quickly as he did, getting her to the hospital.

The doctor had to do an emergency operation on Olympia to remove her child from her tubes. While the doctor was operating on Olympia, she started bleeding internally; she was losing blood fast. Her blood pressure had dropped profusely. The only thing he could do to stop her from losing so much blood and her life was to perform a partial hysterectomy, meaning that Olympia would never be able to have a child. When the doctor left the room and told Olympia's husband, Douglas, what he had to do to save Olympia's life, he understood because he didn't want to lose his wife. He knew long time ago that they had only fifty-fifty chance of Olympia carrying a child. When Olympia came out of surgery, she was drugged up, but she still knew something was wrong; she felt empty inside even though she didn't really know that she was pregnant. Douglas looked at his beautiful wife with admiration in his eyes; he couldn't bring himself to tell her that she wasn't going to ever be able to have children. He just couldn't because even though he wanted children, he knew now that the woman he loved was never going to be able to carry his children.

Olympia was still asleep off the heavy sedation the doctor had given her, so she didn't know that her sister, Darcy, was right there by her side; she loved her sister, and they would do anything for each other. Douglas told Darcy what happened, and she leaned on him and cried. She felt bad for her sister that she wasn't going to be able to be a mother, so she decided right then and there to carry her sister's child for her. Darcy didn't want to tell Douglas what she decided to do; she wanted to talk to her sister first to see if she wanted her to carry her and her husband's child for them. The only thing Darcy could think about was that she and her sister were going through all this turmoil because of Angel some way or another. She will pay for what she put them through. Darcy was still sitting at her sister's side, two days later; she hadn't even been home to shower or change clothes. She hadn't even gotten a bite to eat because she wasn't going to leave her sister's side again. When Darcy's husband, Romeo, called her cell phone, it went to her voice mail every time because she couldn't get reception inside the hospital. She didn't care if he called her or not because they weren't getting along as husband and wife anymore. Darcy had begun to get tired of her husband, Romeo; he was spending too much time in the streets. He was beginning to look like he was messing around with some of his own products; he tried to lie to Darcy that he wasn't using, but she knew better as he was aging faster than his normal age, and for Romeo to be only twenty-five, he looked to be twice his age. Darcy's plans were to leave Romeo. They had a good run; everything was going fine until he fucked up, sneaking behind her back, selling drugs and to make matters worse, he spent weeks at a time away from home. Darcy made her mind up to move on; she didn't need no dope fiend for a husband because when he does make his mind up to come home and if she's not there, Romeo took things out of their house and lied about them. Darcy felt really bad because she was going through things with her own marriage, and she hadn't talked to her sister in a couple of days. She made a promise to herself that she would never spend another day without talking to her sister because of some man.

Three days later, Olympia was getting discharged from the hospital; she wasn't the happy person she used to be. She wasn't responsive to anyone, and she wouldn't talk at all; it was like she went into a shell. Darcy and Douglas tried everything they could to bring Olympia out of the bad state of mind she was in. The only thing she would do was sit and stare out of the window. She had lost a tremendous amount of weight because she wouldn't eat anything; she had completely shut herself down. Darcy told Douglas what she was thinking about at the hospital about carrying their child. They had tried everything to get Olympia to respond to them. So Douglas asked Darcy to go and tell her sister, Olympia, what she just told him to see if she would respond to what she had to say. When Darcy went in the bedroom to talk to her sister, she was sitting there by the window in her chair, looking like she had just given up on her life. Darcy took her sister by the hand. She told her that she loved her and that she would do anything for her if she just let her know what it was she wanted her to do; Once Darcy saw that her sister never took her eyes off the window, she laid her head on her lap, and she just started crying hysterically; then all of a sudden she felt her sister, Olympia, rubbing her head. She looked up just in time to see her sister smiling at her. Darcy told Olympia, "If I knew the only thing I had to do was cry, I would have done that days ago." They both hugged each other, crying of joy. Darcy was so glad to have her sister back that she told her that if she still wanted a child, she would love to be their surrogate and carry their child.

Olympia was more than happy that her sister wanted to carry her child for her; she even wanted to move Darcy in with her and Douglas since she had planned on leaving Romeo anyway. That way, once she got pregnant, she wouldn't be stressed out dealing with Romeo's crazy ass.

Once Darcy decided she was ready to move on, she went over to her condo and packed up her things. When she was about to leave the house, Romeo came stepping in the door, smelling like day-old fish. Darcy hated the sight of Romeo; he wasn't the same man she married, nor was he the man he portrayed to be. Romeo was a straight up dope fiend to Darcy. She wanted him out of her life like yesterday. Darcy told Romeo that he could have everything in their house; she didn't want anything that would remind her of him. Romeo really didn't want to lose Darcy; he knew he fucked up. The monkey was on his back, and he couldn't shake him off now; he was going to lose the most important thing in the world to him—his wife. Romeo was high as a kite when he walked in the house. When he saw that Darcy wasn't going to take his bullshit anymore, he went ballistic. He started throwing things through the house, telling Darcy she wasn't going anywhere and she needed to take her shit and put it back in their bedroom. Darcy took her shit back in the bedroom, but she came out of her bedroom with her .357. She told Romeo, "Nigga, I tried to be nice and wanted to leave you everything, but since you want to get ignorant, it's time for you to bounce now. You can go on your own, or I can put two in your skull and you could leave in a zipped up body bag. Your choice!" When Romeo saw that Darcy wasn't playing, that nigga grabbed his shit and hit the door; he never looked back because one thing for sure, he never forgot what his mother told him: a woman scorned is the worst kind of woman.

Chapter 36
King's Dream Girl

RAMON RAJ CARTER (King), being a drug lord at only eighteen, has the biggest entourage of twenty loyal and armed men behind him. He had four henchmen that followed him at all times. One day, in particular, he wanted to go out and eat at a restaurant that was comfortable and laid back without his right-hand men hovering over his shoulders. He wanted them there; he just wanted them to be a little bit at a distance, but Dallas wasn't having it. He and his brothers were there to protect him, and that's what they were going to do. King decided to finally go and visit his mother's club, Club Sexy. He had being hearing from his soldiers that if you wanted to have fun, Club Sexy is where you wanted to be; King told his soldiers that they were going down to Club Sexy for some fun and relaxation. Everyone got dressed in jeans and timberlines with white T-shirts and snap-back baseball caps. When they pulled up in front of Club Sexy, they were hopping out of different color Hummers. While King and his soldiers were sitting at the bar, in walked the dream girl that King had been dreaming about; she came through the door with three of her friends. She looked just like a Greek goddess to King; he had only had one sexual experience with a female in his life, and that was with Precious before Bow Legs killed her.

King watched her as she sat down at a table by the dance floor with her friends; he couldn't keep his eyes off her. When she walked, it was like she owned the floor. King hadn't seen a woman that beautiful since he left Columbia. Aphrodite was a princess to King; she looked just like royalty to King. He wanted Aphrodite to be his one and only woman. He wanted to go talk to her, but he didn't want to chance saying something stupid to her, so he sent a drink over to her after he asked the bartender what she was drinking. When the bartender told King that Aphrodite was drinking apple martinis, he said,

"Yes, she's my kind of girl. She doesn't drink the hard shit." When Aphrodite turned around to thank King for the drink, he almost melted to see she had the prettiest dimples he'd ever seen.

King was about to go over to Aphrodite's table when a group of niggas came in the door; they were being rude. When he saw that they were headed straight over to Aphrodite's table, with her and her friends, he immediately got angry. King was just hoping that none of them was Aphrodite's man because he really didn't know how he was going to handle that situation. Just when King was getting ready to go to the bathroom, a fight broke out between the rude niggas and one of Aphrodite's friends; the guy they called Gunner was Aphrodite's friend babe's boyfriend. He would always follow them and start shit with babes.

Babes told Gunner to step off, and he threw a drink in her face. That's when the fight kicked off. King stood there for a moment, trying to see what else was going to happen before he intervened. What he saw next sent a cold chill down King's spine: one of the niggas that was with Gunner started swinging because bottles were getting thrown in their direction. When he punched Aphrodite in the face, King lost it; he ran over to the table where the guy's were at and punched the guy so hard in his face until Gunner stopped the fight with his girlfriend and swung on King. That's when you could hear gun fire coming from Kings men Tec-9 all you could hear was "Rat, tat, tat, tat, tat!" The whole club went ballistic. King grabbed Aphrodite by the hand and led her out the door with him and his entourage of soldiers. He wanted to make sure he got her to safety.

Once King made it safely to his Hummer, Aphrodite was stunned because she let him have his way with her, and she didn't know him from Adam, but somehow she felt safe being with him. When King's driver Diego pulled off the lot, he asked him where he wanted to go. King told Diego he wanted to go to his condo on the outskirts of Chicago, but he had to make sure Aphrodite was cool with it before he took her to his condo to talk. King wasn't ready to take her home just yet, not without finding out about her first. He was glad the turn of events turned out the way they did because if they hadn't, he wouldn't have had the pleasure of this beautiful princess sitting in his ride beside him; Aphrodite asked King what his name was and why he traveled with so many guys with automatic assault rifles? King had three marksmen, who were Dallas, Diego, and Detroit; they could shoot an ant on cotton and burn his ass alive. Right before King and his men made it to the freeway, they heard tires bursting and rubber coming up on the side of them. What the assailants didn't know was that all four Hummers were customized to be bullet-proofed with the windows included; the Hummer also had a gun-slide doors put in also where King's men could slip any kind of weapon out that sliding door, and you wouldn't even see it coming. King had Aphrodite to exchange seats with him so he could open the sliding door to return fire. When she changed seats with King, he pulled his AR-15 from under the seat and was ripping that Ford Explore to shreds; he hit it twice in the gas tank before it exploded.

King told his other soldiers on the radio that if these niggas want to get ratchet, let's show them how to party Columbian style. Every one of King's men was firing from their Hummers; it was stray bullets flying everywhere. They had enough ammunition in them Hummers to start world war three in the streets of Chicago; the people that was driving on the freeway was in a frenzy. All you could hear was "pow! pow! pow!" and "boom! boom! boom!" It was like they were shooting cannons; Aphrodite was scared shitless. She didn't know what the hell was going on. She just wanted to go home because to her, these niggas were on some gangster shit, and she didn't want to end up dead for something she didn't know nothing about. King and his soldiers stopped shooting when they heard the police sirens at a distance; they got off the freeway not to far from King's condo. Aphrodite told King she could get out at a service station and call one of her girlfriends to pick her up because they probably was worried about her anyway. King said, "No, I'll take you home only with one acceptation: if I can come by your crib to see you tomorrow." Aphrodite agreed; she would have agreed to a blood transfusion just to get away from King and his soldiers.

King stuck to his word; he made sure Aphrodite made it home safely. She had never been so glad to see her mother even though her mother was an alcoholic and treated Aphrodite like shit. But she was still her mother, and she loved her. King and his soldiers made it back to King Tower's, but King was distracted by the thoughts of being with Aphrodite; she was five years older than King, but it didn't matter because he just looked at it as being matured. In King's mind, age really wasn't anything but a number. King felt like he lost oxygen to his lungs when Aphrodite was around. Without her, he felt like his heart would erupt. He didn't want to be without Aphrodite; she was Hawaiian and black, just like his mother, Angel. Aphrodite was five feet eight inches tall; she had slanted hazel brown eyes with a Carmel completion; she had long silk black shoulder-length hair with a body like a goddess. She had small ample breast with nice round hips and ass. King couldn't control his emotions for Aphrodite; he wanted her bad. The next day he called Aphrodite and asked her out on a date, but she was too afraid to go out with him. King promised her that he wouldn't let anyone or anything hurt her; she smiled at the fact that he was so interested in being with her. She thought that he was cute and young, but she really liked his mannerism; he was the perfect gentleman to Aphrodite, so she accepted his invite to go out with him on a date, but she made sure to let him know that she didn't like all the drama that came along with his lifestyle. Even though she didn't know what he did for a living, she did know he had drug dealer status.

King and Aphrodite became a couple after two weeks of dating. King was spoiling the hell out of Aphrodite; that's what drug dealers did, and she knew it. They did everything possible to keep their women happy, but King wasn't trying to make her think that he would buy her the world on purpose. He had genuine feelings for Aphrodite, and he wanted to express what he was feeling for her from his heart; he was working on Aphrodite from the inside out. He didn't want any part of her body untouched. He was going to make Aphrodite his girl even though she was older than him. That didn't mean shit to him; he was more than emotionally attached to Aphrodite, and he really felt like they belonged to each other.

King dropped Aphrodite off at home one day. When he walked her to her front door, they could hear loud noises coming from inside the house; it sounded like someone was getting smacked around. Aphrodite knew it was her mother and this Jamaican cat named Buddha; she was messing around with Buddha and he only came around when he wanted Aphrodite's mother Karen to do unspeakable shit to him. Aphrodite burst through the door; she went in swinging on Buddha. He had Karen by the neck, pushing her head into the floor because she wouldn't give him a blow job. Buddha stopped hitting Karen and tried to hit Aphrodite, but King told him, "You don't want to do that, baby boy!" Buddha told him, "Young blood, you need to leave before I burst a cap in your ass." Before Buddha could say another word, King hit Buddha in the mouth with a right hook, dropping Buddha to the floor instantly. Buddha got up from the floor and drew his .45 automatic and pointed it directly at King. King told Buddha, "If you point a gun at a nigga, you better be able to use it. Otherwise, I'm coming back with vengeance." Buddha backed up out the front door, still pointing his gun at King; once Buddha was out of view, he broke to his car.

King made sure that his girl and her mother were fine before he left. Right when King made it to his Hummer, shots started ringing out in the air. Buddha was firing at King with his .45 automatic. What Buddha stupid ass didn't know was King traveled with an entourage of soldiers; Buddha had started a war with the wrong people; he wasn't even supposed to be on that side of town. He was supposed to be at the airport, meeting up with his drug connect, Cuba. Buddha had written a check his ass wasn't ready to cash. Buddha was rolling on the freeway with his music playing loud and smoking on some hydro when he felt someone hit his expedition from the back; he looked in his rearview mirror to see three black on black Yukons; he started speeding down the freeway past the airport. He was going so fast he almost lost control of his expedition. King and his soldiers were firing 9 mm at Buddha, ripping his windows out his truck with force; they were shooting 9 mm Magnums with sixteen rounds with extra clips with CZ 75 Magazines.

Buddha was driving like a bat out of hell, trying to get away from King and his soldiers; when he hit an alley to his right, he ran right into a police raid that's when he decided to sit right there where it was safe with all the police being on the set. Buddha had to make a mental note to come back on King's set with his soldiers to blow King and his soldiers off the map; he wanted King to know that this shit wasn't over. He wanted a war and a war was what young King was going to get.

Chapter 37
Baby Girl's Final Decision!

GLORIA (**BABY GIRL**) was still seeing Brad; he was falling fast for her. She wasn't feeling a love connection with Brad, but she did care about him. She had been on two dates with Steven. She enjoyed his company; he made her laugh. He was so funny to Baby Girl because he made her feel things that she wasn't able to feel anymore. Steven would send Baby Girl roses every day until the point that she had run out of room to put them. She did accept them because they brought light to a very dull day. Baby Girl was sitting back in her office when in came Brad; he was dressed to impress, and Baby Girl couldn't help but smile because she knew that Brad had it bad for her; it couldn't be helped. Shit, she was gorgeous! Brad wanted her to go with him to dinner at his mother's house. He had been bragging on her to his brother; he wanted to show off his show piece before his brother left going back to the military. Baby Girl agreed to go only because she finally decided to tell Brad that she didn't see him as her future man because for number one, Brad was too aggressive for her; he needed to know her every move like he was working for the feds. Baby Girl knew Brad was legit; she did her background check on Brad. He was clean, and he hadn't even had a parking ticket; he was just too over jealous for Baby Girl's liking. Brad told her that he had a boutique coming by her office at five to size her up for what she wanted to wear for dinner. He also told her she could get whatever she wanted because she didn't have a limit; she could shop until she dropped if that's what she wanted to do.

Ava and Denise felt that Brad was a suitable guy for her, and if she didn't want him slide his ass over to them; they all broke out laughing like crazy because they both knew Baby Girl had her eyes on Steven. She really wanted to be more than just a show piece hanging on a man's arm; she deserved more, and she was going to definitely have it. She had to choose between two different men. Brad was nice; he spent a lot of time with her, and he had mad skills when it came to the bedroom action, but when it came to being romantic, Brad was lost; he thought romancing Baby Girl was showering her with expensive gifts. She didn't mind the gifts; she just couldn't take Brad's bitching about her hanging out with her girlfriends, staying out till wee hours of the morning. Brad told Baby Girl that no respectable woman stays out till wee hours of the morning unless she's looking for something, or she's found what peaked her interest. Baby Girl had gotten fed up, trying to defend her womanhood to Brad; he had gotten to the point where he wanted her to call him when she wanted to take a piss.

Baby Girl told Brad she was a grown-ass woman that didn't need his smart-ass remarks, and if he had to treat her like she was his last chance at happiness, he could take the next train straight to hell. Brad didn't know what to say after she read his ass his rights and to be honest, he really wasn't trying to smother her; he just didn't want to lose her. Brad really did love her; he was just holding on too tight to someone that he wasn't sure he had from the beginning. When Baby Girl did finitely meet Brad's brother, she thought that he looked very familiar; she couldn't shake the feeling that he could be related to her mother in some kind of way. She wanted to ask Brad if his brother's father's name was Cane Carter, but she thought that maybe she would never get enough courage to ask him before she left Brad's mother's house. Brad and his mother left the dining room to talk amongst themselves in the kitchen, leaving Baby Girl and Reginald alone. Baby Girl tried real hard not to stare, but she just couldn't help herself; she had seen an old picture that her mother had of her dad that her aunt Marie had of her grandmother Gloria and Cane together. Baby Girl took a chance and asked Reginald anyway. She wanted to hear what his response was going to be.

Reginald wasn't shocked that Baby Girl asked him that question because she had been staring at him all through dinner, so he knew it had to be something very heavy on her mind. When he told her that he really couldn't remember his father, he was told by his mother that his father stopped coming around when he turned four years old, but he still sent money to his mother to take care of him until he graduated out of high school. Baby Girl was blown away when Reginald told her that his father was from Hawaii; he told her that his father used to live in Chicago a while back, but his mother hadn't heard a word from him in years. Baby Girl asked Reginald if he didn't mind her asking what was his father's name. . When he told her Cane Carter, you could have knocked Baby Girl over with a feather; her mouth flew wide open. Reginald asked her if she was all right. She said, "Yes, I just got choked up. My wine went down the wrong pipe. That's all."

Baby Girl couldn't believe she was sitting in the same room with her uncle, her mother's brother from another mother; she only wished she could tell her mother, but for now, she will keep it a secret. When Brad came back in the room, he was standing in the doorway, looking at Baby Girl like she had done something wrong; what she didn't know was Brad had been standing in the doorway all the time, ear hustling to their conversation. When Reginald got up to go fix him and Baby Girl another drink, Brad snatched her by her arm and accused her of trying to hit on his brother. Baby Girl snapped out right then and there on Brad; the situation got so out of hand, Brad's mother wound up calling Baby Girl a cab; she didn't want Brad acting a fool in her house again, so she had to defuse the situation quick because Brad had a very bad temper.

Baby Girl left in a cab never to talk to Brad again; she thought that he was a bipolar patient or something because he was switching back and forward like he was crazy. Before Baby Girl's cab could reach her apartment, Brad was blowing her cell phone up; she picked up and told Brad that she didn't want anything to do with his crazy ass and to keep his distance from her or she would kill him. Brad didn't remember what he had done to her; after he took his medication, he was truly bipolar for real. He hadn't taken his meds in three days, so his balance was off.

When Baby Girl arrived at home, she called Steven to see what he was up to; she didn't want to sound angry, but she did. Brad had her ass heated; she wanted to split his wig back, but she kept her composure and left. She knew Brad wasn't the man for her. She knew she had to work side by side with Brad in the courtroom, but that's it. Brad was now history; she was going to start dating Steven if he would still have her. She didn't know that Steven knew something had gone wrong in Brad's mother's house; he followed Brad and Baby Girl from the time Brad picked her up from her apartment; he also saw her when she got into a cab and left. He knew she was at home because he was right outside her house when she called his cell phone. Steven made sure he would only be a phone call away when she needed him he asked her if she was all right. She said yes and said she just wanted to talk that's all. Steven asked her if she wanted company or did she just want to talk on the phone; either way he was cool with it. Baby Girl told Steven she just wanted to talk because she didn't think that she would be good company right now at this time.

Baby Girl and Steven talked on the phone until three in the morning; she fell asleep on the phone. Steven just listened to her light snoring on the phone until he fell asleep himself. When Baby Girl woke up at seven thirty the next morning, Steven was still asleep, holding his phone until he heard Baby Girl's voice; he was still outside her house, asleep in his car. When Steven realized he was still outside, he knew he had it bad for that woman so now that Brad was out of the way, he can start making plans to woo the woman he fell in love with at first sight. Baby Girl had been kicking it tough with Steven; they were planning a trip, but she didn't really want to leave town, knowing her little brother may need her assistance. She asked Steven that if they went on a trip, would it be close enough for her to get back home quick if she needed to get back quick. He said, "Sure, because we're taking my private jet, so don't worry if we have to be back ASAP. Trust me! I can make it happen." Baby Girl had made her final decision; she was now dating someone who appreciated her for who she was and not for what he wanted her to be.

Baby Girl and Steven had come back from their trip from the islands; when they got to her apartment, her front door had been kicked in and her clothes were all covered in bleach. She could smell the bleach as soon as they entered the apartment. Steven couldn't hold her back; she was running to her bedroom because she had more than a million dollars stashed away in her closet, inside a gym bag, that she was to supposed to put in the bank two days ago, but she had forgotten. When she saw the money was still there, she knew that shit had Brad all over it even though he bought most of her clothes; she wasn't mad because she could replace what his stupid ass messed up, Brad was sitting in his car, fuming when he saw Baby Girl pull up with Steven; he said to himself, "That's why that bitch was acting brand-new with me. She has already replaced me with the next nigga. I'm going to kill that sack-chasing bitch if it's the last thing I'd do. I'm going to make her life a living hell; she better watch her fucking back."

Chapter 38
King's War with the Jamaicans

KING AND HIS soldiers were gearing up for the war with the Jamaicans. Buddha had sent a warning to King that his days as Chicago's drug lord were numbered. King didn't take lightly to Buddha's threats; the guy Buddha sent the message by was now tied up in one of King's warehouses. Frank Nettie and Bow Legs beat him to a bloody pulp. Buddha knew something had happened to his nephew because he hadn't come back to check in yet; his brother was going to tie Buddha a new ass hole as soon as he finds out that Buddha sent his son on a suicide mission that he didn't have anything to do with. Buddha started getting nervous because he knew he fucked up royally; this whole war thing happened because Buddha was somewhere he wasn't supposed to be. He had rounded up ten of their soldiers to back him up; he knew he had to get his nephew out of the situation he put him in before his brother found out. Buddha's nephew begged him to let him go deliver the message even though he was only sixteen. His brother didn't want his son being in drug wars until he knew for sure he was ready, but his son wanted to prove to his father that he could handle himself. Buddha knew he had put his nuts in a sling going behind his brother's back, sending his son to King's Tower; he just had to think of a way to get his nephew out of there alive. King didn't give permission for the young boy to be killed, but he did tell Bow Legs to convince him to give up the whereabouts of Buddha. Bow Legs and Frank Nettie beat Buddha's nephew Demetrius until he faded into unconsciousness; the young boy was going to remember that ass-whipping the rest of his life. King and his right-hand men Dallas, Diego, and Detroit went to the archery store. King wanted a crossbow that could pierce a bird at a hundred yards; he wanted one that had performance and accuracy to put a whole straight through a niggas rugged edges. King wasn't going to be playing around with

Buddha and his army of soldiers. King had every gun known to man; now he was adding on crossbows. When King left the archery store, he had purchased twenty Vortex Kolorfusion crossbows. Buddha had been waiting on the time to attack King Tower's; he couldn't wait until it got dark to take out King's men that were on top of the tower. He was going to rescue his nephew even if he had to kill everyone in all six buildings. What Buddha stupid ass didn't know was he was being watched the whole time. King had his undercover cops Williamson and Johnson sit on Buddha's every move; they even followed Buddha to his brother's place. They watched when Buddha and three other guys came out of the garage, carrying all kinds of artillery, putting it in three black Tahoes.

King put in a call to Williamson to see if he had made any progress in finding Buddha. Williamson let King know that he was sitting outside the King Tower's three car lengths down from Buddha and his soldiers, getting ready to run up in King's shit. King told Williamson to sit tight and not to do shit, and he could handle it from there on out. King didn't have to tell Williamson to sit tight; he wanted to see what this young boy could do stepping in grown men's shoes, but it was one thing Williamson could say about King, and that was his young ass had his shit on lock; he couldn't say that all the years that he was a police officer, he never ran into a young nigga like King that became hood rich in such a short time. King had his men on high alert; they had some fire power for a nigga's ass. They had everything from Glocks to 357 high-performance hand guns to .45 Winchester Magnum hand guns to Glock 17 for easy and quick; performance just what they needed for high pressure situations, and not to mention the twenty crossbows he purchased earlier. Buddha's time had come for him to bum rush King Tower's; he had his soldiers running up to the King Tower's, firing their weapons only to get dropped by returning gun fire. King's men were dropping Buddha's men like flies on shit; what Buddha and his crew had wasn't shit compared to what King and his men were using; King had rocket lungers too. Buddha felt like he was being defeated; he was returning fire, but his shit wasn't powerful enough for King's men. Buddha should have thought twice about going on some other nigga's turf. In order to get ass, you have to bring ass to get ass. Buddha wasn't ready; he didn't think the magnitude would be as big; he didn't think King ran his tower with so many soldiers to be a young nigga; he thought he could punk them, get his nephew, and bounce. King spotted Buddha behind a car; he started firing crossbows at Buddha, hitting him in the leg. Buddha was terrified because all his men were scattered all over the ground with enough bullet holes in them; if you were to pour water down their throat, it will come out each hole like a water hose. Buddha crawled back to his Tahoe, got in, and sped off; not only didn't he get his nephew out of King's grip, he got another one of his nephews killed in the war he had with King and his soldiers. Buddha knew he had to get out of dodge quick before his brother found out he had one son dead and another one being held hostage. Buddha didn't have a clue he was being followed by King's dirt cops, Johnson and Williams. They followed Buddha's Dum ass straight to a hotel room where he checked in for a while to take care of his leg. While Buddha was in the bathroom, checking on his leg, Williams and Johnson snuck into Buddha's room, sitting on his bed; when he entered the room and saw Johnson and Williams, he started backing up into the bathroom. Williams told Buddha if he sneezes he would blow his brains all over the bathroom wall.

Williams didn't like Jamaican guys anyway because one day, his nephew was walking home from school and got caught up in a drive by shooting with some Jamaican dudes and some game members; he was very bitter about what happened to his nephew. He decided that he will kill Buddha and let King get the wrap for killing Buddha. Williams had it bad; he told his partner he could stay if he wanted to, but if he didn't want to be a part of what he was going to do to Buddha, he could leave. Johnson told Williams they were partners no matter what; that's all Williams needed to hear. They grabbed Buddha out of the bathroom and commenced to beating Buddha; what Williams did next shocked the shit out of Johnson. He went out to the car and came back in the room with a big 10-inch blade; he stabbed Buddha in the abdomen and pulled the knife all the way up Buddha's abdomen until his guts was hanging from his abdomen. Buddha died instantly with his eyes wide open, looking up at his predators. Williams split Buddha like he was a fish.

King and his soldiers won the war, but will they get away with what went down at King Tower's? It was police everywhere, locking up everyone to find out what went down at King Tower's; it was more dead bodies in the street. It looked like a dump yard for dead people. King didn't worry about getting locked up because he and his soldiers hid all their artillery when the police did a search on King Tower's; they couldn't find anything to prove that they had anything to do with what went down at King Tower's, so they all were released in Baby Girl's custody. Baby Girl dropped King back off at King Tower's and headed home; once King made it inside, he and his soldiers regrouped and started up their meth lab before they could get everything in order to start cooking up their drugs. A big fire broke out in the kitchen; shit started popping like crazy. The smoke was so thick they couldn't see they started crawling trying to get out when they heard the front door was being hit with something hard; when they saw it was Dallas, they were glad to see him come to rescue them and get them to safety. He saved their life because all of King Tower's doors were made of steel.

The fire department came right on time before the building completely burned to the ground. King knew he had to talk to the fire chief because if he didn't, he would have known that they were cooking drugs in that building and that's what started the fire; King paid off the chief, and the fire was pushed under the rug. Once again, King had his way until the police found Buddha's dead body in a hotel room, with King's name carved into his chest.

Gloria (Baby Girl) and Little Ramon (King) stacking paper continues!

About the Author

Brenda (Gean) Wright was born and raised in St. Louis, MO. Her greatest accomplishment was opening up her own Daycare Center. She grows up without her mother who passed away when she was twelve years old. Her father is also deceased. She graduated from Sumner High School. She went on to college and took up Medical Assistant and furthers her education in childcare.

She's happily married to her husband (William) for fifteen years. She has two children (James) and (Christina), two step children (Orlando) and (Reshunda) and nine grandchildren. She spends my time writing in her laptop when she's not keeping children. Her hobby is cooking and baking. She loves to cook and bake cakes and cookies for sale. Right now she's in the process of going back to school for a degree in Masters in Business Administration.

CPSIA information can be obtained at www.ICGtesting.com
Printed in the USA
LVOW121100280912

300635LV00002B/76/P